Sun Kissed & Salted

by Angela Blair

SEA PONY

B O O K S

BAKER CITY, OREGON

Edited by Roisin Heycock and Luisa Colon
Copy Edit by Brianna Shepard
Proofread by Brenda Lange
Consultation by Robert Hall and Paul Weisser

Library of Congress Cataloging-in-Publication data:
Names: Blair, Angela, author
Title: Sun Kissed & Salted/Angela Blair
Identifiers: LCCN 2025904479 (print) LCCN 2025904807 (ebook)
ISBN 979-8-9928261-3-5 (pbk) ISBN 979-8-9928261-1-1 (ebook)

SunKissedAndSalted.com

HUMAN
AUTHORED
AG Authors Guild
6218223

"It is never too late to be what you might have been."

— George Eliot

Special thanks to Jade and Ruby, who light up my life. To my faithful mother and father, Barbara and Jon, and my forever friend, Luana. To the precious people who have encouraged me to follow my dreams, some of whom are beloved beta readers: Juliana, Rebecca, Shirley, Sherry, Amanda, Jasmine, Allana, Randy, Fina, Melody, Katie Bee, Brian, Corrine, Ben, Diva, Bruce, Dori, Lisa, Kathleen, Mark, and Stephen. To life and all its marvelous and miraculous ways. To the freedom and light guiding my way each day and the undying love pulsing through the universe.

Contents

Spoke 1

Dario. 7

Box of Buttons. 23

America in the Dust. 47

Wrong Turn. 55

High and Mighty 63

Stomping on Teen Street 69

Powerless 83

Tokyo Lights 93

"H" is for Human 101

The Cracked Drum. 113

Money, Murder, and the Moon. 129

Bread, White, and Blue 139

The Cult 151

Lament in Los Angeles. 175

Diana 199

Lifted. 209

Holy, Wholly, Holey 225

Arms 241

Jackson 263

Sweet Destiny 269

Time is Never Late 281

Collecting Keys. 291

Family First 307

Surrender 327

900 Miles 343

Home 351

Spoke

Chapter 1

After the crash and a silent pause in blackness, I began to see myself lying in the street from a bird's-eye view. People started to gather around my broken and bloody body, afraid to get too close. As I rose into the air, I began to see the tops of the palm trees that lined the boardwalk, the long stretch of sand, and the ocean in the distance. Embodying the lightness of air, I recalled the recurring flying dreams of my youth.

It was summer in Los Angeles, 1988, when I moved to the beach and started taking art, operatic voice, French, and photography classes at Santa Monica College. I had graduated from high school in 1986 without plans for college, intent on pursuing a career in show business. I gave up on becoming an actress; the sexual predators scared me off, and having no legit connections in the business made it too hard to catch a break. Instead, I was excited about reinventing myself, exploring, and hopefully saving enough money to travel the world.

Salty air swept in through the window of my basement apartment on Venice Beach as I stretched my body, barefoot, early on a Sunday morning. I always enjoyed watching the legs of people walking by and imagining what the rest of their bodies looked like as the click, stomp, or shuffle of their shoes hit the pavement. In the dim light of my apartment, the whiteness of a blank canvas called to me from a corner of the room. Suddenly inspired, I grabbed my bicycle, lifted it up the stairs and headed to the art store to buy some new paint.

I rode away under sunny skies in my yellow two-piece bathing suit with black and white checkered Vans on my feet, sporting teased up hair and homemade earrings made of crystals. Listening to *Dark Side of the Moon* on my Walkman, I felt the wind tickling my skin as I entered the intersection of Electric and Westminster Avenues. Carried away by the female vocal solo from "The Great Gig in the Sky," I may have had my eyes closed when there was an abrupt impact propelling me up and over the car, landing on my face and right knee in the middle of the street while the cowardly driver sped away.

In the split second that it took to disrupt the course of my lighthearted day, time ceased to exist, and to my amazement, something supernatural alleviated any pain that would be expected from such a horrible accident. In fact, the experience was mystical, providing my mind with perfect clarity. I was alert, invisible, and slowly floating higher and higher into the air.

People who got close enough covered their faces in horror at the sight of a young woman with a torn-up face, who was as still as a corpse, so vulnerable in her yellow bathing suit. Yet, I felt exhilarated.

My mind was functioning just as it always did. I was still Alika Jones—the same girl I had always been, except that I felt a freedom which filled me with wonder. Detached from my physical self, I felt no pain whatsoever. That slender, tan body on the street wasn't me at all, just a form for me to inhabit. As I rose in the air ever so slowly, I felt no regret, no resentment, no anger, no sadness. Instead, I was excited about whatever was going to happen next. All around me, there was a feeling of safety, love, and peace. I didn't even think of the word *death*.

I had always enjoyed adventure. I often turned a simple event into something fun—perhaps to the point of dangerous. I was a thrill seeker. But this experience didn't have an adventurous, "on the edge" feeling. I was already over the edge, an untethered and pure soul. After being in that lofty space, I started to feel that I wasn't alone. I couldn't see anyone or anything other than the world below me, but I felt a presence. And not just a singular presence, but a unified multi-presence of sorts.

Then a message entered my consciousness, whispering, "Not now. It's not your time."

The "voice," for lack of a better term, said this with a gentle kindness I had never known before. Tranquility consumed me. Without a doubt, I had just experienced a conscious contact with a great power. And even more so, it *loved* me.

Soon, I awoke in my body without having had a chance to say goodbye to the mysterious presence. When I opened my eyes, the crowd that had gathered around me pulled back in shock.

"She's alive!"

The onlookers were stunned as they started to ask me questions.

"Can you hear me?"

"What's your name?"

"Don't worry, help is on the way."

"Can I call someone for you?"

I couldn't talk. My face had been ripped open at the mouth, right through my cheek, exposing more of my teeth than anyone cared to see. My skin was peeled back on the right side of my forehead revealing my skull, and blood colored my complexion. Despite this, my eyes were wide open, taking in the scene. I blinked, trying to clear the blood from my eyes. The onlookers panicked, but still I was calm, and amazed to find I was still experiencing zero physical pain. I felt protected, as if that presence were still with me.

Then the paramedics arrived, and I vaguely remember being lifted onto a gurney and into an ambulance. I must have blacked out while riding to the hospital, because the next thing I remember was being in the emergency room with a doctor flashing a light in my face. I still didn't feel any pain.

I remember my mother—who never left the San Fernando Valley if she could help it—recoiling and gasping as she lifted the gauze that covered my face. *Do I look that bad?* I wondered.

"Can you hand me a mirror, Mom?"

When I looked at my reflection, I had to agree that I did look horrifying.

But I couldn't be bothered with the implications of disfigurement. In my tranquil state, it didn't seem important. The doctor told my mother that he had called a plastic surgeon from Beverly Hills to see if he could come over to help.

"Thank you," my mother said, "but I can't afford that."

Shaking his head, the doctor replied, "No need to worry. There are surgeons who will do pro bono work now and again. I know this man. He'll fix up your daughter's face, trust me."

I didn't wake up again until there were stitches across my face and a cast on my right leg, thigh to ankle. My kneecap had been shattered, so surgery was required to insert bolts, pins, and wires to hold it in place. Miraculously, there weren't any other serious injuries.

I healed in peace in my cozy apartment, reading books and listening to music by the sandy shore, swaying on my crutches as I watched the sunset. It was a good place to be. I had some money in the bank from tips I had saved from the restaurant where I worked, and all I needed was nearby: friends who could keep me company, coffee shops where I could read my poetry at open mic nights, and a local lover who still cuddled my banged-up body. And when I was lucky enough to be caressed over my stitches, I would drift away in my mind and wonder why I wasn't finished here on Earth.

Was it to see myself from a new perspective—perhaps as God sees me?

I had caught a glimpse of something awe-inspiring that nearly welcomed me into a blissful eternity. I settled on the presumption that I still had a lot to learn, and for me that came the hard way. But that glimpse—that peek into what is next—kept me seeking something I didn't understand but didn't fear. Each day while I healed, I would meditate on that element of humanity which is simply a part of the whole, a spoke in a wheel that was constantly turning.

Dario

Chapter 2

Living by the beach felt glorious. The near-death experience from my bike accident was a transcendent event that I carried with me as I continued to heal. I wrote in my journal furiously and continued my art classes at Santa Monica College while privately philosophizing about the existence of a supreme being. I read Rumi, Rilke, and Kahlil Gibran, wrote poetry, and wondered about my purpose in life.

What would I call the force that spared me from death?

When the stitches were taken out of my face, you could hardly tell I had been in a life-threatening accident. That generous plastic surgeon had almost completely restored my face, aside from a faint scar on my forehead and on the side of my lip. The important thing was that I had survived. And survival mode was where my mind stayed, stuck for years to come, before I understood what a miracle it was to have made conscious contact with the divine. I was vulnerable to the dark allure in the world. It would grab me, and I would go with it willingly.

Seven months later, when the cast was taken off, I abandoned my crutches and began working again at the Broadway Bar and Grill, a hot spot on the 3rd Street Promenade. Black pants, white shirt, and black tie in place, I served customers with flair and earned big tips. I begged for extra shifts to save money that I would need to visit Kari, my best friend from high school, who was in college spending a year in Kenya. I had always wanted to travel abroad, and I thought that Africa would be an excellent place to start. I had almost saved enough money for the trip when I met Dario.

I spotted him outside smoking a cigarette before he strolled into the restaurant with swagger. I persuaded the hostess to seat him and his group of friends in my section. Carrying an acoustic guitar on his back, wearing a black velvet jacket and vintage shoes, he possessed a magnetic charisma that had me mesmerized. I couldn't stop staring at him with his dark hair, dark eyes, prominent cheekbones, and full lips.

I was shaking with excitement, my heart racing. It was obvious to the whole party that I was captivated with this strange man. The jolly group teased me a bit when, in an alluring accent, he introduced himself as Dario Moretti, shaking my hand with his fingertips as if he were a king.

"*Ciao, Bella,*" he said stripping my uniform off with his eyes.

What was it that had me excited but scared simultaneously? I felt like I had walked into a sexy vampire novel and couldn't resist the dark charms dangling before me. Was I willing to go down that mysterious and dangerous road? For lack of better judgement, I was.

They all drank beers on tap and ate the highest priced items on the menu. Dario was precise when he ordered a pescatarian meal, insisting that there be no butter, or anything with dairy. He talked with his friends about his hometown near Rome. I had never met an authentic Italian before, and it made me tingle between my thighs. When I laid the $350 check on the table there was an awkward moment when Dario didn't pay his share of the bill after coming up with only loose change in his pockets and his friends had to cover him. I intentionally ignored the red flag waving. He flattered me and we flirted with each other all evening. Instead of leaving with his friends, he waited at the bar until my shift was over and escorted me home.

As soon as I opened the door to my apartment, he pressed me against the wall and carefully took off my uniform, caressing me all over, exhilarating my skin, and nibbling my neck. I was left submissive and malleable in his arms. I was his.

His physique was flawless, so in between our moments of passion, I broke out my Polaroid camera and took numerous nude photos of him. Using my coveted black and white film, the instant photos looked soft on the edges, sensuous, surreal. Resembling classic Italian sculpture, Dario was like a real-life *David*, and he had no qualms about posing for me. We barely slept that night, and when the dawn shone its light from below the horizon, Dario picked up his guitar. A sensuous buzz rolled over my skin leaving me heated under the sheets.

Amazed by the strange chords he played in the stillness of the morning; I was swept into a dreamy place that only music could take me. Dissonant, deep tones lingered in the air filling my basement apartment when shoes started to shuffle along the boardwalk.

"I've never heard anyone play like you before," I said, faintly, as if coming out of a daze. "Would you make the soundtrack for my slideshow? I'm almost done shooting the final project. Your music is perfect," I said, leaning in for a kiss.

"I'll make you the best fucking soundtrack you've ever heard, *amore*," he said as he leaned me back and smothered my small breasts with kisses.

The next day, at my friend's studio down the street, Dario recorded a three-minute guitar instrumental in one take. The track had open chords and unique rhythms as he slapped the front of his guitar and vocalized what sounded like a jungle at night. Dario's music was mesmerizing, and I just knew he was born to be a rock star. I was utterly infatuated.

Photography had become my passion. I won first place with a self-portrait in the art exhibit at school that year. In it, I peered into a shattered mirror I had found on the pavement with a mural behind me depicting a waterscape, while the sunset created a warm glow on my face. My hand reached into the broken mirror as my long, newly auburn hair blew in the wind and my eyes searched for an answer to the perplexing question of life's purpose.

But for my final project, I had a beautiful mixed-race model from my neighborhood, who had long dark hair and beautiful curved eyes. The slide show portrayed her internal struggle of being lost in the world as I shot dramatic close-ups under streetlights along the boardwalk. I directed her emotional expressions as she emerged from shadows and ultimately lifted herself from the water in my bathtub as if she was being reborn. Gratified, I was pleased with my show. The images experimented with lighting, composition, and perspective, complemented by Dario's intriguing music that heightened the swell of drama portrayed on my model's face. It was a smashing success and the pinnacle of my semester.

By that time, Dario had moved in with me. He insisted that I have my hair cut into a shoulder-length bob like Faye Dunaway in *Bonnie and Clyde*. He also picked out my clothes each morning, dressing me like a doll in my long flowy skirts pushed down around my hips exposing my torso. It was fun to be his model dressing up in vintage minidresses, or wide-legged black satin pants with a golden glittery halter top as we strutted down the Venice boardwalk like the new "It Couple." Dario had an entitled air about him, as if people were fortunate to have him in their presence. He made me feel important too, often swooping me up in his arms and carrying me along the beach while showering me with kisses.

It was the summer of 1989, and a perfect day at the beach, when Dario whispered in my ear, "*Amore*, come with me to Italy."

Exhilarated by the suggestion, I felt torn.

"But I'm saving money to meet my best friend in Kenya."

Determined to go to Italy in November for his brother's wedding, he asked how much money I had saved up. When I said that I had about two thousand dollars, he told me about a scam he often used to double his money. After buying physical travelers checks, he would sign them with a thick rubber band around his arm, hidden under his sleeve, which would produce a slightly shaky signature emulating a forgery. Then he would cash the checks, report them stolen, and get his full amount refunded from American Express.

"You can only do it once," he said, "and I've already done it. So have all my friends in New York. It's easy, *amore*. None of us have ever gotten caught."

I was reluctant at first, the red flags were multiplying, but after Dario persisted and I rationalized that it wouldn't be hurting anybody, I finally agreed to do it. When my $2,000 became $4,000, Dario and I made international plans.

While we drank beer and threw back shots in a Hollywood bar to celebrate, he said, "Marry me, *amore*."

Without hesitating, I said, "Yes!" and after hours of drinking, we decided to elope in Big Sur.

Dario had always wanted to drive along Highway 101 to witness for himself the stunning coastline that he had seen so many times in iconic films. As we drove, we marveled at the beauty of California and the Pacific Ocean, stopping several times along the way to make love on a blanket laid on the sand. The weather was perfect with a cool breeze wafting through the windows and clear sunny skies lighting up the sparkling ripples across the expansive blue mass of saltwater.

We ascended the mountain curling along the shore witnessing the rocky terrain where the waves crashed with excitement against the boulders surrounded by smooth shards of jade. After passing through the winding roads along the extraordinary cliffs, we checked into the historic Deetjen's Big Sur Inn, made famous by Henry Miller and Jack Kerouac, and hit a bar in town.

We were drinking martinis when we mentioned to Dave the bartender that we were getting married and needed an officiant.

"You're in luck," he said. "I'm ordained as a minister by the Universal Life Church. I'll marry the two of you."

"*Buono!*" Dario shouted. "You're a perfect minister. *Saluti!*"

He told us to go to the courthouse in Monterey the next day.

"You'll need a witness, so I can bring my girlfriend if that's okay with you. And for you two lovebirds I'll do it for 100 bucks," Dave said. "Next round is on the house!"

The next evening, on the edge of a cliff, Dario, resplendent in his black velvet jacket and I, in a short, vintage, red lace dress and red platform heels, gave each other simple bands made of local jade we had found in a souvenir shop. It didn't occur to us that the rings were thin and frail and sure to crack one day. After we said, "I do," we slid on the rings and sealed our vows with a long French kiss. As we embraced, a strong wind blew off my netted pillbox hat, sending it into the sea— perhaps symbolizing that I had lost my mind. As our hair wildly flapped about, the bartender took pictures of us with my 35-millimeter camera while the sun set over the ocean. As the headlights from my car created a warm glow around our beaming faces, the lighting and landscape made our wedding photos seem magical.

How apropos it was that a bartender married us, for it soon became apparent that it wasn't me that Dario couldn't live without, it was alcohol. He drank more than anyone else I have ever known, including me. I was a happy drunk, but he would eventually become a monster. When we got back to our hotel room that night, I thought it was time to make love and seal our vows, but after we ran through another bottle of vodka he started mumbling in Italian and without warning, walloped me across the face, knocking me to the ground.

As I sat up, confused and crying on the floor, he lay on the bed and lit a cigarette. He had displayed so much fury with that one slap. I was scared, but I just sat there stunned. I was transfixed, drunk, and wondered why he was so angry as my face stung. Not thinking of myself, I wanted to help *him*. My new husband was a tortured soul. The red flags had become crimson.

The next morning, Dario didn't remember what had happened, and I rationalized that it was a one-time thing. Our heavy drinking was indicative that we were both emotional escape artists. I had met my match. I resolved that my new husband had undisclosed trauma at a young age—our pain connected us with a glutinous bond. Spending our honeymoon roaming through the redwood forest, leaning back over fallen trees, naked, watching clouds pass, I abandoned myself to the unknown.

We decided to drive cross-country to New York, where he'd show me his old stomping grounds, and catch a flight to Italy from there. Before leaving California, we registered our marriage in the county clerk's office, then swung back down to Los Angeles to stop by my mother's house and tell her the news. She and her new husband Ron were surprised when I showed up married. My mother disliked Dario from the start; his narcissism and pompousness irritated her. But I didn't pay attention to any of that because unknowingly I was riding a manic wave, totally unaware that I was in a world of my own, oblivious of the reality surrounding me. I was a hot air balloon ready for takeoff.

Ten minutes into our stay, Dario said to my mother, "Don't you have a beer or something?"

"No, we don't have any alcohol," my mom replied.

"I'm going to need something to get me through this boring visit," he said under his breath before getting up.

Offended, my mother shot back, "You could just leave."

As I got up to go with Dario, my mom pulled me aside, "Alika, stay here. I want to talk to you."

"I'll be right back. I'm going to the liquor store," Dario said. "Then we should go."

And out the front door he went.

"What have you done, marrying this guy?" my mother snapped, "And without telling me? What's gotten into you?"

"You wouldn't believe what a great musician he is, Mom. He's gonna be a star," I told her. "We're going to travel through Europe. You know it's always been my dream to travel."

I should have trusted her eyes, which were literally pleading with me not to go. She rarely told me what to do or gave me advice, but this time she desperately wanted me to take her seriously because she knew in her gut what kind of man Dario was. I didn't care and I craved the excitement, refusing to listen to reason. As in the child's game Truth or Dare, I tended to always choose dare—avoiding the truth.

When Dario pulled up in front of the house, I gave my mom and Ron big hugs before getting in the car.

"I love you!" I shouted out the window before we drove away. "I promise I'll write."

That was the last time I saw my sweet mother for years. I was hell-bent on living on the wild side, and nothing was going to hold us back from the wreckage we would create. Grabbing a handful of cassette tapes and my boombox, we filled my car with gas, headed east, and left nearly everything in my apartment behind. I packed only a few dresses, underwear, my passport, a toothbrush and toothpaste, soap, a hairbrush, and my camera, all of which fit in a foot-long, bone-colored, hard-shelled cosmetic case from the 1950s.

The lights and towering skyscrapers of New York City excited me. Dario wanted me to meet his old bandmates, plus prices to Europe were cheaper from the east coast, so we began our adventure by crossing the country.

My faded blue Toyota was already stressed from the trip through the mountains, but it was in the desert heat of Arizona, at over 110 degrees, that it broke down. A mechanic at a small repair shop in the middle of nowhere offered to trade it for a 1976 gold convertible

Cadillac Eldorado if we could come up with an additional $1,500. It was sleek, and we were mesmerized, wanting to travel in style. We needed all the cash we had to buy gas and our airline tickets to Europe, but I had a credit card that my mother had given me for emergencies years ago. Dario insisted this *was* an emergency and convinced me that this is what credit cards were for. As I handed the card over to the mechanic, I could feel my morals disintegrate, knowing that I would not be the one to receive the bill. Since we maxed the card out, I threw it away, along with my mother's trust.

Cruising down Route 66 in the Cadillac, we crossed deserts, hills, and valleys watching lightning storms in the distance. We blasted our Public Enemy, Joni Mitchell, and Miles Davis cassette tapes with the top down and our arms out waving in the wind. It was blazing hot in New Mexico, the Texas panhandle, and through Oklahoma. As the desert receded into the background, we drove past farms and cattle ranches. The cool nights were a relief while we slept in the roomy back seat, spooning our skinny bodies under the stars.

We survived mainly on coffee and cigarettes. Dario insisted that I eat like him. I craved a traditional American breakfast with sausage links, hash browns, buttered toast, and eggs over-easy at the diners along the road, but he wouldn't have it. As I did with all his other commands, I obeyed. Dario talked about all the great Japanese, Indian, and Thai restaurants we would eat in when we got to New York City, saving his stomach for his favorite pescatarian meals. He would often talk about how eating meat was disgusting. It wasn't that he was an animal lover, he just had a propensity to hate certain things with a passion. In particular, he hated working any job unrelated to his music because he thought he was above it all. Dario thought of himself as entitled to be served and worshipped because of his superior talent and wit. Because I was lacking self-worth, I saw it as the confidence I wished I had.

Approaching the outskirts of St. Louis, we thought we had hit a milestone and would surely roll into New York within a couple of days when the Cadillac overheated. Since the ignition had failed and smoke rose from the engine, we felt we had no choice but to abandon it on the side of the road. Hitchhiking the rest of the way, we carried only the guitar and my bone-colored case. Catching rides from truckers, we eventually made it to the Big Apple via the subway once we got close enough.

It turned out that Dario had a drug of choice: heroin. It was with his friends in the Lower East Side where he taught me to smoke the brown powder by putting it on tinfoil, lighting it from underneath, and sucking in the smoke from above. An immediate flush of calm soothed my soul. All sense of time disappeared as my worries and concerns vanished. Skin felt exhilarating. Anything soft was a delight. Unlike the effect of alcohol, Dario's anger disintegrated when we were high, and we felt like we had caught a piece of heaven joining us into one being, a feeling I wanted to last forever.

After days and days of being in a haze, his friends ran out of dope, and Dario persuaded me to sell my camera for a handful of little powder-filled baggies. That crimson flag had become the color of dried blood. I was numb to my sense of self, without a spine to hold me up. Then we got high for a week with his old bandmates while we waited for our flight to Germany, the cheapest country to fly to in Europe.

Our flight was leaving the next day, but because the heroin ran out and Dario got into an argument with his friends, we needed to find somewhere else to crash. When I called my mother to ask for money, of course she chewed me out about the credit card bill and refused to send me anything. Aching in body and mind, I felt terrible. But she did tell me that Kalani, my best childhood friend, had moved to New York City and gave me her address.

Unannounced, Dario and I knocked at her door.

"Kalani! It's me. Alika!"

When she cracked open the door and peeked out, she said, "Hi, Alika. Your mom told me what's going on. *You* can come in, but he can't."

I was shocked, and Dario was pissed. I felt split in half.

"He's my husband, Kalani. We got married."

"I know. I'm sorry. But he can't come in."

I didn't know what to do.

"Kalani, please! We just need a place for one night. We're leaving New York tomorrow, so it's not a big deal."

"You can come in," she said. "I want to talk to you."

By now, Dario was fuming.

"I thought you said she was a good friend," he sneered. "She seems like a bitch!"

Her warm brown eyes pulled me inside, and Kalani double locked the door behind us. Kalani looked beautiful with her long, soft blonde hair and healthy, graceful face. She was a sensible person, always strong for me when I was troubled.

"Alika," she said, "You must leave this guy. I don't trust him for a minute. Stay with me. Just get away from him!"

"I can't. He is my husband, Kalani. Please let us sleep over just for tonight. We leave for Berlin tomorrow."

"You don't look good, Alika. You look sick. You need to get off the drugs. Stay here and clean up. Please don't go to Germany with him. Dario can take care of himself. He's just using you!"

"We're in love!" I pleaded, my voicing cracking with emotion as I looked down at my dusty feet in flimsy flip-flops. "I must stay with him. I'm going to meet his family in Italy. Now they're my family too. I love you Kalani, but I can't leave him, I'm married."

With a defeated look on her face, Kalani said, "I love you, Alika. I'll always be here when you're done with this guy."

As Dario and I walked away from her apartment building, I felt riddled with rejection. I knew she was right. Kalani was always right. But I was committed to being Dario's wife. I believed things would get better once Dario made it in the music business. He was so talented and bound to be a star.

Dario called some of his other friends, but those bridges had already been burned, so we stayed in a flea-bitten room that only cost thirty bucks a night, where drug addicts slept until their high wore off. We curled up, shaking, feeling sick, and I wondered how my life had come to this. The mattress was dingy and smelled of sweat—stained with jagged orange rings. The blanket was musty, and the floors hadn't been cleaned for what seemed like a century. The brick walls had been tagged with spray paint, the windows so dirty with a grey film that nothing could be seen outside of this tiny room. It felt like the lobby on the way to hell. This would be over tomorrow, I told myself. We would catch our flight and be free from the grime on a clean, shiny airplane, eat a vegetarian meal and drink unlimited alcohol. I told myself everything would be okay, everything would change tomorrow, before throwing up into the garbage can.

Box of Buttons

Chapter 3

Deep memories cross my mind now and again. They are the fabric of my early identity, bound by threads that still hold me together. My earliest fond memory was of our playground. It was a field around the corner from Grandma's house, where people would abandon their old, rusted cars and semi-trucks. It was where my cousins, sister, and I imagined rolling down the highway and talking on CB radios. With deep voices, we would say, "Ten-four, good buddy," and "Roger that." Those were the only truckers' terms we knew from TV, but they made us feel like we were the real thing. Blowing our pretend horns with a big, bellowing sound and bouncing on the springy seats kept us engaged in our exciting adventures as we crossed the country. It was then, at four years old, that the travel bug bit me.

Before we started kindergarten, my four cousins, my sister Tess, and I were just old enough to wander the neighborhood. Kids rode their bikes in the streets and bounced freely on their pogo sticks. Pacoima, on the outskirts of Los Angeles, was a place where most kids were born to immigrant parents from Latin America. My Grandma, Virginia, had entered the United States from Mexico as a young woman and settled down in the 1950s to raise her four children.

In the late '60s, after her children married and had children of their own, Grandma provided that critical childcare that her sons and daughters needed to work full-time jobs. Her second son, Ricardo, was the man I called dad.

Grace, my mother, was just a child when her parents died. Her oldest brother Bill, a Navy officer who was stationed in Hawaii during the Vietnam War, assumed custody of my mother and her three sisters, moving them from Florida to live on a military base. That's where my teenage mom met a handsome sailor named Danny Jones. I always imagined that I was conceived on a beautiful, secluded Hawaiian beach, impassioned by young love. Now, I think it may not have been so romantic, because Bill, who was Danny's superior officer, forced him to marry my mother after she became pregnant, unwilling as he was. My parents gave me the Hawaiian name Alika, which means "truthful" and a French middle name, Cheri, which means "dear" or "darling." Are we given names that we are meant to live up to?

I was a year old wearing a Hawaiian printed dress and a bow taped onto my fuzzy head when Danny was discharged from the Navy in 1969. Paradise, its sacred air fragrant with flowers and sea salt, yet thick with resentment for the white men, was left behind as the three of us departed from Honolulu. When we landed in Los Angeles, dry heat replaced the tropical mist, and shoe scuffles on concrete replaced our bare feet in the warm sand. We moved in with Danny's parents in the San Fernando Valley, but after a few months, Danny said he was going outside to smoke a cigarette and took off in the new Mustang that my mother had bought for him with her inheritance money. My father drove away like a horse set free from captivity and never returned, leaving my mother to fend for herself in a large and strange city. She started working as a cashier at a large grocery chain when she met Ricardo, the store manager. My mother was a stunning young woman: blonde, kind, wholesome, and naïve. Those blue eyes had his heart racing. Awestruck with her movie star beauty and gentle nature, Ricardo proposed to her even though she already had me *and* was pregnant with my sister.

My first memories are at Ricardo's mother's house, where we lived. Grandma Virginia kept her humble home impeccably clean; her pride in it was undeniable. I remember her waking us kids up early in the morning and brushing the sheets with a broken broom made of straw. It had just enough of a handle for her weathered hand to hold as she swept the sleep away and patted our behinds out of bed. She then vacuumed the whole house before making us breakfast, which was often homemade flour tortillas that she would toss like Frisbees onto the breakfast table. We would lather the tortillas with butter and sprinkle them with sugar before rolling them up like thin burritos. We'd bite into the tips as the warm butter dripped from the bottom and down our wrists and we would lick it up, sure not to miss a drop. The sugar rush had us bouncing on the springy vinyl cushions on either side of the table, which made us feel like we were on a seesaw. The breakfast nook looked like a booth right out of a restaurant, and the cushions glowed with sparkles. After breakfast, we would rush outside to play in an old, gutted camper in the backyard where we would pretend to be grownups on vacation, fighting over who got to be the "driver."

After a long day of playing pretend, barefoot in the backyard, Grandma would insist on giving us baths. I always felt so clean after Grandma bathed me in the kitchen sink, until I got too tall, and I would share the tub with my sister. She would thoroughly scrub me with a rough washcloth and an abundance of suds that piled up like fluffy hills. We would blow bubbles at each other and laugh before she'd dry me off with a huge towel and douse me in baby powder. She would pat me with the powder until thin clouds of it floated in the air and I looked like I was covered with snow, though I had no frame of reference other than Christmas cartoons.

I only knew the dry dirt and tumbleweeds in the field across the street. There were giant cement cylinders scattered throughout the field, where Tess, my cousins and I would play hide-and-seek. Though it appeared to adults like a neglected empty lot, in the eyes of a child it was a magical place full of danger and excitement, where we would bravely fend off the rattlesnakes with our rocks.

Without fail, we all went to the large Catholic church that had two tall bell towers on each side, which rang every Sunday. Grandma didn't drive in the early '70s, so we would walk to church six long blocks away. The weather in Pacoima was usually very hot, with the sun bearing down like a weight. The resonating sound of the church bells called for us to scurry in and begin Mass.

As we entered, footsteps and the echoing sounds of kneelers hitting the hard surface of the floor reverberated throughout the huge church. The drone of a Latin chant from the priest sounded archaic yet drew us into the present moment. Hundreds of candles glowed along the walls under a dozen statues of saints. Coins were tossed in a metal cup before each candle was lit, especially under the Virgin Mary, generating more echoes under the high, arched ceiling.

The first thing we did was dip our fingers into the holy water held in a receptacle that looked to me like a birdbath. We would bow with a bent knee and touch our foreheads, then our heart, then each shoulder in the shape of a cross—a ritual that made me feel connected to something I didn't understand. Grandma meant everything to me, and church was important to her, so I cherished every moment.

One thing I was able to grasp was the call and response from the priest to the congregation when he said, "Peace be with you," and hundreds of people would reply in unison, "And also with you." People would shake each other's hands, reaching over the pews as they repeated the phrase. Although a formality, this was a special moment of sharing peace, when adults I didn't know shook my little hand with a smile, and I shyly returned the gesture. The scents of their perfumes and colognes, fused with the burning incense, made me feel lightheaded.

After Mass, Grandma would take her flock of grandchildren to a Mexican bakery. I always chose *concha*, or sweet bread, with pink streaks of sugar across it. On our way home, we would go to a used toy store where wooden bins were filled with baby toys, dump trucks, stuffed animals, board games, bikes, Barbies, and practically any toy imaginable. Grandma would buy us dolls for a dime and handballs for a nickel. One time, she bought me a small Native American doll with braids and a faux leather dress adorned with fringe and a geometric design painted in faded greens and whites. I tilted her head back and forth so that she batted her tiny eyelashes. Because of her brown skin, she made me think of Grandma as a child.

When we arrived home, Grandma would change us into some play clothes and send us with our new toys into the backyard, where we would chase each other, pretending to be our favorite superheroes while she prepared lunch. I always had to be Wonder Woman, while my cousins would take turns being Superman, Aquaman, or Batman. My sister, Tess, would usually play the villain, an appropriate role for her as she would soon become the antithesis of my free-spirited nature and the main character of my living nightmare.

Whenever I wanted to be alone, I would go into Grandma's hall closet, where she kept her sewing supplies. There was a box of buttons that I used to play with for hours. There were buttons of all shapes, sizes, and colors. The metallic and wooden buttons, the plastic buttons, and the fabric-covered buttons gave me something to sort, something to organize, something to imagine personalities for. There were endless combinations, and the diversity stimulated my imagination. Plus, it was a nice break from playing Barbies and G.I. Joes with my cousins, who were all boys and rudely pretended that our dolls were humping. I sympathized with my Barbies who were violated before my eyes, pounded by a toy soldier.

I liked to sit cross-legged in the hallway, next to the AC vent where it was cool, and peer through my Viewfinder, fascinated by the slides that showed the Seven Wonders of the World, castles, and beautiful landscapes. I was entranced by those images, which lit up and switched to a new scene whenever I pushed the lever. The Viewfinder made me dream of going to faraway places. It was a window to the world that I didn't see on TV, which usually played cartoons in the morning and news at night.

Sometimes my grandfather, always aloof and hardly ever around, would watch *Wild Kingdom* while sitting on the floral sofa behind the coffee table with large glass grapes placed in the middle. My little hands would clasp those glass bulbs tightly and I'd look through them as a lion captured a gazelle and ripped it apart, exposing its insides. Watching the kill in Technicolor heightened the contrast of the blood that stained the lion's fur. Identifying with the prey—caught and devoured—I would cry for the gazelle. I felt powerless like her but didn't know why.

At times, my older cousin would dare us to go into the bathroom in the dark and play a game called "Bloody Mary." We would have to face the mirror and repeat "Bloody Mary, Bloody Mary, Bloody Mary," over, and over again, until we saw her ghost. It was frightening because we would see our own distorted reflection in the dark as our eyes adjusted, and fear made us look demonic. I didn't want to be considered a chicken, so I would do it. I think that image of the demon in the mirror stuck in my mind, and I became afraid that it was that image that people saw when they looked at me too closely.

Eventually, my mom, Tess, and I moved in with Ricardo, who had bought a yellow house with white trim nearby in the San Fernando Valley. Ricardo had dark hair with a pronounced forehead, a thick mustache, and sideburns. He was on trend with '70s fashion, often wearing printed button-down shirts with big collars and fitted pants with a thick leather belt. He listened to popular music, wearing his bulging headphones to tune out the rest of us, drinking six-packs of Budweiser while reclining in a giant bean bag chair smoking Tareytons. The red-and-white labels on the beer cans and the cigarette packs always matched. After drinking for a few hours, he would throw things like plates that crashed against the wall as my mom cried, and I would retreat to the hallway and watch.

Whatever demons he had haunting him found an outlet whenever he was drunk and would assault me with degrading insults.

"You're stupid!" He'd say, "You'll never amount to anything!"

He would laugh whenever I talked about my dreams of traveling the world.

"Who do you think you are? Someone special?"

The struggle to accomplish my goals started there, and I wrestled with it for decades. His harsh words crushed my spirit almost daily. Being so young, I absorbed whatever my dad said about me. I felt a sense of worthlessness swirling around inside my innocent brain, and those filthy lies became my truth.

Tess was still going to Grandma's house while I was at kindergarten. My babysitter, Wanda, would often pick me up after school while my parents worked. She was a teenager from the neighborhood with long sandy hair, freckles, and a leather purse with dangling fringe that I liked to touch as we walked. Wanda often took me with her to her friends' houses after school instead of taking me directly home. I vividly remember a wild pool party where everyone was drinking, smoking, and skinny dipping. A muscular teenage boy lifted me onto his shoulders in the pool and my clothes got all wet. I wanted to grow up fast and be just like all of them—happy, free, and having fun.

But the oppression of alcoholism ruined everything.

As the confrontations with Ricardo worsened, my mother filed for divorce. My mom, Tess, and I temporarily stayed with a friend of hers while the separation was finalized. I remember Ricardo visiting at bedtime once, and sitting on the side of my bed as he sang the song, "Did You Happen to See the Most Beautiful Girl in the World?" My dad's serenade made me long for a sincere and healthy connection with him. At first, I hoped that he was singing to me—that I was his most beautiful girl. Then I realized that he had my mother in mind. It was my mother who walked out on him, she was the one he loved and needed, not me. It never would be me.

Eventually, my mother was able to buy a small, neglected house for $26,000 in the flats of Encino, a neighborhood in the Valley where many rich and famous people lived in the hills, most notably Michael Jackson and the Jackson family. The little house was a fixer upper, but it was hers. The weeds in the backyard were so overgrown that they towered above our heads as Tess and I played tag and I begged my mother to never cut them down because we thought of them as a wild jungle. There was a malformed tree with bulbous shapes on the trunk that Tess and I named the "Boobie Tree," which stood next to a rusted swing set. The infestation of cockroaches was extreme, but we grew accustomed to them scurrying away when we opened a cabinet door in the kitchen, or whenever they blatantly walked across the TV screen. The living room carpet looked like moss, I thought, with varying shades of green. We acquired a curved mustard yellow couch, velvet and voluptuous. The dense wooden coffee table had compartments for my mom's *Cosmopolitan* magazines, and the bookshelf held our 8-track stereo and huge twin speakers. The only books the shelves ever held were the row of large encyclopedias my mother eventually bought from a traveling salesman. They provided all the information in the world.

My mother, who was a resourceful and responsible woman, set out to raise Tess and me on her own, with her union job as a cashier. It was her first and only job, which she held for thirty-five years. Mom often rang up Mrs. Jackson's groceries, which was always a full cart load to feed her large family, bringing to light the humanity of the King of Pop and his brothers and sisters sitting around a large dining room table.

I remember ironing my mother's uniform before she started off for work while she rolled hot curlers in her hair. The smell of the warm fabric and steam heating my face felt like a ritual as the cloth flattened beneath the iron. She would hurry over with her blonde curls bouncing on her shoulders as I proudly handed her the dress, perfectly pressed, and she would thank me with her sweet smile as bright blue shadow covered her eyelids and tan pantyhose hugged her legs, the smell of the freshly ironed uniform lingering even after she fled out the door.

Sometimes, Ricardo would come over just to punish me and Tess when we got into fights and my mom didn't know what to do with us. We dreaded when he would call us each into our bedrooms alone with him. I was first as I was the oldest, and with his thick leather belt in hand, he told me to take off my shorts and panties. Crying, wearing only my yellow T-shirt that had iron-on magenta letters that said "Boogie," I obeyed while he laughed at my tears.

"I haven't even hit you yet!" he said, amused.

Bending me over his knees, he would spank me with his belt on my bare bottom. Stiffened up like a plank, I stopped crying as the belt made its marks. Over time, I felt something inside me harden from the damage of being exposed and mocked, which to me, was far worse than the lashings.

"There," he would say with an accomplished look on his face. "That wasn't so bad. Was it?"

Did Mom even realize what he was doing?

"Fighting" was the usual cause of these punishments. Typically, a little sister is not known for being the root of violence in a family, but Tess was a mysterious case. At a very young age, she became overwhelmed with rage and would attack my mother and me like a maniac. She looked like my sister with the same soft, light brown hair and blue eyes, but she didn't feel like one. Almost every day, she would jump me, even in front of my friends. She was little but surprisingly strong, knocking me to the ground, scratching my arms until they bled, pinning me down and spitting in my face, laughing like a lunatic. I tried not to hurt her when I fought back but I learned early on that self-defense was critical for survival.

Tess would speak in deep voices as she pulled my mother down by the hair and kicked her, hissing obscenities.

"Fuck you, bitch, for bringing me into this world!"

Once to defend my mom, I punched Tess in the stomach hard enough to knock the wind out of her, to the point that she started to turn blue. After that, I never hit her again, afraid that I might kill her. In family counseling, Tess would sit in the corner silently with a maniacal look on her face, amused by our displays of distress. My mother and I had no idea what to do, how to help her or ourselves. This went on for years.

To afford living in Los Angeles, my mother worked overtime every week, leaving me to clean up after Tess's destruction. My little sister would fly through the house like a tornado, tearing everything off the shelves and out of the drawers, leaving carnage in her wake. Not wanting my mom to come home to the wreckage after a long day at work, I would clean up the mess while my sister watched and laughed. I restacked the *Cosmopolitan* magazines, organizing them with my favorites like Farrah Fawcett on top, dreaming that I might be on the cover myself one day with a smile like hers on my face. Instead of reading books for kids, I read articles about makeup and beauty and how to please a man.

My only solace was spending time with my best friend, Kalani. We connected in second grade and were practically inseparable after learning that we both had Hawaiian names. Because my name meant Truthful and hers meant Heavens, we naturally had a precious bond. Kalani had long blonde hair, warm brown eyes, and fine facial features, in contrast to my wavy, shoulder-length brown hair, blue eyes and bangs. We were both tall for our age and skinny and had so few clothes that we shared T-shirts with each other to instantly produce variety in our wardrobe. As latchkey kids, we were free to roam as we pleased, roller skating to the local park and all around the neighborhood because it just didn't matter when we went home. We started the Pinky Tuscadero Club. Pinky was Fonzie's girlfriend from *Happy Days*. She was tough and didn't put up with Fonzie's shenanigans, while still being smart, witty, and beautiful. She had her own gang, and we wanted to be part of it. We agreed to wear something pink every day, even if we'd have to share a pair of socks.

We played records and danced to our heart's delight, taking turns pretending to be the male and female roles in love song duets. Thankfully, I had a lock on my bedroom door, so my sister couldn't bother us as we danced in front of the mirror and blasted the soundtrack from *Grease* and our favorite Donna Summer hits. Kalani and I dressed in matching Halloween costumes every year as vagabonds, aliens, or gypsies, unaware that we were portraying the outcasts we felt like inside. Kalani was my refuge. She made me feel valued, like I belonged in the world.

Going to her house was especially fun for me. Because her father was in the theater business, artists and actors were often gathered there singing and playing piano. Her house had skylights, dogs, plants, and big pillows strewn throughout the living room to sit on during parties. But Kalani didn't have a mom, like I did, and her dad was always so busy that we both felt a missing component in our lives. Our friendship gave us both what we really needed: love, trust, and togetherness.

When I wasn't with Kalani, I busied myself with work. I was a very industrious kid, mowing lawns for five dollars a pop, packing, then delivering items for the Avon lady, and operating my own aluminum can recycling business. The employees where my mom worked played baseball games, competing against other stores, and the beer cans I collected at their games were a goldmine. I would take home large black trash bags full of cans on my bicycle after stomping them flat so I could fit as many as possible in the bags. Sometimes they would get stuck on my shoe, curving around my heels, and I would walk around for fun as if I had high heels on. By the time I was twelve, I had a newspaper route. I woke up before dawn and went to the nearby 7-Eleven to buy powdered donuts and chocolate milk, which I devoured while folding up the pile of papers left for me on the sidewalk. Then, I tossed them onto porches from the bags hanging on my trusty bicycle before heading off to school. I used the money to buy '70s pop records I heard on the AM radio. My mom had only a few 8-track tapes: Barry Manilow, Supertramp, Chicago, Neil Diamond, and Helen Reddy, which I nearly wore out. But when

Saturday Night Fever hit the scene, my mom bought the tape, and the Bee Gees became the soundtrack for doing chores. My mom and I would clean the whole house together, "Staying Alive" day by day.

My greatest source of inspiration was the YMCA summer camp at Big Bear Mountain—Camp Round Meadow, which I attended year after year. It was there that I learned what peace and harmony felt like as the hippie counselors sang folk songs around the campfires at night. The shade of tall pine trees, their thick gnarled bark, the piles of dry needles, and the cones I kicked around connected me to the earth. I especially loved the group activities, including hikes, early morning polar bear swims, performing skits at night, and playing tag in the forest. Hidden in the boulders, I shared my first kiss with a counselor in training. David, with his long, wavy blonde hair, was in middle school—that made it even more exciting. Fellow campers gave each other friendship ties that we fastened onto our camp bandanas and wore loosely around our necks. The atmosphere of the mountains, with its fresh air and seclusion, had a way of creating bonds that we just didn't experience in the city.

To pay for the camp fees, I would sell chocolate bars and cans of peanuts for the YMCA in front of the grocery store where my mom worked. I was an outrageous salesperson and would go to any lengths to capture the attention of potential customers. I would dance, sing, jump up and down, compliment, coerce, joke around, and give away small bottles of water to entice interest. Every summer, I earned enough money for both my sister and me to attend Camp Round Meadow.

I felt extreme gratification helping my mother with an expense she couldn't afford while also getting what I wanted: a connection to nature, people, and a release from the hum of the city traffic.

It was always a thrill to see Grandma at holiday dinners at my aunt's house. I'll never forget the warm smell of her skin. She always welcomed me with wide arms, calling me *"Mi hija,"* making me feel special as I put makeup on her and gave her funny hairdos while my aunts were cooking. She had moved to a nice trailer park near the coast after Grandpa died. We all learned, after his death, that Grandpa had kept a secret second family in another city not far away. It was no wonder we rarely saw him.

I would also see Ricardo on Thanksgiving and other major holidays. He had remarried and now had two small boys of his own. Grandma's family basically adopted my mother, sister, and me after the divorce, probably because my mom was the sweetest woman alive. All her sisters were on the east coast, and she had no other living relatives. But I didn't know all that. This was the only family I knew.

I was nine years old when I learned Ricardo was not my biological father and my world spun in the other direction. He and my mother sat us down on the couch to tell us the news.

"I'm not really your dad," Ricardo said to both of us. He had on his work uniform, as did my mother who was sitting next to him looking afraid and unequipped to handle big life events. "You have a father, named Danny, who wants to meet you."

My mother waited silently, anticipating how we would react.

Tess stormed out of the room.

"You're not my dad?" I asked, thoroughly confused, with tears beginning to fall down my face. I felt betrayed and upset that I had been lied to all these years. But something clicked. It was no wonder I thought he didn't love me.

Danny, a handsome stranger with a slender build, who looked a lot like me with blue eyes and nice teeth, lived about an hour away near the airport in a small apartment with his pregnant wife. He picked me and Tess up on a Saturday morning. It was awkward. We were all nervous and barely talked while playing cards around the coffee table. Later, we ate bologna sandwiches and potato chips for dinner, listening to the airplanes pass overhead, and then watched sitcoms before Tess and I fell asleep on the thin mattress from the sofa bed in the living room. Sunday morning was downright uncomfortable when Danny called in to a Christian evangelical program on TV, wanting Tess and me to talk to someone on the phone about being saved.

"Do y'all accept Jesus Christ as yer lord 'n' savior?" a woman on the other end of the line asked me with a thick Southern accent.

I looked hesitantly over at Danny, who was staring at Tess and me, obviously urging us to say yes. I wanted him to like me, and there seemed to be no other way out of this.

When I said, "Yes," Danny jumped up and down, waving his arms in the air.

I wanted so much to be accepted and adored by my father, which seemed unlikely, as he was constantly distracted by his new wife. She seemed to wear a permanent scowl, appearing threatened by me and my sister. It was no wonder that even though I was now saved, I still didn't feel safe. And Danny did not come back to pick us up the following weekend, nor any weekend after that. A strange mixture of sadness and relief swirled inside. Was having a dad more trouble than it was worth?

Fourth grade was a big year for me—King Tut, *Star Wars*, sign language, new grandparents, and homegrown corn cobs were new experiences that propelled me into my 10th year of life. By entering an essay contest, I won the trip to the Los Angeles County Museum of Art to see the King Tut exhibit. All the gold shining through the thick Plexiglass casings was fascinating. When I saw the iconic death mask, I thought of how much this boy king was honored. I was amazed that he was only a 10-year-old kid like me when he ruled a nation, rejuvenating the love of the people that had been tainted by his father. I supposed even boy kings had daddy issues.

It was 1978 and Star Wars had just come out. I only needed five quarters to see the movie, and Kalani and I saw it over and over again. Enthralled that I was chosen to play Princess Leia in a class skit, I got to say, "Obi-Wan Kenobi, you are our only hope." Saying that line made me think that hope was precious, so I hung on to it and put it in the pocket of my heart. Turns out Luke Skywalker had his own unique daddy issues as well. This motif, well played out in script and song, resonates for so many. I was just one in a billion over the course of time.

I also learned the American Sign Language alphabet from my teacher's assistant, Mr. Goodman. He was a kind, deaf man who took roll call by spelling out our names with his hands. Kalani was in my class, so we sat next to each other, spelling out secret messages in sign language while giggling all day about our teacher, Ms. Ricci, who had a thick New York accent and wiry salt and pepper hair. Her peach-colored lipstick was usually smeared on her front teeth and the skin hanging from her upper arms jiggled as she snapped her fingers trying to get the class's attention. Kalani and I would sign jokes about her and talk about the cute boys in our class with silent speed and clarity when we were under our desks during earthquake drills. The joy never ended with Kalani. We were forever friends, inextricably bonded by love and laughter.

On the last day of school and ready for summer, I carried home some ears of corn that my class had grown in the school garden. Just as I was shucking the corn in the kitchen, there was a knock on the door. When I opened it, I found a smiling middle-aged woman.

"Hello, Alika. I'm Kate, Danny's mom. I'm your grandmother."

I was stunned, unsure what to say.

"Hello" came out of my mouth. "Do you want to come in?"

"Yes, please. I hope you don't mind me dropping by. Danny gave me your address. I've wanted to meet you for ages. I haven't seen you since you were a baby."

Kate's smile was intense and unsettling. Her teeth were yellow, and she smelled like cigarettes.

"My mom isn't home from work yet," I said as she sat down on the couch. "Do you want to see my corn?"

Just then, Tess peeked into the living room from the hallway.

"You must be Tess," Kate said. "I'm your grandma. Me and your grandfather, Burl, live not too far away in Ojai. I'd love it if you came to visit this summer."

When Tess didn't reply, I broke the awkward silence.

"I'll tell my mom you came by," I said, nervously fiddling with the silky threads under the husks of my corn. "She won't be home for a few hours."

"Here's my phone number," Kate said, as she handed me a piece of paper. "Have Grace give me a call. I guess I'll get going now. It sure is nice to see you girls. Don't forget to have your mother call me."

As I closed the door behind her, I was intrigued by the thought that there might be, not one, but *two* grandmas to love. When I told my mom about Kate, she agreed to let me and Tess visit her the following weekend, and I felt the hope in my heart begin to grow.

Kate and Burl lived in a modest home surrounded by trees and hills about an hour and a half away. When I met my grandfather, I couldn't help but stare at his hands. He was missing all his fingers, which made his thumbs look huge.

"Whatcha lookin' at?" he asked hoarsely, pointing his right thumb directly at me. "I lost 'em in the war. Bet your bottom dollar I can do just about anything with my hands that you can." He took a drag from the cigarette he was holding in his nubs. "I built the shed in the back. Wanna see it? We have a pool table and lots of card games to teach ya. Ever play poker?"

"No," I coughed, feeling like I was going to choke on the smoke in the air.

"Let's go," he said, picking up his beer can.

"Burl," Kate called from across the room, "you take them to play some games. I'm gonna start some supper. Have you girls ever had chicken fried steak?"

"No," my sister and I said in unison.

"Well, you're in for a treat," Kate replied, squashing the tip of her cigarette in a nearby ashtray before putting on an apron. "Go on now, git. Burl's got lotsa tricks up his sleeve."

We had a lot of fun playing pool and card games together in the shed, which felt more like a clubhouse to me with a refrigerator filled with soda, a transistor radio playing '70s pop, and curtains that looked cheerful and homemade. And true to Kate's word, her chicken fried steak was delicious! The fried crunchy coating held a hamburger patty and was smothered with thick, creamy country gravy that also lathered the mashed potatoes and lined the edges of fresh corn on the cob, which tasted almost as good as the ears I brought home from school.

After dinner, when we were all sitting around the living room, they told us they were from Oklahoma and that Kate was half-Cherokee. That made me proud. I had learned in school about Native Americans, and I always wanted to be like them and to live in harmony with the Earth.

Throughout the whole stay, Tess hardly said a word, which puzzled Kate and Burl. They asked me questions about her that I didn't know how to answer while she sat on the couch, twirling her long stringy brown hair, frowning, and mumbling to herself. However, on our next visit a couple weeks later, they finally witnessed her rage.

It happened when we were all watching a show on TV together called *CHIPs*, which starred a white, blonde-haired, highway patrolman and his dark-haired, brown-skinned partner. It was a lighthearted series, but Burl exhibited a bigotry I had never encountered before. As he pointed his enormous thumbs at the TV and banged his fists on the table, he started furiously yelling, "These fucking Mexicans are taking over the country!" He then rambled on and on about things my 10-year-old mind couldn't comprehend.

Kate was laughing nervously as she sat in her chair, smoking one cigarette after another, while my sister and I shrank into the couch. It was so uncomfortable that we eventually went outside, where my sister lost control.

Tess started chasing me around with that maniacal look in her eyes, arms raised in attack mode. Desperate to protect myself, I ran to the shed in the backyard and slammed the door shut. I pressed my body against the door with all my might as she pounded herself against the other side, trying to get in. My newfound grandparents tried to calm her down, but she swung her fists at them wildly until Burl grabbed her and held her firmly against his chest, while Kate called my mom.

I could feel this new world crumbling down—card games and homemade dinners disappearing like a puzzle coming undone. We would return to frozen meals heated up in the oven and served in their thin, flat aluminum containers, watching my mom sleep on the couch after another exhausting day at work while the laugh tracks roared throughout the silly sitcoms on TV, and no one to talk to at home because Tess mostly talked to herself.

Before Mom arrived, Kate pulled me aside and said, "You're welcome to come back anytime, Alika. But your sister should stay back home. It'll be best."

But I doubted we'd be back; Tess and I were a package deal. Plus, I felt conflicted. Kate was nice enough, but Burl scared me with his confounding hatred. Did I even want to come back? After all, Virginia was a Mexican woman, my beloved grandma who had more love in her boney pinky finger than anyone else I knew. How could anyone hate her? It was apparent that my family, exemplified by Tess and Burl, was stricken with mental illness.

Could something be wrong with me too?

America in the Dust

Chapter 4

It was November of 1989, and the Berlin Wall had just fallen when Dario and I caught our flight. In those days, passengers could smoke cigarettes on the plane and were served free alcohol. Dario and I laughed loudly with the other drunk passengers, obnoxiously excited about crossing the Atlantic after our last treacherous days in New York City.

"*Amore*, you need to learn some Italian. My sister, or *sorella*, speaks pretty good English. But my parents, not at all. *Buongiorno* is good morning, of course, *buona notte* is good night. How are you, *come stai?* Let's hear your accent."

I repeated all the phrases imitating Dario's inflections and developed an ease on my tongue. I enjoyed speaking in Italian. I found it much easier to pronounce than French. It was fun learning the lyrics to Dario's favorite Pino Daniele song and singing them together.

"My friends are going to love hearing this! You got it down, *Bella! Ti amo, tesoro mio.* You are my treasure."

"I love you too, *Bello*."

Arriving in Berlin was exhilarating. The city was alive with people from all over the world, celebrating in the streets. Artists, musicians, and performers of all kinds formed parades by day and inhabited abandoned buildings in what had been East Berlin by night. I was fascinated by the ornate buildings and relished the ambiance of a truly international cluster of people who took over the war-torn part of the city with the fervor of freedom.

That's when Dario and I started performing together. He taught me his songs and how to harmonize with him, and we quickly became a tight duet. I was infatuated with Dario and his music—or rather, I was possessed by some deep unnerving force that I thought was love. I was determined to do whatever was necessary for him to achieve his dream of stardom. My personal dreams of success had fallen like The Wall. While the others around me experienced the fresh feeling of liberation, taking pieces of rubble from the wall like souvenirs, I experienced a subconscious crumbling of my sense of self and immersed myself in being Dario's wife.

Despite this, busking in the streets gave me a new joy. Swept up by the music and harmonies, I danced to the rhythm and gave it my all. With Dario being a great songwriter, we always captured the attention of passers-by, and they often put money in our hat appreciating our talents and passion. I felt one with the magic of music; that unifying power of song connected us with the audience as we naturally entertained the crowds. Dario was on fire playing his guitar, my body moving with flair, when we met Lina. She was a beautiful and tall young woman, a free spirit who joined me dancing in the city square. We had fun twirling each other, ending our improvised routine with a dip in the center of the crowd.

Graciously, she invited us to sleep at her apartment on the west side. Relieved not to be sleeping on the floor of an old, abandoned building, we spooned on her soft couch and awoke to her offering us hot coffee and pastries. To our astonishment, Lina undressed and poured beer over her body standing on a raised tub next to the sink in her kitchen. She doused her head and washed her hair while we sipped the hot coffee from frail teacups, and we marveled at the sight of her perfect form raised up on the platform. It was like art in motion. I couldn't resist her cheerful smile and delightful demeanor when she took my hand and invited me to join her. The smell of warm hops tickled my nose and the beer sliding off my skin felt silky as we giggled and washed each other. Lina and Europe had me mesmerized. Adventure waited around every corner as she took us to dance clubs at night and then to the lake in the countryside in the morning. Nudity at the lake was commonplace. The transparent energy of a hundred naked bodies of all ages and sizes dipping in and out of the water opened my eyes to a kind of acceptance of the human body that I had never considered before—a far cry from the judgmental air in America I had been used to.

The wedding we had traveled all this way for was soon approaching so it was time to thank Lina and say goodbye. After hitchhiking through Germany and Switzerland, we eventually arrived at Dario's hometown of Chieti, east of Rome on the Adriatic coast. Chieti was nestled in the hills, beautiful with ancient buildings, stone pathways, and a variety of cathedrals capturing different historical eras. Dario didn't think much of it, but I was taking in the charm while soaking in the depth of history.

When we stopped in the city square, he met some childhood friends who greeted us with open arms. We all smoked cigarettes while Dario told them stories about America. I felt celebrated as his friends were impressed that he had acquired an American wife. Dario had taught me some Italian phrases on the plane, which I was beginning to string together like "pleased to meet you," and "do you have a light?" I did my best to communicate with his friends and was happy to make them smile with my attempt at an Italian accent as this expressive language rolled off my tongue.

By the time we reached Dario's parents' apartment, we were starving. He had raved about his mother's cooking, and when we entered, I could smell the delicious aromas coming from the kitchen. His mother, Lucia, beamed when she saw me. She called me *figlia*, which is "daughter" in Italian, and then his father, Pietro, looked me up and down with suspicion. They didn't speak English, but Pietro proudly showed off the few words he did know and quickly warmed up to me as I eagerly spoke bits of Italian longing to win him over. Lucia, who was a kind woman with a constant smile, black hair, and plenty of cushion around her hips, kept an impeccably clean home, reminding me of Grandma. She often gave me warm hugs and pinched my cheeks. Pietro had a full head of silver hair and was a handsome, sharply dressed man, with an obvious arrogance about him. Dario's older sister, Gia, joined us on her lunch break from work. She was a beautiful woman, whose oval face resembled her mother's, with dark hair to her shoulders, shining brown eyes, and a tender spirit.

As we sat at the table in their tiny kitchen, drinking red wine, Lucia brought over a pasta dish with freshly picked tomatoes and black olives that gave a new meaning to the word *delicious*. After lunch, we sipped espresso, made from the two-tiered pot on the stove, and devoured Lucia's homemade pistachio cookies. I was ignited as everyone spoke with so much passion, but then Dario and his father began arguing about something I couldn't understand. Lucia cried, and Gia pleaded with them to stop. The flailing arms and the intensity of Pietro's anger was shocking. I realized that this aggressive pattern had haunted Dario's family for years. Pietro clearly disapproved of everything about his son, disregarded his musical talent, and was convinced that he was wasting his life. As Dario told me later, Pietro wanted him to get a "real job," like his older brother, Matteo, who had followed in his father's footsteps by joining the *Carabinieri*, the Italian paramilitary police.

After the fight, Gia drove Dario and me in her vintage Fiat to her home in the country. It was just outside of town, where she had a rustic garden and tomatoes drying on the balcony. It was obvious how close Gia and Dario were from the intimate way they spoke and embraced each other. I knew then that she was his most sacred love, and I could never measure up to her. Though I grew to love Gia, I felt small when compared to her. Her grace and beauty, her poise, and poetry of motion left me feeling "less than" and I knew Dario thought so too. I was scrappy, uncultured, and uneducated. I wondered what Dario saw in me. Was it my loyalty that was the clincher?

We had made it to Chieti just in time for Matteo's wedding that weekend, which was held in the beautiful courtyard of a Roman villa. The ancient stone walls and vines that clung to them had me swooning in the romance of it all. After vows between the bride and groom were sealed and the reception began, we all drank prosecco and toasted the couple with great cheer.

Dario prided himself on his ability to expose the ugly truth about people. Tonight, his target was Matteo's new wife, and he degraded her with insults in my ear. Her snobbish, "holier than thou" attitude rubbed Dario the wrong way. Perhaps as a mirror reflects our own image, Dario saw himself in her and didn't like it. In typical fashion, Dario drank more than his fair share of the free alcohol, and he and his brother, who appeared to hate each other, got into a huge argument that left the bride in tears. Mayhem ensued when Pietro got in the middle of it as Lucia wailed. There was an uproar and guests stood on their feet shouting in disapproval, insisting that Dario leave the reception immediately. Like a typical caricature of pissed off Italians, the scene became quite comical.

Gia and her husband, Niccolò, Dario, and I dashed out of the building as people started throwing things. After a short drive, we arrived at some ancient ruins which were deserted, apart from a large family of cats. With my red platform heels in hand, I ran barefoot as we all raced to see who could get to the top of the hill first. Exhilarated and drunk, we all laughed and howled at the waxing moon that lit up the sky and watched the silhouettes of cats creep by on walls surrounding the abandoned village until dawn broke over the horizon.

Constantly on the move like a shark, Dario longed to return to London, where he had lived prior to coming to the States. He felt that Italy was a backward country that didn't appreciate a cutting-edge musician like himself. As he said goodbye to Gia with tears in his eyes, he kissed her on the lips. His sister was the only person in his family who believed that he would become a rock star one day. She was his muse and confidante who never gave up hope.

With my bone-colored suitcase in one hand and my thumb stuck out on the other, I hitched us a ride while Dario smoked a cigarette out of sight. I was the lure who would catch the car, and then he would run up and persuade the driver to take us further north by speaking in Italian, and further on our trail, in French. As we got closer and closer to England, I felt the gooseflesh on my arms from the cold fast approaching, which would signify not only the changing weather, but the bitter future as well.

Wrong Turn

Chapter 5

During my 6th-grade graduation, in 1979, while my classmates and I were innocently dancing to Michael Jackson's "Off the Wall," I had no idea that my life was about to veer off track as the tune sweetly bounced along and I proudly swayed my hips to the beat. I was in the front row of the class and happy that my mom could see me wearing my best lightweight floor-length dress, which resembled a 1970s patchwork quilt. The lyrics of the hit song foreshadowed the seemingly endless "party" I was about to embark on. Living crazy *was* the only way.

After a summer of running barefoot with Kalani and the other neighborhood kids, racing to prove who was the fastest, we took the big leap into life as teenagers. We had squeezed out the last of our childhood days sharing bicycles and roller skates, records and funny dance moves, dime store candy and soda pop. Woefully, Kalani and her father prepared to move to North Hollywood before summer's end, which felt like the other side of the planet. My heart was broken when we enrolled into different middle schools, and I was left to sail in the sea of teens alone without a compass, in a rickety boat, and without a life jacket.

As I walked onto the campus of Sequoia Junior High School with a mixture of fear and excitement, big kids were filing into the main entryway wearing cool clothes, which made me realize that I needed to step up my game. If I didn't get some Jordache jeans and Chemin de Fer sailor pants, I would die! Being among these teenagers made me realize that being cool mattered, and that peer pressure, even subliminal, was a real thing.

Eventually I joined the kids who smoked Marlboro reds as we walked nearly two miles to school each morning. The shock of my first cigarette, repulsive as it was, gripped me nonetheless and left me wanting more. We would meet at the railroad tracks and tobacco evolved into marijuana. Being high and feeling the rush of a shift in body and mind had me hooked from the start. I liked feeling different, escaping my typical insecure thoughts when comparing myself to my peers, and relaxing into a peaceful bliss where almost everything was funny.

Like clockwork, we roared with laughter and taunted the middle-aged flasher who tore open his trench coat nearly every day when we reached the little league field on the way to school. The first naked man I had ever seen was near the playground in the park when I was in elementary school and my ball rolled into the bushes. He had his pants down and his hand on his stiff, red penis while he watched the children play. I was terrified and ran away leaving the ball behind, panicked, and never told anyone. But this man hiding out at the baseball fields by the railroad tracks was a joke. We gave him a name and called out "Harold" when we reached the bleachers. Without fail, that clown popped out from behind a shed near the batting cage, coat spread wide open exposing his scrawny nude body. He had a head of wild hair, and wore a perverted smile while silently standing on the other side of left field for about ten seconds before he ran away.

My mom was as strait-laced as they come, so there weren't any drugs in my house. However, many of my new 13-year-old friends stole pills, marijuana, booze, and cigarettes from their parents. They were the coolest kids in school, passing out pills like Black Beauties, Quaaludes, and Pink Hearts during class. Water bottles were not yet the norm, so we would sip the metallic tasting water from the communal fountain to swallow our pills and wait for the effect to carry us into euphoria. A group of us were slouching in our seats, writing notes to each other, and feeling our faces melt, when the math teacher, Mr. Lamb—who always wore corduroys and plaid shirts—called out, "Are all of you kids on drugs?"

Living crazy didn't stop when the school implemented a strict dress code, which wouldn't allow girls to dress too sexy. I wore Dolphin shorts like everyone else, but they were banned when the bottom crease of our exposed butt cheeks got out of control. It seemed like the more clothes they banned, the tighter our pants became and the more of our tummies we revealed.

It was December 8th, 1980, when news spread that John Lennon had been shot. Experiencing grief for the first time, I mourned with the world over this shocking and senseless murder. We all felt as though we knew John, he gave us so much of himself through song and spirit that even at thirteen years of age, I knew what he meant by "Imagine" and he made me feel that I wasn't alone in my dreams for a peaceful planet. Tears streamed out of my body, like all the water inside of me was pouring out. True sorrow flooded the world that day, and as the hours passed, I realized I didn't feel like a kid anymore.

That spring, on a typical scorching day in the Valley, a group of us were having a water fight after school when one of the girls said to me, "Hey, it looks like you sat in the dirt or somethin'."

Soaking wet from head to toe, I ran to the girls' bathroom and twisted my body around to inspect my rear end. To my surprise, the whole curve of my lavender Dittos was dark with blood. I rushed home as fast as I could, found my mom's tampons, and popped one in. With a deep, uncomfortable, pinched feeling, I entered womanhood by myself, without ever telling my mother that it had happened. I yearned to be an adult, but this made me feel even more vulnerable than before. I felt exposed as a woman, raw, and tender like a beating heart.

Ms. Dearmore was the first teacher who ever saw talent in me. Drama class changed my world when I learned that I was a born actor, who loved everything about performing—from memorizing lines, rehearsing, to working as part of a team. There was a freedom about becoming another character, connecting with the emotional bond of human nature. Two months into the class, she entered me in a citywide competition, where I performed a solo pantomime that I had written and choreographed myself. The skit portrayed a dream in which I lived in a magical world where I could eat anything I touched, consuming everything in sight, and it ended with me waking up and discovering that the dream wasn't real. I won first place in my category, but this fantasy world I created only foreshadowed my actual behavior as a teenager. I was obsessed with always wanting more and craved escape from normal life.

In the spring semester before graduation, Ms. Dearmore cast me as Professor Van Helsing in a school production of Count Dracula. Rehearsing every day after school, I took on the character and played the hero who slays the vampire. Eventually, I met my metaphorical vampire in the flesh and married him without a second thought. Many years later, I discovered that, like Van Helsing, I also could triumph over evil. Art, after all, imitates life, and like a mirror, life imitates art.

But it was one fateful day at the end of seventh grade, that the beginning stages of alcoholism reared its ugly head, and I got my first taste of self-sabotage. Why, the day before the opening night of the play, did I bring a stolen bottle of Jack Daniels to school? My brain said that it had to be me when there was a dare amongst us kids about who would be brave enough to steal a bottle of liquor from the grocery store. I had to be the one to prove to the gang that I too could contribute to the drugs and alcohol that we shared with each other. I thought that I needed to carry my weight, so I walked in and slipped that bottle into my backpack and cruised out of the store with my heart pounding, holding my breath while I hustled onto the school grounds. I gave my group of friends the combination to my locker, and we all took turns swigging down the whiskey between classes. When kids started falling in the hallways and throwing up all over their desks, it was all traced back to me. The principal had no tolerance for my behavior, and no matter how much I begged him to let me do the play, his mind was set. So, I was kicked out of school right before my debut as the lead performer.

The shame I felt when I saw Ms. Dearmore's face after she heard the news tore me to shreds. The disappointment in her deep brown eyes pierced my heart when she tilted down her head and said with her African American twang, "Alika, I hope one day you'll understand what the word integrity means."

I had never heard that word before and its meaning would be lost for decades.

I was transferred to Portola Junior High, which was south of Ventura Boulevard, where all the rich kids lived. Obviously, I was a misfit from the get-go. I pleaded with the new principal to put me in drama class. She did, but the production of *Grease* had already been cast, and the only place left for me was in the chorus. I was so jealous of Mandy Goldstein, who got to play opposite Tony Benducci, the cutest boy in school. After singing along to the soundtrack with Kalani for years, I was steaming. I knew that play by heart. Mandy looked nothing like Sandy, and I did—my hair was dyed blonde from my mom's Clairol Nice-n-Easy, while Mandy's full head of black hair and mouthful of braces made me cringe as I watched her rehearse. Mandy was so tall that she towered over Tony, who had the resemblance and the charisma to fit the role perfectly. Mandy was the best singer in school, but it didn't matter to my envious mind. Having to take the back seat and nurse my wounded ego was torture.

Portola was farther away from home than my previous school, so I had to take a public bus. Near the bus stop, there was a stretch of electrical towers bordered by a strip of high bushes where I would walk from the boulevard to reach campus. One day, a cocky boy named Adam started teasing me in a crude flirtatious way, daring me to go into the bushes with him. Because peer pressure was taunting me, and not wanting to seem prudish, I followed him. After pulling down his zipper and parting the opening in the center of his boxer briefs, he told me to get on my knees. When I did, the smell of tender sweaty skin pervaded my nostrils. He told me to open my mouth. There was already a tiny drop of cum on the tip of his penis that tasted salty when I licked it. But when I looked into his intense eyes, I remembered the man in the park as a child and lost my nerve. I didn't know what to do anyway.

I got up and hurried out to the clearing, his friends jeering at me as I scurried away to class, feeling dirty and humiliated. I avoided Adam by walking the long way to school and stayed away from him and his gang of friends on the quad, thankful none of them were in my classes.

Nearing the end of 9th grade, I had shaken off the incident in the bushes and developed my first crush on Malcolm Solias. He was one of the rich kids and the best musician in school. I was mesmerized when he played electric guitar in drama class and watched him as he hung his arm over his girlfriend so casually, as if his life was golden. He was smart, came from a solid family, had lots of friends, and was talented. With his long, curly brown hair and olive skin, I thought he was so cool and sexy. But I remained in the back seat, watching the year I graduated from middle school roll by, without a band of friends to get into trouble with, feeling lonely, and standing on stage in the shadows of the spotlight.

High and Mighty

Chapter 6

Busking in between rides to buy cigarettes, espresso, fruit, and dark chocolate, Dario and I arrived at the English Channel, where we had to wait for the ferry. The marvel of the 31.5-mile Channel Tunnel had not yet been completed, so we boarded the boat and played our music as I passed our hat, gathering francs and pounds all the way to London.

Dario had an uncanny ability to memorize phone numbers, which came in handy at a time when there were no cell phones or social media, and email was barely a thing. As soon as we arrived in the city, he phoned an old friend. Emile lived near Portobello Road in a row house jammed with French artists and musicians who needed a place to sleep. Staying there was a communal experience. Since everyone there pooled their resources—whether those were food, tea, or the crucial spliffs, Dario and I contributed the sounds of our music.

Winter was unbearable in London, making busking outside nearly impossible. I had to start working, so I got a job as a waitress at the American Bistro near Soho in the center of the great metropolitan city. I knew my way around a restaurant and made decent tips, but one day a friend—also our drug dealer—came rushing in and flagged me down.

"Someone is trying to sell your passports in the pub on Portobello!" Jemma exclaimed out of breath.

"What?" I was shocked. "Who?"

"I don't know, some shady Italian guy. I was having a pint when he walked up to me at the bar, asking if I was interested in American and Italian passports for a hundred quid each. Thinking of you two, I asked to see them, and they were *yours*!"

"Fuck! What'd you say?"

I wondered if someone had broken into the flat.

"I told him I would buy them, and I'd meet him back there in an hour, cuz I had to get the money. What do you want to do?"

"Have you seen Dario?"

"No, I looked around for him, but no luck. I'm just glad I knew where you work."

"Thank you, Jemma! Okay, wait for me outside. I need to wrap things up here. Just hold on."

After pissing off the manager of the restaurant for leaving in the middle of a shift, I walked out with Jemma as our breath appeared like smoke in the cold night air.

"Let's swing by your house first. I have an idea."

The "Heroin House," where she lived, always had junkies lying on the sofas and sprawled out on the floor. As we rushed in, I made an announcement.

"I will buy a baggie for each of you guys if you come help me. I need you to get up *now* and follow me to the pub."

Three of them popped up, and one said, "What do you need?"

"Protection," I said in all seriousness, and rushed out with Jemma and the three junkies in tow.

My plan was to have Jemma meet the thief in the pub and lure him outside, where we would confront him and demand that he hand over the passports. When we arrived, I peeked in through the crowd and saw Jemma approaching a guy we had befriended the night before at Emile's house. Massimo. He and Dario had been laughing all night, making fun of their hometowns in Italy.

I breezed by the bar and put on my acting skills.

"Massimo! *Bello!* Funny to run into you," I said as I squeezed between him and Jemma. "Let me buy you a pint."

Smiling as I peered directly into his eyes, I witnessed the shock as his nerves fried.

"*Ciao*, Alika," he said, stunned. "*No, grazie.* I was just leaving."

Looking at Jemma, he tilted his head toward the door.

"What's the rush? Stay," I said knowingly. "But hey, if you have to go, I'll just see you later on at the flat, right?"

"*Si. Si.* Later. See you there," he said, squirming under his coat.

The desperation in a thief's eyes always tells a deeper story, but I didn't have time for pity. No one was going to steal the only valuable thing I possessed. My passport gave me a ticket to see the world, and I had just gotten started. As Jemma and Massimo walked outside, I scanned the room for the junkies and motioned for them to follow me.

It was a Friday night, so Portobello Road was bustling with people drinking pints and smoking cigarettes. I told the guys to approach Massimo as he was making his deal with Jemma and bully him into getting the passports back, but Massimo refused to give them up, so they started pushing him around, and one guy slapped him hard on the face.

Massimo thought he was being robbed when I broke through the junkies and shoved him against the wall.

"You fucker! How dare you!" I snapped. "Give me our passports, or I'll have these guys beat the shit outta you!"

Frantic, Massimo held the passports above his head, attempting to rip them apart.

"Fuck you!" he screamed.

Looking up at the little books I planned to fill with international stamps, I swiped the passports from his hands just as one of the junkies smacked him on the side of the head.

"You idiot!" I shouted, waving my guys off. "You better get the fuck out of town, Massimo, 'cause if I ever see you again…"

As my little gang walked away, Massimo was shouting insults in Italian at the top of his lungs, while the drunken crowd laughed and gawked at him.

Through word-of-mouth, Dario caught wind of what happened and came running to the "Heroin House" out of breath.

"*Amore!* Are you okay? What happened?"

After taking a long drag, I breathed out the smoke. Now high, relaxed, and proud of myself, I said, "No worries. We handled it. Want a hit?"

Stomping on Teen Street

Chapter 7

There were days I explored the streets of London alone, and I would think of my past—the potential I squandered and the missed opportunities, all resulting in the endless rationalizations that swarmed in my head. Drugs and alcohol stunted my growth, but I didn't realize it at the time. I was feral, and being an undiagnosed bipolar woman and an addict, I was always looking for the next high to escape my insecurities.

I recalled finally finding my tribe at Birmingham High School in 1983. The school's campus was swarming with kids that came from a wide variety of backgrounds. Some were bussed in from Black neighborhoods in Los Angeles, some came from the rich areas of Encino Hills, driving Mercedes Benzes and BMWs, and some came from the flats of the valley who walked to school like me.

I began hanging out with the punk rockers, dying my hair fire engine red, and dressing in creatively concocted thrift store fashion. I only pretended to like punk rock music just to fit in with the outcasts.

It was really an eclectic mix of classic rock and R&B oldies, '70s funk, disco, or new wave music that really got me dancing. After going to my first concert in junior high, I was addicted to live music. Hearing Journey play their hits with amplified power filling the large arena had me hooked. Throughout high school, when I couldn't afford a ticket, I'd find a way to sneak in by speedily slipping through the crowd past the bouncer, or through the back doors. Sometimes, I would hitchhike with my friends to the Los Angeles Forum to see hot tickets like Duran Duran, The Police, David Bowie, and Prince, before hitching a ride home, sometimes in a limo. I also loved going to grungy clubs downtown to see X, Jane's Addiction, Souxie and the Banshees, and the Red Hot Chili Peppers before they made it big. Music never ceased to thrill me, and I couldn't stop dancing once a tune started. An explosion of dance moves poured out of me; an endless eruption of energy laid bare on the dance floor every time I went out to the club, concert, or even at times, danced drunk on top of the bar.

The turning point of 10th grade was meeting my best friend Kari, bussed into the valley from the city, I thought she was the best dresser in school wearing her unique take on mod fashion. A stunning Black girl, Kari was intelligent, passionate, and fun. She was the first person since Kalani I could laugh with for days. We were in drama class together and were both passionate about human rights. We attended protests in the city, went to music festivals, and made speeches in sociology class together defending the Black Panther Party.

Sometimes Kari smuggled weed into school from the city. During lunch, she would buy an apple from the vending machine, carve a tunnel in it with a pen, and then use it as a pipe. Once, our friend Jacqueline joined us to smoke in the bushes and she had so much hairspray in her new wave hairdo that her bangs caught fire. That Aqua Net was powerful stuff. It defied gravity by holding mohawks straight up in the air and made '80s hair big and trendy. It was so effective that the fire hazard was worth the risk.

In the mornings, I would often spend so much time on my hair and makeup that I would miss the public bus and would end up hitchhiking to school. One day, when I was at the bus stop with my thumb out, who but Malcolm Solias stopped to give me a ride! After that, he offered to give me a ride every morning. We started dating in 10th grade and soon a friendship blossomed into love. It was when he invited me to his parents' beach house for the 4th of July that, after walking on the sand and holding hands, we kissed for the first time. As fireworks exploded in the sky, our kiss lit up the whole world. With our bodies tingling and our vision fuzzy, we felt a profound connection that deeply rooted our friendship into something romantic.

It was pure love, and we lost our virginity together. We would sneak into each other's bedroom windows late at night to make love, absorbed in the bliss of sexual exploration. Malcolm was tender and considerate, creative, and kind. But I couldn't protect this young love—I was a loose cannon, with too much pain and confusion inside. His parents knew it before I did. They never liked or trusted me with their precious boy, and rightly so. At times, Malcolm grew frustrated with me because of my flakiness, since I often ditched him for a night on the town with my girlfriends. When my birthday came around, he gave me a box of Corn Flakes wrapped up as a gift with a bow. When I unwrapped it, I saw that he had changed the label to read "Alika Flakes." I tried to hide the shame behind a weak smile, but I knew it was true.

Malcolm was adventurous but as straight as they come, so he was always the designated driver when we partied with his wild musician friends, a bunch of rich kids who always had expensive drugs. Acid, weed, and cocaine were all the rage, and it's a wonder how much tolerance we had. We would trip on acid at parties, at school, and at Grateful Dead shows. I was even thrown into the Disneyland jail once for joining the Electrical Parade when I was high and tripping out of my mind. But ironically, the best acid trip I ever had was on New Year's Eve in 1985 with my sister. By this time, Tess had ceased to be violent and was more like a recluse, so I dragged her into the car on a road trip to San Francisco with a bunch of other kids to celebrate the New Year. The Grateful Dead show was sold out, resulting in thousands of people camping and frolicking around the park outside the arena. Tess and I dropped a tab of acid that opened our hearts as if a slice of heaven had connected our souls. We laughed and cried, apologized to each other, and cherished each other's company as never before—or ever again. We got a peek that night into what life could be like outside of the confines of mental illness, when fear and anger disappear, and love rules the day. I saw the pure soul of my sister that night and mourned her when the wretched illness that plagued her would again take her prisoner.

The summer before my senior year, I participated in a three-day counselor training program for the YMCA camp in the mountains near Big Bear Lake, hoping to rekindle my love of camp from years past. That's when I met Jessica and her 21-year-old coke-dealing boyfriend, also in the training program. I came to learn that they were just on mountain getaway cost free. Instead of embracing the wholesome energy of the summer camp that I had cherished so much as a kid, the three of us snorted lines on boulders in the forest that whole weekend. Jessica, who was a year older than me, was a voluptuous young woman with wavy dark hair and sultry brown eyes that sparkled with excitement.

We both had troubled childhoods, and bonding with a girl as wild and wacky as I was comforted me. We could connect on an emotional level in ways that I couldn't with my high school friends, who generally came from healthy homes. Jessica and I took the Los Angeles club scene by storm, which in the mid-1980s was raging. We got jobs as go-go dancers at Power Tools, a hot club in downtown L.A. located in the ballroom of an old fancy hotel. Dressed like angels, devils, or whatever characters fit in with the theme of the night, we consumed free drinks and drugs *and* went home with hundreds of dollars in our pockets. I don't know how we survived the '80s with the abundance of free cocaine and the crazed nights out on the town. I was constantly lying to my mother about my whereabouts and sometimes didn't even know where I was when I woke up the next morning.

One day our friendship leveled up when we shared a tender kiss, and I realized that I loved Jessica. She sparked the fact that I wasn't exactly straight and that I was open to loving both men and women. At times, when she slept over at my house, we explored each other's bodies in my twin bed, under the covers, quietly, so no one could hear. We kept our sexuality a secret from our families and friends, but we explored our erotic fantasies by seducing older guys from the clubs together, engaging in *ménages à trois* at their homes, away from our high school lives.

Because of this, Malcolm and I broke up during our senior year and Jessica and I went to the prom together as a secret couple. Since she'd already earned her GED but never went to a prom, I arranged a single friend from my school to take her, while I took a sweet gay friend from drama class. We rented an old beat-up white limo from Rent-A-Wreck, dressed it up with streamers all over the outside, and hired a bartender buddy to be our chauffeur. There was no radio or tape player in the car, so we brought a huge boombox to blast mixed tapes from the front seat and stocked liquor in the back. Jessica and I designed our own '80s inspired metallic dresses and paid a seamstress from the local dry cleaner to make them for us. Mine was a shiny, silver, strapless minidress with detached sleeves that ended with poofy curves over my shoulders and had a train down to my calves. Jessica wore a long, gold, fitted strapless dress covered in black lace cinched at the waist. We looked amazing! It was prom night on a budget, but we made it work. Stealing kisses all dressed up in silver and gold, alone in the elevator at the Bonaventure Hotel, was the highlight of the night.

Starring each year in Birmingham High's big theatrical productions and participating in numerous statewide thespian competitions made me certain that I would become a famous actress after high school. I had no plans for college.

Malcolm would go on to a private art school because he had a serious interest in photography at a time when developing film in a darkroom was still magical. I often modeled for him when we were on good terms, although I didn't feel beautiful. Whenever he pointed the camera at me, it was so close that my feelings of unworthiness caused me to tense up. There was something different about a camera, like it was peering inside me, whereas on the stage, I felt open and free to express myself. I was like the film that Malcolm spent so much time developing in his darkroom—an opaque, blurry image in the process of being defined.

I was surprised when Birmingham let me graduate after spending so many days getting high at the beach instead of sitting in class. Somehow, I managed to maintain a "B" average by showing up for the tests. At the graduation ceremony, I wore a black robe and received a diploma, while passing out magic mushrooms to my friends in preparation for grad night. My mom was there with her new fiancé, Ron, who was also a lifelong employee at the same grocery store, and she looked proud of me. Had she only known that I had a bag of shrooms in my purse. Mom and Ron had been having a love affair for months before they broke the news that they intended to get married. I was happy for her; she had been alone for so long. He was kind and good for her, and the timing was perfect because I planned on moving out right after graduation.

Convinced that acting was the career for me, I joined the California Youth Theater, a troupe that consisted of kids from the Valley with big dreams. We created an original musical called *Tiff*, staging it at the Taper Two Theater. It was near the Hollywood Bowl, where I auditioned under those famous arches, facing the rows of seats that climbed up the hill. I felt I was destined for greatness, but as fate would have it, I mostly met a slew of perverted "producers" and "directors," who claimed to be part of the industry, lying through their teeth about how they were going to make me famous.

"You've got something special," they would say. "You have the 'it' factor."

I wanted nothing more than to believe them, but after locking me in rooms and making me choose between sex or ruined dreams, my hopes began to fade. *Tiff* wrapped, and the troupe fell apart after the director caught AIDS—which was ravaging Los Angeles at the time—so I gave up on the whole idea of becoming an actress, but deep inside I still yearned for the spotlight.

That summer, Jessica and I had a fight and parted ways. Something unclear happened, which stemmed from jealousy and insecurity causing our falling out. Too many lovers, too many drugs, and not enough sanity were our downfall. I wanted to move out of my mom's house and Malcolm wanted to reconcile our relationship, so we tried to live together. He had an apartment off campus near his college, and I bought some plants to liven it up. I named the tallest plant Robert in honor of the singer of Led Zeppelin. We enjoyed the feeling of adulting, showering together, and sleeping in the same bed night after night. But the symptoms of my then undiagnosed bipolar disorder started to ignite, and before long he would find me wandering the streets around the neighborhood unable to sleep during a manic episode. There were times when I would hide in a dark closet and cry for no apparent reason. I didn't understand what was happening, no one did, but I didn't want to find out. I just wanted to escape reality, and I couldn't control my alcoholism, my attraction to drugs, or my promiscuous nature.

Malcolm hung onto the hope that our relationship could work, but it was my infidelity that ruined us. It wasn't until decades later, when I got a grip on my mental illness and alcoholism, that I realized I was sorry that I had taken him for granted. I had missed an opportunity to experience a rare and beautiful love that could have lasted a lifetime, and instead was always chasing the next "high." Regrettably, I had to find a new place to live.

Luckily, Kalani and I found each other again and decided to become roommates. Through the grapevine, we heard about a mansion in Bel Air that was renting rooms, and we moved in, sharing a bed for only $300 a month. There was a mixture of tenants, including Playboy bunnies, models, and an English professor at UCLA. Charles, a real estate developer, owner of the mansion, and Hugh Hefner wannabe, wore a short robe every day and barely left the house. He threw large parties every weekend and Kalani and I were required to dress up and greet people at the door while checking them off the guest list.

At times, we joined the guests for after-parties at elite dance clubs. Once, I danced next to Prince while "Let's Go Crazy" played, which at the time felt like the highlight of my life. Since dancing to his music synchronized with my natural sensuality, I went all out on the dance floor in my high heels and black-and-white polka dot mini dress with long flared sleeves. I had seen his epic *Purple Rain* concert that year, masturbated to his music countless times, and just couldn't get enough of him. Everything felt right when I was in a club, so on this night, dancing next to Prince under disco lights, I was on top of the world.

At one of the parties, a modeling agent told me I should do some test shots and take modeling seriously. After the results from the shoot came back, he offered me a contract and said he would pay to have my dried-up, bleached hair shaved off, as well as plastic surgery to lift my slightly lazy eye. He said he had already secured me the cover of a European magazine and would pay me $10,000 up front. I was excited that someone believed I could be a professional model, and initially, I was ready to jump at the chance. But fear started to creep in, and I became reluctant to cut my hair off and get the surgery. Vain insecurity won the argument, and I declined.

On New Year's Eve, Kalani and I had the massive house all to ourselves after the last group of guests went to the Playboy mansion around the corner. Blasting Stevie Wonder, we rang in 1987, dancing freely around the living room that overlooked the lights of the city.

But after a few weeks, our stay there ended abruptly when Charles demanded that we join an orgy in his bedroom. Kalani refused and persuaded me to do the same. She was my sounding board and often held me back from getting too hedonistic. In fact, Kalani probably saved me from catching a venereal disease, or two. But after we moved on from the mansion, couch surfing and sleeping in my car for a bit, we parted ways because we just weren't compatible despite our deep friendship. Without her, I would have to navigate through rocky waters on my own.

I soon began juggling two jobs, one as a cocktail waitress at the Moustache Café on Melrose and the other as a cigar/cigarette girl at the Palm in Beverly Hills. For $350 a month, I found a charming studio apartment in Hollywood near Mann's Chinese Theater, so I was able to walk to work after my car died. Eventually, I bought a Ford Pinto for $200 from a junkyard that had a hole in the radiator, and I had to fill it with water frequently so it wouldn't blow up. I didn't even think about the danger.

That summer, I wondered if my grandparents Kate and Burl were still alive. Neither my mom nor I had their phone number, but I remembered where they lived so I headed over on my day off from work. When I showed up on their doorstep, Kate was happy to see me but informed me that Burl had died of cancer. When I asked about Danny, she said, "He lives in the shed in the back. He's working right now at a bar nearby. Wanna see him?"

Did I want to open that can of worms?

I did, so Kate drove me to Duke's Biker Bar and waited in the car, so I could surprise him. After passing a bunch of motorcycles on the way in, I sat alone on a barstool, wearing large sunglasses that covered half my face.

When Danny saw me, he slowly walked over from behind the bar.

"Well, hello," he said. "You must be new in these parts. What's your pleasure?"

"Vodka soda with a lime," I said, putting on a slightly British accent.

"Fancy," he said, scooping up some ice.

I wanted to spy on him to see what he was like, but it didn't take long before he started hitting on me, which made my body feel like it was burning up. Embarrassment has a way of generating internal heat.

"We don't have many young women as sexy as yourself around here," he said as he handed me the drink. "Where are you from?"

After squeezing the lime and taking a sip of my drink, I flinched. "Wow! You make them strong."

Slightly licking his lips, he said, "Well, I'd like to show ya around town, get to know ya."

I couldn't take it anymore, so I took off my sunglasses.

He stepped back. "Do I know you?"

"I'm your daughter," I said in my normal voice.

"Well, I'll be damned! Alika Cheri? I don't believe my eyes!"

He turned to a bunch of bikers at the other end of the bar. "Hey, guys!" he called. "This is my daughter!" Then, looking me in the eyes, he said with a smile, "The drinks are on the house."

I was on my second drink when Kate came in and sat down next to me. Danny gave her a can of Pabst Blue Ribbon which he knew she liked, the cheapest beer in America. The three of us planned to have dinner together that night. Kate would make her famous chicken fried steak.

I wanted to ask Danny why he was so happy to see me. In fact, I wanted to ask him a lot of things. To start, I wanted to know why he left when I was a baby. I wanted to ask him why he had stranded us in his parents' house back in 1969 with a lunatic of a father, who I later learned threatened to bomb the grocery store where my mom worked because she was dating a "Mexican." But it was Danny's sexual comments at dinner that crushed any hope I had of developing a relationship with him.

The reason he had left my mother, he said, was because she didn't like to give him head. I was disgusted by his crudeness. As he left the house later that night, he mounted his Harley and said that he was going on a date with a girl about my age.

With a wink, he said, "I hope she swallows."

Shocked, I had no words before he sped away.

As I drove back to Los Angeles, disappointed and sad, I could only think that I surely would have been molested as a child if I had grown up with Danny. I realized that it was best that he had left us.

When I stopped to refill the water in my radiator and blasted my Prince cassette tape, I suddenly felt the urge to masturbate. After finding a secluded cul-de-sac somewhere in the industrial area of

Oxnard and dreaming up a sexy scenario about Jessica, Malcolm, and me in bed together, I wondered if somehow my sexual addiction had been inherited.

Driving along Highway 101 catching peeks of the Pacific Ocean, I decided to move closer to the beach. My lease in Hollywood was almost up, and it was time for a change. Time to make some decisions, start taking classes at community college, and take up a new art form. I could feel the gravity of self-discovery heavy on my heart. Who was I anyway? Certainly, college would provide some clues. After all, whoever I was, my whole life was still ahead of me.

Powerless

Chapter 8

Life in London had begun to sour. Dario and I needed a change and we set our sights on Japan. We loved Japanese food and had heard many stories about how work came easily to foreign musicians. A friend of a friend had connections in Tokyo, so we made it a point to get to know her at her Japanese clothing shop, which was down an alley from Portobello Road.

When we got there, a cute young woman named Miko greeted us at the door. When she told us that she was the owner, Dario put on his charm, which quickly had her giggling at his compliments and laughing at his jokes. Dario always carried a guitar strapped to his back and she was impressed by the music we played for her. When we expressed our desire to visit Tokyo, she graciously said she would contact her friend, who was a director for music television there.

The thought of living and working in Japan was so exciting to us that we immediately started saving money for the tickets. We were making more quid busking down in the tunnels of the Tube in between my shifts at the restaurant. Rotating about a dozen original songs (Dario didn't do covers), we would sing until we had enough for food, cigarettes, and some booze. We stashed my restaurant pay tightly folded in our shoes for the plane tickets because there was nowhere else safe enough to hide it at Emile's house. However, our stay there ended abruptly when he kicked us out after another one of Dario's senseless, pint-fueled fights. Having nowhere else to go, we stayed at a squat, which was an abandoned house in Battersea, south of the Thames.

It was squalid. There was no electricity or hot water, and our fellow squatters were mainly petty thieves. Somehow the gas stove still worked, and there were a few pots and pans lying around the kitchen, so we could always boil some pasta and pour in a can of chickpeas, using the juice in the can as our pasta sauce. Because it was freezing at night, we often burned old wooden furniture in the fireplace to stay warm. We would toss in pieces of end tables and chairs that we didn't need and light the room so we could see to roll our spliffs with hashish while we sat on the floor.

My mania had me feeling that I was still on the adventure of a lifetime. In fact, I felt high even before we smoked. At a time when I still thought I was deeply in love, an otherworldly environment had saturated my brain, which made the spontaneous and downtrodden life we were living seem thrilling. Life was an adventure nonetheless, no matter how cold it got in wintertime.

Coby, a tall teenager with long, blonde, wavy hair and an angelic face, worked as a cook at the vegan café that Dario and I frequented in Covent Garden. A brilliant fine artist, he recently came to London from the far reaches of northern England to attend art school. However, he dropped out because he couldn't conform to the culture of the modern art scene at the university, which was more conceptual and negated his old-school approach to art. Since he was homeless, like us, we invited him to stay in our room at the squat. He delighted us with his humor and wit and became our only true friend in that stark and harsh metropolis. Because he was a few years younger than us, we took him under our wing. To stay warm, Dario and Coby often spooned me, like bookends, as we slept on an old mattress at night.

Because Dario and I were still short of the funds we needed to get to Japan, I answered a newspaper ad for a modeling job. It was high noon when I arrived at a typical English brick and mortar building in a working-class neighborhood in southeast London. As I naïvely walked into a cramped room, I was greeted by a middle-aged man who had photography equipment strewn all about.

Extending a handshake he said, "Hello, you must be Alika. I'm Thomas."

"Hello, Thomas. Mind if I have a seat? I've been walking miles in these darn heels. I didn't realize you were so far south."

"Of course," he said, showing me a clearing on the sofa. "Beer okay with you?"

"Yes, thank you," I said. "I am parched."

After chatting with him for a bit, I asked, "So, what is this audition for?"

"A magazine ad," he replied. "There's a new brand of moisturizer, and we're looking for a fresh face."

When I was nearing the end of my drink, I began to feel heavy and disoriented. Meanwhile, Thomas was just sitting calmly, eying me from his chair as he swirled the ice in his glass.

"I don't feel so good," I said. "I think I'd better go home."

But as I tried to get up, I fell to the floor. I soon realized that I couldn't feel my body. Losing all sense of physical control, I felt like a lump, paralyzed from the neck down. I could see and hear, but I couldn't move.

"Now, now, my dear," he said, "don't worry about a thing. It will wear off in no time."

Then he undressed me on the old, smelly carpet.

Frightened, I kept repeating "No, no! Please don't do this!"

But unaffected by my pleas, he pulled me by the arms, dragging me into a back room.

Thick black curtains hanging along the walls made it seem like we were entering a cave. There was a platform that looked like a stage, and a tripod with a video camera propped up in front of it. As he lifted my body up onto a padded bench, I began crying, powerless and ashamed that I had been so dumb. Then he turned on the spotlight and camera and proceeded to take off his pants.

Lying on my back, certain of my fate, I pleaded with him not to enter my vagina, telling him that I was married. He was leaning on his knees when I begged him to turn me over and do it in my backside.

"Oh, all right," he said, "have it your way."

As if I could have my way.

I could see us in a mirror that he had set up next to the camera. My torso was face down longways on the bench, and my head was hanging heavily over the end of it, with my rear end prominently raised up on a cushion. I watched the anguish on my face captured on tape.

"You're a pretty little lass," he said, slapping my numb ass.

I have no idea how long the torture lasted. There were gadgets, sex toys, and bits of costumes on and off me for hours. Time had stalled, and I was stuck in a nightmare that I couldn't get out of.

When he was done, he turned off the camera and said, "I'm going to get a nice price for these videos. You were great."

As I lay on my stomach helpless, alone in the room with the stark spotlight still in my face, I wondered what was next. After I heard the toilet flushing down the hall, he entered the room with my coat, dress and panties, flipped me over, and put my clothes on. He tossed me over his shoulder with my high heels hooked on his fingers and carried me to his car. It was parked outside in a dark alley, and he tossed me onto the back seat.

I was beginning to feel a sense of my body but was only able to barely lift my fingers. I couldn't see where he was driving, only the passing streetlights and the black sky out of the side window.

My legs were still dead weight, but my arms had an inkling of feeling coming back to them by the time the car had stopped. He opened the door behind my head and dragged me off the back seat by scooping me up from my armpits, placing me into the gutter at a bus stop.

As I lay against the curb, he bent over me and whispered in my ear, "If you so much as peep about this, you will be done in. I work with very dangerous people, so don't get any ideas, lass."

As he drove away, the smoke from his exhaust pipe blew into my face.

Alone in the dark, I began sobbing uncontrollably. Humiliation had a new meaning. Feeling like a piece of trash in the street, I just wanted to disappear.

Suddenly, I felt my legs twitch. I tried moving my arms to lift myself, but I could only place my hands on my chest. I became keenly aware of my chest rising and falling, and thought, I am still alive. Fighting gravity, I turned onto my side and waited, watching the cars roll past.

Behind me on the sidewalk, I heard footsteps scraping the cement.

"Shame some people just can't handle their liquor," someone said as they passed by.

In a quiet, defeated voice, I managed to say, "Help."

But no one heard me.

I passed out—I have no idea for how long. When I woke up, two lights were beaming in my face. As the bus roared away, someone shook me and said, "Love, this is no place to pass out. You could get yourself killed."

I was trying to gather my words as they lifted me out of the gutter and onto the pavement. Before I could respond, they walked away, muttering, "Damn drunks!"

Managing to gather some strength, I finally sat up. Noticing for the first time that I smelled of urine, I practically choked. Using the pole from the stop sign as leverage, I struggled to stand up. I was missing a shoe, and one did me no good, so I removed the other shoe and walked barefoot with great difficulty. My legs were still weak, and I fell again. Somehow, I eventually reached the pub across the street.

With mascara and snot streaming down my face, I wobbled inside. Leaning against the wall, I could see the bartender, but my cry for help was barely audible.

"We don't need the likes of you in here," he shouted. "Be on your way!"

I stumbled toward the bar but fell again before I could grab it.

"What'd I tell you? You've had enough. Get out of my bar!"

He picked me up under my arms and dragged me out the front door, where he lay me down on a bench.

"You just need to sleep it off. Watch yourself. It can be dangerous out here."

"I need help," I managed to say.

"That's right ain't it?" he said as he walked back inside.

Shortly afterward, a police car pulled up.

As two officers approached me, one said, "Shame, isn't it?"

The other officer nodded.

As they lifted me up and put me in the back seat of their car, the first one asked, "Where do you live, lass?"

Distraught and with a sunken heart, I just managed to say, "Battersea."

"What are you doing way out here? This is no neighborhood for a young lady like yourself to be getting sloshed alone. What happened to your shoes?"

I began crying silently. Everyone's assumptions that I was drunk had worn me down. I had no energy to explain what had just happened to me. I was still scared by his threat, and everything was still foggy. I just wanted to disappear. As we drove along the Thames, I thought about the countless women who had been raped throughout history. I was just one more.

"We're in Battersea, love," the officer behind the wheel said. "Where are we headed?"

"On the corner by the bridge," I said in a broken voice, finally able to string some words together.

"Is this it?" he asked.

"Yeah," I mumbled.

Pulling up to the house, the driver said, "Now you stay out of trouble all right?"

They lifted me up the front stairway and knocked on the door.

When Coby opened it, the second officer said, "Does she belong to you?"

"Yeah," Coby said, looking alarmed.

"Well, keep an eye on her. She's pissed drunk."

Muttering amongst themselves, they got back in their car and drove away.

Dario was furious.

"You bring the cops here?" He slapped me hard across the face. "How can you be so stupid?"

But then Coby got between us.

"Hold off!" he said.

I began to cry again, collapsing in Coby's arms.

"Where the hell have you been?" Dario shouted, as the rest of our roommates gathered around. "What the fuck happened? You had me worried! Where are your shoes?"

"I don't know," I mumbled.

"I don't know why you're such a fucking idiot!" Dario raged on. "Did you even get the job?"

"There was no job," I said, still in Coby's arms. "There was no fucking job!"

Tokyo Lights

Chapter 9

Walking among the skyscrapers of Shinjuku, in the center of Tokyo, I watched the snow elegantly drifting down before it melted on the pavement. Dario and I had traded one winter for another, but it didn't feel as cold as London. Tokyo was crowded, vibrant, glowing with digital billboards, and bustling like New York City, but without the human diversity or the grime. Businessmen looked like clones in their dark suits, each carrying a briefcase and wearing a tie, always in a hurry to get somewhere.

It was the tail end of 1990, when foreigners, or *gaijin*, were still a rare sight. We caught many glances from passersby, although eye contact among strangers was rare in Japan, it was because we were dressed ready for the stage. My shiny gold, lamé minidress disguised the horror my body had been through. Relocating helped me to bury the trauma in London and the thrill of a new place in the world distracted me from the emotional pain.

Miko was a woman of her word who referred us to her friends in the art scene. The first person we met was Asami, a beautiful young woman, quiet and thoughtful, who would be managing a big New Year's Eve event in a few weeks. Her fiancé, Hiro, was an energetic fellow with blue tips dyed into the edges of his hip haircut. He was the director at a music television station. Asami and Hiro both spoke English slowly, but well enough, and began to teach us key Japanese words and phrases that we would need to get around. *Kawaii*, or "cute," was a word I heard a million times when they introduced me to their colleagues. My pixie cut, big aqua eyes, and tall, thin body made me perfect for commercials and magazine ads.

Dario and I stayed in Asami and Hiro's small apartment, sleeping on thin floor mats in the living room that we rolled up each morning. Our hosts were fascinated by American and British music, which we listened to most evenings as we drank Japanese beer and Irish whiskey, sharing funny stories. We never came across drugs, so life felt fresh, exciting, and hopeful again.

On New Year's Eve, we rang in 1991, celebrated for being unusual, bold, and beautiful. Asami had booked me as a model in the fashion show and hired Dario to play guitar in the band. The scene was so hip and flooded with international artists that I felt like I was in the pocket of creativity. I accepted numerous jobs in video and print ads, jazzercising, posing, and dancing in music videos through Hiro's connections. I felt valued and Dario and I were able to afford expensive restaurants for the first time in our lives together. But after two months, our stay with our new friends came to an end. They wanted space for themselves since they were planning to get married soon and desired the quiet life that they had enjoyed before our arrival.

We had heard of several *gaijin* houses, a type of hostel, where people traveling from abroad roomed together. We found a nice one on the outskirts of the city center. Young people from all over Europe, Africa, and Australia shared common spaces: a gathering room with a television and stereo, a kitchen, and a bathroom with multiple stalls. Otherwise, we all rented out narrow individual spaces, the size of large closets, where we slept on customary thin mats.

Black men were all the rage, wanted by young and wealthy Japanese women who would buy them anything they wanted in exchange for sex and companionship. Those guys drove expensive new motorcycles, wore gold and diamonds, and liked to come to the hostel to party and brag. Other *gaijin* told stories about how they walked out of retail stores with anything they wanted because the clerks didn't do anything about it. Staring or accusing someone of stealing is very rude in Japanese culture, and the thieves would get away with it every time. That didn't sit right with me. I had no interest in becoming a thief, so I had to find a job.

Because money slipped through our fingers in this expensive city, we were low on funds, so Dario came up with a plan. A guy from the house had a Korean girlfriend who worked at a burlesque club in the center of the city and said that they were looking for a *gaijin* dancer.

"It's like theater, *amore*. You just need to take your clothes off a little," he said with a pleading look in his eyes. "Just a bit of stripping. No big deal." It hurt that Dario thought of me as his meal ticket. He never tried to earn a dime unless we were busking. But I needed a job, and I did like dancing more than most things in life.

The next evening, we headed for Roppongi, the center of Tokyo's night life, which was filled with lights and huge neon signs. Different from any other city I had seen in the world, Roppongi had suited businessmen sleeping on the sidewalks, curled around their briefcases or just sprawled out and hammered in subway stations. Strangely, it was not unusual for them to go out drinking after a long day at work, find a public place to crash, and then go back to work the next day.

When Dario and I arrived at the door of the underground club for the audition, the bouncer let me go inside, but kept Dario out.

"I'll be here when you come out, *amore*," he said with his guitar on his back, lighting a cigarette.

As I walked down the stairs covered with red carpet, I brushed my right shoulder against the red velvet swirl wallpaper. When I entered the basement bar and showroom, I saw dozens of small round tables and chairs crowded in front of a stage with thick red curtains. A man and woman who were smoking and drinking in the corner called me over.

"*Kawaii desu ne?*" the woman asked, as the man nodded in fervent agreement. "Work now!" she said to me.

She called loudly for someone to come translate for her. A young woman came over from behind the stage, bowed to them, and then to me. After the woman in charge said a few sentences in Japanese, the young woman said to me in choppy English, "You start tonight. We make costumes now and rehearse. Come with me." She motioned for me to follow her to the green room.

Six half-dressed young women, who I later learned were all Korean, were crowded into a small room surrounded by mirrors, racks of robes, and various elaborate costumes. One was plucking the hair from her calves with tweezers, but most were putting on makeup and wigs.

"*O-namae wa?*" the young woman asked.

"*Watashi wa* Alika," I said.

"*Konnichiwa* Alika!"

They all responded cheerfully, except one woman who was sitting in the corner. She was the only one who had very large breasts, and she barely looked at me.

The other girls giggled and began talking with each other as my escort took my coat.

"My name is Yu-Jun," she said. "It is a pleasure to meet you, Alika."

"Thank you, Yu-Jun. It is my pleasure," I said, drawn to her beauty.

I quickly learned that the show had a series of acts, or choreographed performances, that were at times group numbers, pairs, or solos. Yu-Jun filled me in on all the details of how the last *gaijin* performer was fired for being too drunk on stage.

"No whiskey when working," she warned. "You will perform in middle of chorus line, have solo in middle of show."

I picked up the choreography quickly and was good at improvisation. Being sensual came naturally, so I didn't even have to act when I was paired with Yu-Jun in a lesbian number. The scene grew heated, even during the rehearsal when she portrayed a servant undressing me, taking off my Victorian outfit.

When the show began, a crowd of men in suits, already drunk from the bottles of Jack Daniels atop every table, roared when I entered the stage. I was someone new, someone exotic to them, and I ate it up. I fanned my feathers and swayed my hips, topless with a sultry smile. From one number to the next, the men grew more intrigued, but it was when Yu-Jun and I played the servant scene that they went crazy—especially when I leaned back on an ottoman, and Yu-Jun acted as if she were licking me between my legs. When I pretended to have an orgasm, the men stood up, hollering with excitement.

After the last act, we performed the traditional chorus line, took our bows, and blew kisses at the audience. When the curtain closed, I felt elated. It had been so much fun! After a short while, the woman in charge came backstage smiling and put the equivalent of $300 of yen in my hand, smiling and very pleased with me,

"Very good," she said. "Come back tomorrow."

Dario often made vegan soups with mung beans and vegetables for us to eat when I returned to the *gaijin* house after work. Like his mother and sister, he was an extraordinary cook and delighted our housemates with his knack for flavor, feeding them in exchange for spliffs, which he shared with me late at night. But hard drugs were expensive and difficult to come by in Japan, so Dario set his sights on Thailand, a heroin junkie's haven.

After three months, our visas in Japan were going to expire, and we were saving our money for flights to Bangkok. We both looked forward to the hot weather, a warm ocean, and the Thai cuisine. For the next two weeks I continued working at the club, which was the highlight of my day. I especially relished the intimacy with the other dancers. Although we were all acting, I genuinely enjoyed caressing female bodies and simulating kisses onstage.

Sex with Dario had ceased to exist since arriving in Tokyo, and his affections were rare. As I had feared, he was especially cold after the police had dropped me off at the squat on that horrible night. We were a sexless married couple, and I presumed he thought me tainted. But the sensuality of exotic dancing filled me with pleasure. At times, I even felt myself orgasming in the middle of it all. During our last dance together, Yu-Jun and I locked our eyes in passion under the hot lights and gave each other a deep, sincere kiss goodbye.

"H" is for Human

Chapter 10

Cheap tickets, free liquor and food, and smoking on flights characterized jet travel in the early '90s, so for vagabonds like us it felt like royal treatment. We planned to stretch our yen as long as we could, doing nothing but getting high, swimming, and soaking in the sun. Landing in Bangkok, the heat eased the tension in our skin after spending too much time in the north, and we broke a long-awaited sweat.

When our taxi dropped us off at a bustling market, we devoured some street food and asked around for a cheap place to stay for the night. An English-speaking vendor recommended a popular hostel nearby, so we hopped on a *ricksha* that took us there in ten minutes. I had never ridden on a *ricksha* before, so it gave me a thrill to bounce along on the springy seat as our driver dashed through traffic, peddling his bicycle in front of us.

Shortly after we checked into the International Hostel, we were invited by some loud, tattooed Australians in the room next door to celebrate my twenty-first birthday by smoking some pure Thai heroin. After they all sang a languid birthday song, Dario and I lounged on the floor. The drug acted as an aphrodisiac, generating laughter and tickles which brought on those loving sensations that we had been missing, making me feel that the amorous tides might be turning.

The next morning, after the desk clerk told us where all the best beaches were, we headed for the coast. Our first destination was the island of Ko Samui, where we drank juice from cracked coconuts and rolled in the waves. That afternoon, we rented a bungalow for 20 baht—about $1 a night—right on the sand, with mosquito nets and a soft bed that looked out onto the Gulf of Thailand. Every day for the next three weeks, local families sold us fresh fish, tasty noodles, and ripe mangoes from huts spaced out along the shore.

Time did not exist for us. A perpetual euphoria reigned supreme on what felt like a second honeymoon. The beach became our love land as we ran around half naked and lay on the wet sand with the soft waves caressing our legs. We were living in ecstasy, and it felt like it would never end.

However, after several of Dario's drunken escapades had made us unwelcome guests, we began island hopping, first to Koh Tao, then to Ko Phangan, and finally to Thong. Often, I didn't remember what had happened the night before, but it never surprised me when I learned that Dario had insulted someone in charge or simply flown into an unprovoked rage. At the time, I never analyzed why I tolerated Dario's abhorrent behavior. I was still on an adventure, and I was married—for better or worse.

After four months on the islands, far from a phone, listening only to the breezes, the lapping waves, and the entertaining rhythms of the Thai language, we returned to Bangkok and found an international call center to phone my mother and Dario's sister.

"Hi, Mom!"

"Where are you, Alika? I've been worried sick! Are you still in Japan? Why haven't you written?"

"I'm in Thailand, mom. Our visas were up in Japan, so we had to leave Tokyo, but we're going back there soon."

"You're still with Dario?" she said, sounding disappointed.

"Yes. We've been having the time of our lives! Thailand is so amazing!"

"What are you doing for money? How can you just keep traveling like this?"

"Yen lasts a long time here. It's so cheap. We've been living on the beach for months."

"Will you please remember to at least write to me more often," my mother begged. "I can't stand it!"

"I'm sorry, Mom. I will. I promise. Oops! Gotta go. My time is running out. I love you."

"I love you, too. Take care of yourself, Alika. You can come home anytime you—."

With that, the line disconnected.

For a second, I imagined what my mother must have been going through, not hearing from me for months at a time or knowing where I was in the world. Crossing my heart, I vowed to send her more postcards. I wouldn't tell her how I felt deep down where my denial resided. I had to keep my feelings on the surface, or I might have had a mental breakdown too far from anyone who cared.

When Dario appeared from the booth where he was talking with Gia, he abruptly told me, "I need to go back to Italy, *amore*. I need to see my sister," He placed his hands on my shoulders. "Her house is where I need to go to get clean. Why don't you go back to Tokyo and make some money. I'll go to Italy, and I'll meet you in London in a couple weeks."

Feeling crushed by this news, I started to cry, not knowing how to exist without him.

"We'll be back together soon," he said. "I promise. At the club, you can make the ticket money to London in a week. Gia is sending me money to help with my ticket. *Ti amo, amore.* Don't cry."

As he embraced me, I leaned on his shoulder and wondered if he would really meet me in London. Why couldn't I go with him? I knew deep down he would always love Gia more than me. I felt rather jealous of her really, because Dario treated her like pure gold, and me like the gold tricking fools.

After we picked up his money from Western Union, we booked our flights at a travel agency near the hostel. I already had a return ticket to Tokyo, and Dario bought his flight to Rome. With the little money we had left over, we got high and wandered the city for the next two days. In the chaos of the crowded streets, we came across a Buddhist sanctuary where two monks in orange robes were playing basketball.

Ever since he was a kid, Dario had been a huge fan of the NBA and loved to shoot hoops. So, we approached the monks, using gestures offering to play a game of two-on-two, and they happily agreed. I always had some athletic ability, and Dario had been on his high school basketball team, so I played defense and passed the ball to him to make the shots, which in hindsight represented our lives together. The monks moved surprisingly well in their robes, but Dario and I were totally synchronized, just as when we played music together, so we celebrated our victory and bowed respectfully to the monks as they bowed to us, sweaty and smiling.

When it was time to go to the airport, saying goodbye to Dario tore me up. For the past two years, we had been inseparable. I was hooked like a fish, dangling without legs to hold me up. I had forgotten what it was like to be alone. Dario's flight was first, but before he left, he gave me a kiss and the last tiny baggie of heroin. My attachment to Dario became my connection to that bag. I thought I would fall apart without being numbed, so I hid it under my hat.

When I arrived in Tokyo, I saw customs agents patting people down as they came off the plane. Suppressing the gripping fear in my belly, I summoned the guts I needed to fool them with my little bag of smack still under my hat. When it was my turn to be searched, they told me to hold out my arms while they patted the sides of my body and legs. When they motioned for me to take off my hat, I removed it with both hands and made a quick sweeping motion to hide the baggie in my left palm and then slipped it inside my pocket. Like a master magician, I extended my hat with my right hand to show them that it was empty, while diverting their eyes with a flashy smile.

"*Konnichiwa*," I said, greeting them in Japanese.

As I walked away, my heart was pounding in my chest.

After I passed through customs, I felt the stress draining out of my body and was exhilarated to walk out of the airport unscathed. The risk was both thrilling and stressful, but I needed that bag. Counting the yen I had left, I realized that I only had enough for the train ride into the city and a few days at the *gaijin* house.

I planned to go to the club that night, hoping they would take me back. First, I was dying to break open the baggie. I needed some tinfoil and matches. There was a little market near the *gaijin* house, where I knew I could get some foil, because if I asked anyone at the house, they would certainly want me to share. My little stash had to be kept a secret, so I could stretch it out for at least a week. I was lucky to get a tiny room in the corner on the bottom floor of the house, which had a low window where I could blow out the smoke. Hopefully, nobody would smell it. This bag was mine, and only mine.

When I went to the club that evening, the owner wrapped her arms around me, beaming.

"*Irasshaimase!* Alika!" she said, welcoming me back. I knew I was popular with her clientele, many of whom had approached me after the shows hoping for some extra favors which I always refused. I chose to say nothing to Dario, but had he known about these men, would the extra money be more important than my loyalty?

"*Konnichiwa*, Alika." Yu-Jun said, jumping up and down while clapping her petite hands. "How are you?"

"Sad, Yun-Jun," I said. "But happy to see you."

Getting back to dancing took my mind off Dario. As I soaked in the sublime moments of adoration and praise, the music and the lights transported me to a fantasyland where sexuality flowed through me like a river. Night after night, the girls and I celebrated sensuality and the freedom to express it.

At the *gaijin* house, I made a huge pot of mung bean soup like Dario taught me. Saving my money, I ate a bowl once a day before going to the club. I carefully measured out one small line to smoke per day after work, so that I would have enough until I left for London. After eight days, I had earned enough for a flight and some extra pocket cash.

Before leaving Tokyo, I called Gia, who said that Dario had already left for London the day before. He was clean and would meet me at the squat. I wanted to be clean again, free from the torment of addiction. My little bag was empty. I had smoked my last hit.

With my bone-colored case, I set out for the airport, knowing that it would soon be summer in London. Dario and I would surely be playing music together. I would see Coby, and the little family I knew would once again laugh together and take long walks across town to our favorite pubs.

The excruciating fifteen-hour flight wasn't the usual gleeful experience that Dario and I had drinking and making merry. Instead, I was going through withdrawal and feeling terrible. I was trembling all over, which only got worse on the train from Heathrow Airport to Paddington Station. Pain had a new meaning on the plane and then the train ride was right out of hell.

When I arrived at Battersea Park, I struggled to cross the bridge over the Thames and walk to the squat. I was completely empty, and so very tired.

The front door was unlocked, and no one was home. There was no pot of tea and no warm welcome. It was still daylight, but all I wanted to do was lie down and sleep. I went upstairs to our old bedroom and curled up beneath the blanket without a pillow. Sadness overwhelmed me, but right now nothing mattered. I just had to sleep.

After a while, I felt someone shaking my shoulder.

"Alika! Hi, love!" Coby said. "Want some food? I brought you some tofu and veggies from the restaurant."

"Coby!" I exclaimed in a daze. "Where's Dario?"

"He went to rehearsal today. He'll be back soon for dinner. C'mon, eat something."

I heard people talking downstairs.

"Who's here?" I asked.

"Some new blokes moved in while you were gone. I missed you. You're always the only lass around here."

The snow peas and bamboo shoots were delicious. It was nice to eat something other than my perpetual mung bean soup, and I felt better after my rest. When Dario returned from his rehearsal, he stormed in and lifted me up with his arms.

"Amore!" he said, kissing me all over my face. "My God, you're as light as a feather!"

I felt hollow.

"I met a guy who runs a place where you can dance," he said, sliding me down onto his lap. "It's all set up. I've been playing with these amazing Senegalese musicians! That's where we're going next, *tesoro mio.* To Africa!"

Africa. That is where I had wanted to begin my world travels light years before I met Dario. Africa. Sun, music, and a culture I dreamed to be a part of sounded heavenly. An adventure I longed to experience with Kari. I wondered what she was doing now.

A few days later, when I was feeling stronger, we went to meet his friend in Soho. After we walked up a narrow stairway, we arrived at a peep show that had no stage, no bright lights, and no glittery costumes. Instead, there were rows of plexiglass boxes, each one with a naked girl in it wearing high heels. They all looked half dead as they swayed their hips.

The man in charge looked me up and down with a sigh.

"She's bloody skinny, man!" he said to Dario with a Jamaican accent. "But you're right, she's pretty enough. She can start tonight."

"Cool," Dario said. "What time do you close?"

"I shut the doors at 4 a.m. I've gotta get home before the sun rises, man, or I'll burn up like a vampire," he laughed.

"I'll be here to pick you up at four o'clock, *amore*," Dario said. "Make that money!"

And down the stairs he went.

"I'm Oliver," said the boss. "What's your name?"

"Alika."

"Oh, American!" he said, surprised. "Why on Earth are you in a place like this?"

I had no answer, as he reached for a pipe, lighting up some crack cocaine.

"Want a hit?" he said, extending the pipe toward me, "It'll get you in the mood."

After pausing for a moment, wondering if I wanted to go down that rabbit hole, I reached for the pipe sensing that smoking it would make this place more bearable. Blowing out the smoke gave me a rush that woke me out of my stupor and revved me up like a race car. I passed the pipe around to the other girls, one of whom, I learned, was his sister Jalissa.

"Oliver," she said, "she looks rather gaunt, don't you think? She needs a look. I've got some extensions. That'll fix her up."

Jalissa rubbed my head to loosen my short hair. The touch of her long nails reminded me of Grandma when she bathed me. I almost cried as I recalled being so clean. But the crack cocaine shifted my brain, and I started crunching my teeth. I was consumed by the insatiable feeling of wanting more. I smoked every time the pipe made its way around the circle of women, enduring the yanking as another girl helped Jalissa to speed up the process until I had magenta braids falling down my back.

As I worked night after night, dancing in my plastic box, I watched the men desiring me, perhaps pitying me, and I didn't care. I just smoked, danced, and saved money for a ticket out of there.

One night, Oliver suggested that I meet with the "Johns" behind the scenes.

"We'll make a lot more money that way," he said.

"But I'm married," I replied. "What do you think I am?"

"You're a tart," he laughed. "Whether you know it or not. Dario doesn't even know what he's got. Why are you with that wanker?"

"I love him."

"Love's a losing game, Alika. Sounds like it should be a song, doesn't it?"

The Cracked Drum

Chapter 11

Catching our flight out of Heathrow couldn't have come at a better time as I felt the life being sucked out of me from the drugs, depression, and malnutrition. I was slowly wasting away as, day by day, I went from the squat to the peep show, and back again. Desperately in need of a change, it was a great relief to leave London behind.

Staring out the small oval window of the airplane, I recalled living in Venice, California, still in my cast after the accident. One peaceful evening, my friend led me through a past life regression by laying me down on the floor, and through a guided meditation, I was lifted out of my body and up into space. After floating in the darkness and seeing our blue planet at a distance, I was told to return to Earth. As if in a lucid dream, I vividly remember becoming an African woman tending a field with a baby on my back. I was topless as I touched the growing grains and could feel the sun on my chest. I had a loving husband who kissed my shoulders as I baked some stuffed patties in a clay stove for my family. Then we danced barefoot under the starlight around the fire. As the flames crackled, a supreme serenity enveloped me, and I felt like my life was complete.

As Dario and I descended the stairs from the airplane, excitement ran through my veins. When my feet touched the tarmac in Dakar, Senegal, it felt as though roots were shooting out from the soles of my feet, and I even struggled to move my legs. I felt deeply connected to this land, like we had a history. Beads of sweat started to pour down my neck under the long magenta braids that felt so heavy in the heat. Exchanging 1,000 British pounds for West African francs, we entered the bustling city of Dakar with no plans on where we would stay.

I carried only my bone-colored case, and Dario his guitar, and a swarm of men quickly surrounded us speaking rapidly in a variety of languages. There was one man who stood out from the crowd. He had the biggest smile and the funkiest teeth, so Dario pointed to him and asked him to take us to a bar, speaking French.

Amadou, a tall, thin, and enthusiastic man about our age, became our guide during our stay in West Africa. We all became fast friends, laughing as we drank multiple bottles of La Gazelle beer. I tried to keep up as he and Dario spoke French, but I knew only a couple phrases. I longed to understand the jokes they were laughing about, and pitch in when I had a question, but I was only ever able to throw a word around in between their dialogue. I did catch that Amadou had invited us to his home in a village called Kaolack outside the capital city. Jovial and drunk on good beer, we ended up hopping into the back of a small pick-up truck and traveling for two hours until we reached his village in the desert.

Children came from every direction as we strolled toward the market and into the village center. They jumped up and down and reached their hands out to touch us. Wide-eyed, laughing, and shouting words I didn't understand, they were shocked to see foreigners in their village. Kaolack was not a tourist destination. Far from the coast, there were no hotels, and in 1991, we might have been the first white people some of these children had ever seen. Small homes made of mud and cement blocks sprawled around the market. Women wearing long, brightly colored fabric, some carrying vessels of water, some baskets of fruit on their heads, looked at us sideways with suspicion. The bazaar was just as vibrant as the women's clothes, with fresh fruit and vegetables of every color spilling out from crates on the ground. As we devoured fresh mangos—just as tasty as the ones from Thailand, but with a slightly different flavor, Dario translated many of the things Amadou was saying. He informed us that we would be visiting his cousin's mango farm in the coming days where we could eat mangos to our heart's delight.

Amadou soon introduced us to his family and friends. We quickly learned the traditional greeting, *"salam alaikum,"* and the response of *"wa alaikum salaam."* We must have repeated this a thousand times during our stay in Senegal, where over 95% of the country practiced Islam. While we learned many Arabic phrases, Wolof was the predominant indigenous language, and most people were excited to teach it to us. Wolof was a joy to speak because of its lively and animated style, making communication in this new tongue exhilarating. Learning simple words like *waaw*, meaning "yes," and *deedeet*, meaning "no," was so fun because they were accompanied by expressive gestures. For example, people didn't shake their heads when they said "no." They stretched their arm straight out in front of them, and with their pointer finger, abruptly waved it back and forth, sometimes too close for comfort. The word we spoke most often was *jërëjëf*, meaning "thank you," because the people we met were so generous and hospitable, more so than anywhere else we had been in the world.

It was fast approaching time for the afternoon meal and Amadou's wife, Miriama, invited us to join them at their home for lunch. The food was spectacular. We were in culinary heaven because meat was rarely eaten in this village. The whole family squished together sitting in a circle on the floor around a large shallow bowl as Miriama doled out portions of stewed vegetables over couscous to each person with her hand. She gave the best selections to us, her guests first, and then to the growing children, before feeding Amadou and herself. When I bit into the carrot, I realized that I had never tasted a "real" carrot before that moment. Each flavor surprised me with its purity as I fed myself with my hands. Peanuts are a major crop in this region, and a traditional sauce made using these nuts, roasted in the sand, blew our minds. Day after day, we tried new dishes like *mafé* and *thiéré mboum*, which were piles of vegetables over rice or couscous covered in various delectable sauces. We learned how to say *Suur na*, or "I'm full" in Wolof, responding to all the families who invited us to eat lunch multiple times per day.

Speaking Wolof was a joy, but I usually mispronounced and fumbled the words, making most people belly laugh. I communicated via improvisational pantomime, successfully acting out my thoughts and feelings, being creative, and having fun.

The women walked regally and were strikingly beautiful. The bright colors of their wraps swayed in the light wind across their dark bodies. They were stunning, elegant, and artful visions to behold. The community was strongly segregated by gender; women cooked and gathered food and water, while men sat in the shade smoking and drinking hot tea if they weren't out working or hustling money. We often hung out with them, under Baobab trees, rolling massive joints with newspaper. Our friends would lift the pot of tea high into the air and pour it into small cups with impressive aim, so that the tea would cool off on its way down.

The guitar Dario carried attracted the musicians of the village and before long, we were jamming out with the local drummers and singers. Women who had seemed suspicious at first began to warm up to me and taught me popular and traditional dance moves. Soon my legs were flying in all directions, my arms moving in wide motions to irresistible beats as I danced. Parties were held nearly every night, and I was having the time of my life dancing under the bright stars and black sky.

We stayed during the dry season, the hottest months of the year. The scorching sun made my head sweat under the braids, forcing me to beg Miriama to take them out. Relieved to feel the breeze on my head again, I watched Miriama happily weave the magenta extensions into her daughters' hair, creating beautiful hairdos, like intricate sculptures. These girls were envied by the other kids in the village with the bright pink color popping against their deep brown skin.

Education was highly revered in Senegal. While at school, children sat on mats covering the dirt floor under a structure built to provide shade while listening to oral instructions. They learned multiple languages from a young age, and wrote their math equations using small individual chalkboards that sat on their laps. Our friends were eager to teach us the history of their country. As we listened, they taught us about the consequences of the repeated colonization of their lands. It was hard to understand, even though they used combinations of the French, Arabic, Wolof, and English languages. Our friends were keen, sharp, and strong minded. I deeply desired to know more about their philosophy, their understanding of astronomy, and the rich storytelling that entertained the children.

At times we made trips to Dakar to buy gifts for Amadou and his family, since his home was our main residence during our stay. On one trip to town, we naively asked, "Where can we buy Miriama some flowers?"

Amadou laughed and said, "Who are you going to pay, Allah?"

After a few weeks, we traveled south with Amadou, following the river to Gambia, to stay with his fishermen friends on the coast. They steamed a large fish they had caught that day by wrapping it in banana leaves and placing it in a hole in the sand over some rocks heated by smoldering wood. As we sat in a circle on the floor, ready to eat the fish, a woman proudly offered Dario and me each an entire eyeball. I could tell this was a gesture honoring her guests, but we couldn't bring ourselves to eat them. The offended look in her eyes crushed me. It is a look I will never forget, like I had just slapped her in the face.

After being in Senegal for five or six months, the money we had brought from London dried up. However, we were able to stay for another couple of months, living on the kindness of our friends. I continued dancing with a fervor to raging drumbeats and impromptu vocals every night. Never had I felt as happy and connected to the essence of life than those moments of joy that I experienced dancing barefoot in the desert.

One fateful day, Dario got into a drunken fight with Amadou, and we left for Dakar in a public transit van. Dario had become enraged after a drinking binge and now turned his anger at me. He hopped out of the van as we came to a stop in the outskirts of the sprawling city, slamming the door behind him before storming off with his guitar.

"I'm done with you!" He shouted as he left.

At first, I was relieved to be rid of him and his senseless anger, but I didn't know how to be without him. When I exited the van in the center of Dakar, I felt alone among a crowd of strange men staring at me.

It was dangerous to be a young foreign woman alone. Even a man I was familiar with from the market approached me in the bathroom, exposing his erection, assuming he could have his way with me. Luckily, I easily shooed him away. And in broad daylight, a strange man approached me and asked, unexpectedly in English, "Do you know I have the right to rape you?" I walked away, thinking he just wanted to scare me and that if he were serious, he would have attempted it. My fresh wound from London had scabbed over, hardening my vulnerability. Still, it wasn't safe for me to be in this congested city without my husband, money, or anywhere to live.

Dario was the one who got us around by speaking a variety of languages, so I struggled on my own. Because we had lost our return tickets weeks before, and not knowing how to find Dario, I decided to go to the U.S. embassy and ask for help. Maybe this was a sign, I thought, a time to return to the land I came from. After signing some papers stating that I would repay the government for a ticket to the States, I was set to take off for New York City the following day. I was in a state of hiatus, suspended between worlds, and I didn't know how I would adjust to a rigid society all over again.

Wondering what to do for the night, I remembered some friends of Amadou who didn't live too far from the airport. When I showed up asking if I could stay the night, I was welcomed and invited by Fatou and Moussa to join them for lunch. Sitting in a circle, I practically wept at the thought that this would be my last marvelous meal made with the loving hands and unique flavors of this country. After our meal, Moussa gave me a *djembé* drum he had made from the skin of his goat, hoping I would sell it for him in New York and wire him the money. I agreed, pleased I would be able to repay him and Fatou for their hospitality.

After spending the night with the whole family on a queen-size bed, I splashed myself with water and put on a colorful green and white wrap. Fatou generously gave it to me while she washed my dress. After it dried, I put my gold mini in my bone-colored case next to my ticket to the States. I sat in the sun before I left for the airport, watching the children play as we relished fresh-baked baguettes and café Touba, a roasted coffee drink mixed with Guinea pepper, cloves, and other spices. Dipping the crust into the coffee with its multitude of flavors tantalized my taste buds, tipping them over into bliss.

I was reluctant to leave this country, and sad that I wouldn't see the glowing smiles on kids' faces across Senegal anymore—the happiest kids I had ever met, exuding an energetic joy and pure freedom of spirit. I knew in my bones that someday I would return, maybe to live out my last days on earth.

After checking in at the airport, I carried the *djembé* toward the plane out on the tarmac, thinking I would carry it onboard. However, I was shocked when a soldier, holding a machine gun across his chest, demanded that I put the drum on a conveyor belt that was ascending to the storage compartment of the plane. I cried in protest, knowing it would roll off the belt, fall, and crack. But my tears did nothing to move the soldier, and in the end, I boarded the plane sobbing. I knew that Moussa would be so disappointed, since the drum *did* crack, and my friends wouldn't be receiving the money they had hoped for. Ultimately, the drum became "lost luggage," and I never saw it—or the family—again.

There were only a handful of passengers spread throughout the plane, and I was the only woman. As I involuntarily scratched my mosquito bites, I must have looked like a wreck. I was upset about the cracked drum, clearly sad and alone, and nervous about going back to the States.

Smoking was still common on airplanes in 1992, so the cabin quickly became hazy and foul as every man seemed to have lit a cigarette. My nose was running, and tears were quietly streaming down my cheeks. After the plane leveled off, a pilot approached me, leaned over, and apologized about the drum. He spoke in English with a delightful accent. After introducing himself, he invited me to sit in the cockpit with him, the co-pilot, and the navigator. As I chatted with them, I learned that they were all quintessential gentlemen from the Ivory Coast.

As the crew and I followed the perpetual sunset, telling each other funny stories of our travels, a flight attendant served me first-class food and champagne. It's astonishing how at times we can experience the worst and then the best of life, at the most unsuspecting moments.

The flight went by quickly. All too soon, I saw the classic New York City skyline framed by the small front window. I will never forget the sight of the orange, almost red, horizon interrupted by the silhouettes of familiar downtown skyscrapers.

As I stepped off the plane, I already missed the cheerful pilots whose kindness, humor, and class I will always cherish. Carrying only my bone-colored case with my passport, toothbrush, journal, gold dress, and now a few bags of pretzels, I went through customs as a citizen, but felt like a stranger.

Passing through the subway turnstile at JFK Airport, I headed into the city. I didn't know a single soul because I had learned months before from my mother that Kalani had moved back to L.A. After wandering the streets for a while, I hopped in and out of bars downtown, making fast friends with anyone who would buy me a drink.

Just before dawn, I ended up dozing off on a bench in the park off 14th Street and 10th Avenue. As the city heated up, I woke up in a sweat with a parched throat that was pleading for water. It was after I found a drinking fountain that I saw a copy of *The Village Voice* and Madonna's ad.

During the sweltering summer of 1992, when Madonna's *Erotica* album was being released, she advertised an audition. *The Village Voice* was a free, weekly newspaper doled out everywhere across town, and I was struck by the small, inconspicuous ad that was placed in the back of the paper. The ad read something like, "Open Auditions: backup dancers for Madonna's new tour." It gave a date, time, and address somewhere in midtown. And it was starting in an hour.

I rushed over there and got in line, a very long line. It went around the block, but I had all the time in the world. Standing there for at least two hours, the excitement of the audition was accentuated by the dizziness I was feeling from my hangover. Grimy from not bathing, I still had the scent of vodka on my breath, which made me feel queasy.

"Hello," said a teenage girl behind me. "Where are you from?"

"Los Angeles originally, but I haven't been there in years. I just arrived from West Africa last night. How about you? Where are you from?"

"Oh, nowhere special," she said as we scooted up in line. "Just a small town in Texas. That's an interesting outfit you have on. What's your name?"

"Alika," I replied as I scratched the mosquito bites on my thighs. "I cut this wrap a little too short last night in a bar. It was down to my ankles yesterday because women wear long skirts in Senegal. It's a cultural thing. I wish these threads weren't hanging down all over the place… How about you? What's your name?"

"Cindy Lou, but you can just call me Lou." She fidgeted with her hair. "I wonder if Madonna will be here. I've loved her ever since middle school!"

"I actually waited on her table in a fancy restaurant in L.A. once, when she was still with Sean Penn," I said. "They argued the whole time, though. But I get it. My husband and I fought all the time, too." I wondered what he was doing now.

"You don't look like you'd be married," Cindy Lou said as we entered the building.

In a large, bare room, the organizers separated us into different groups of forty or so and taught us sultry choreography to a new Madonna song. After my group learned the routine and practiced a few times, we entered the studio where Madonna and her entourage were sitting on a bench, leaning against the wall. I was suddenly spent from jet leg and a lack of sleep, but after we did our routine, wouldn't you know it? I was the person Madonna pointed to.

Her assistant called, "You. Come over here," in her New York accent. Weaving through the dancers, I walked up to the front and stood face-to-face with Madonna and her entourage.

"What's your name?" asked the choreographer.

"Alika. Alika Jones," I said as my voice cracked. I needed some water.

All the members of Madonna's entourage had that sexy androgynous look. With my thin frame, small breasts, big eyes, and short hair, I fit the bill.

"Well Alika, that's a bold outfit you've got on. Rough around the edges, but interesting."

"I just arrived last night from Senegal."

"Senegal huh?" the choreographer smiled. "What were you doing there?"

"Dancing mostly. Every night in fact. They have the best parties over there."

The girls in the room snickered a bit.

"Well, show us some moves, Alika Jones," the assistant said as she sat on a bench against the wall next to Madonna.

As the music played through the large speakers, I swayed my arms side to side and began to kick my feet to the beat. I closed my eyes and recalled the joy of dancing with villagers who made me feel welcome, smiling as memories drifted through my mind. I began moving faster and faster, I opened my eyes and looked straight at Madonna. I suddenly felt out of control and began to shake. Stunned, my nerves got the better of me and I collapsed to the floor as if I was having an epileptic fit, flopping around like a fish out of water.

The entourage cracked up, and the laughter soon became contagious, spreading throughout the room. I was in such a daze that I didn't realize that everyone—including Madonna, although she struggled not to—was laughing at me. Then the kind assistant helped me up and escorted me out of the room.

Back out on the sidewalk, I cried a flood of tears, not simply due to the embarrassment but also because I felt shattered, alone, and so very tired, not understanding what had happened.

Madonna and her posse had no idea what was going on with me—my lack of sleep, my hangover, and in hindsight, my deeply rooted fear of success that had sabotaged my chance at a leg up in life. All they saw was a scrawny young woman in a cut-up African outfit, gyrating on the floor, looking like a fool. And a fool I was because I ended up taking Dario back.

I called Gia to see if she had heard from him. She informed me that he had traveled north to Mauritania, then Morocco, before finding his way to Spain. She said he was currently in France and would soon be in Italy. Again, Gia would give him the money he needed to come and meet me in NYC.

I had been making friends as though they were temporary tattoos, living on the kindness of strangers, going clubbing, and couch-surfing, when Dario arrived. I met him at the airport and he sprang through the gate in a new outfit, handsome in a deep-blue flowered buttoned-down shirt, new black slacks with a matching vest, and shiny platform shoes. He shone like the sun catching the gleam of sea glass on the shore. He had a pocket full of cash and his new bright idea was to go to Mexico, so we left New York and ended up hitchhiking across the states to get there. His guitar had new strings, and we began practicing again—our homespun sound was bound to entertain Mexican spectators along the beaches.

At times I recall that I gave Madonna a belly-clutching laugh that day. I hope she can recollect it sometimes when she needs a good chuckle. The abandonment, the cracked drum, the mosquitoes—and even my disastrous audition—were all worth the pain, because I had gone out on a limb. I've always thought that is better than staying in limbo.

Money, Murder, and the Moon

Chapter 12

How exactly did a zero save my life?

We all know that when a zero is added to the end of any number, the product is significantly altered. In my case, an $800 wire transfer from Italy to Mexico City mysteriously became $8,000, which in 1993 amounted to roughly 21 million pesos! Dario and I had been in Mexico for about a year, mostly busking in cathedral squares in Mexico City, then on the beaches of Acapulco, and even on public buses.

We both were keen on speaking Spanish and enjoyed our time eating fresh seafood with the local fishermen who carried their catches right off the boat and onto the table to prep them for a feast. We would drink Mexican beer and tequila, smoke marijuana, and sing around a campfire on the sand entertaining our friends nearly every night. The beach was once again our love land where Dario and I enjoyed each other and the freedom we experienced trading our music for fish, drink, and smoke in a land where being poor among the poor was an authentic and delightful experience. Our love life was flourishing once again. We even renewed our vows in a sweet little ceremony after shaving our heads on a whim in Chiapas and taking a second honeymoon leaping naked in the waves in beautiful Chocohuital, which was still quite pristine before becoming a tourist destination. Cuddled on hammocks as the ocean wind blew over our skin, I had hope that our marriage was revitalized.

As fate would have it, nearly a year later, my body rejected all food and drink. I couldn't keep anything down. I was very skinny to begin with, but I had become so thin and frail that even sitting or lying down was painful. I was starving, suffering, and confused. It had all started because of one horrifying night near the end of our excursion in Mexico, when evil was in the air.

On the back side of the well-to-do hills of Acapulco, we sat around a fire in front of our rented shack-like home with some neighbors, drinking homemade mescal out of little plastic bags with holes cut in the corners. An older woman, who had a tiny *tienda* in her home down the hill, sold those bags filled with the devil juice. During the day, we often visited her for snacks and to play music for her grandchildren. There was one 11-year-old boy, Carlos, who was excited by our music and enthusiastic about learning how to play the guitar.

When there was nothing left to drink, we played music for our friends and smoked marijuana until the fire faded away. After our friends went home, Dario leaned a baseball bat against the inside of the door to secure it for the night, as he always did, and we proceeded to get into bed. The air always smelled of the earth in our little rental with the dirt floor and haphazard planked walls around us. The windows were without glass and the fragrance of the jungle, lush with wild banana trees, wafted through them. I lay naked under the sheet in the dark, thinking about how inexpensive acoustic guitars were in Mexico.

"Hey," I whispered to Dario. "Let's buy Carlos a guitar tomorrow. You could teach him how to play."

This must have triggered something deep in his drunken psyche because Dario became enraged. He sprang out of the bed, infuriated, grabbing the baseball bat. He used it to smash one thing after another in the shack. When he came at me, eyes blackened and with the bat raised over his head, I knew in my gut that he was intent on killing me.

At that moment, time stretched.

In a split second, I envisioned myself dead with a cracked skull, naked in a pool of blood on the dirt floor. Then I darted out the door and ran as fast as I could.

Filled with adrenaline, I sped naked through the brush on the mountain as Dario chased after me. Fleeing a crazed murderer was the stuff of movies, not something I had ever imagined myself doing. And yet here I was, running for my life, falling in shallow ditches as dogs barked at me in the darkness. Sharp thorns and jagged rocks tore at my flesh, smearing my arms and legs with blood. Guided only by the light of the moon, I finally outran my madman husband.

I searched frantically for the cave where our friend Guillermo stayed. He worked at the banana boat attraction on the beach, and we had become close as he diligently taught us Spanish. When I appeared at the mouth of the cave, I found him with his girlfriend, Juanita. They were shocked to see my naked bloody body, heaving, and falling from exhaustion.

"*¿Que pasó?*" Guillermo exclaimed.

As they gingerly washed me and gave me some clothes, I told them what had happened in my choppy Spanish.

They laid me on a thin mattress on the floor and I nodded off, hoping that they would stand watch in case Dario found me.

When I awoke, I was sore all over.

My friends offered me breakfast, but after a few bites of bread and sips of water, I felt nauseous. Last night was a horror story, I had never been so afraid. Dario seemed possessed by a demonic spirit. His eyes said murder as he raised the bat over his head ready to smash my skull. I had seen lunacy in my sister's eyes as a kid, but never murder.

If I was finally going to leave Dario, I still needed my bone-colored case that held my passport. Hurting from all the scrapes that scarred my skin, I mentally prepared to face him. Guillermo and Juanita walked me back to the shack, which we approached hesitantly. Had Dario made it home, or gotten lost somewhere in the jungle?

We found him fast asleep on the hammock. He snoozed with an occasional snort as usual. The bat was nowhere in sight. We decided to leave him to sleep it off and I went into the shack to change my clothes and gather my things.

Just then, Dario reached for some water and a cigarette before he saw Guillermo and Juanita sitting on rocks warmed by the sun. "*Buenos días*," he said casually.

I walked out of the shack.

"Good morning love," he said as if nothing had happened. "Why are you all scraped up?"

I broke the news to him, but he couldn't believe that he had almost killed me.

"*Tesoro mio!*" he cooed. "I wouldn't hurt my precious beauty."

He always called me sweet names in Italian after his outbursts.

"If you had your way," I screamed, "I'd be dead in the dirt now. I'm lucky I got away!"

"I love you, *amore*. Come here."

As I walked toward him, he opened his arms and then wrapped them around me kissing my forehead over and over again. Tears started rolling down my face and my breath shuffled as relief washed through me. Craziness ruled my life. I was exhausted and felt as though I was crumbling. But Dario's embrace soothed me. I leaned my head in the crook of his shoulder and cried. He rubbed my back and kissed my head.

What in the hell had happened last night!?!

Rolling their eyes, Guillermo and Juanita said, "*¡Son locos!*" and returned to their cave.

No one had running water on the hill, and soon I was too weak to retrieve water from the well. I lacked the strength and balance to carry the vessel on my head up to our shack. It became obvious that I was ill. Was it the mescal, the water, the trauma, or all the above?

It was time to leave the shack, the hill, and Mexico altogether. That horrible night began to fade. We stopped talking about it because Dario didn't remember. I was left to carry the memory alone.

Leaving the mountainside, we took a cheap bus ride back to Mexico City, performing our music for the other passengers along the way. Many of them had homemade crafts, chickens, or goats to sell. With generous hearts, some of them put change in our hat or handed us some fruit. Often, we found that the people who lived off the land were more benevolent than the people we encountered in fancy city squares, and it was more of a pleasure to perform for them. Their smiles always brightened even my most depressing days.

When we arrived in Mexico City, Dario called his sister, once again, to ask for money. Gia said all she had in her bank account was the equivalent of $800, but Dario begged her to send it, explaining how sick I was. She eventually agreed. We had to wait because the bank made us leave and return three days in a row, saying there was a problem with the transfer. Finally, the bank handed us a huge pile of pesos and a bag to carry all the coins in. We were in shock—we had never had this much cash before!

We instantly knew there must have been a mistake and decided to get out of Mexico as fast as possible. After buying two one-way tickets to Italy for the next day, we got a room in a hotel in the city.

That night, I simply couldn't sleep. My body was in agony. The physical pressure was excruciating, especially when I sat or lay down. I tried to sleep standing up, leaning against the wall, but I couldn't. Instead, I picked out a book from the library in the hotel's lobby: *Crime and Punishment*. Written in 1866 by Russian novelist Fydor Dostoevsky, it temporarily took my mind off my pain and hunger. I was so wrapped up in the intense story that I forgot my own torment for a while. It was like a relentless masseuse painfully digging into deep tissue to relieve muscular tension—fictional anguish was my cure to get through the night.

After what seemed to be an endless flight, we finally landed in Rome. I was bony, hungry, and dehydrated. Dario had to carry me in his arms across the city, where we boarded a train to Chieti. Three hours later, we arrived at a farmhouse on the Adriatic coast. The farmers—Gia's friends Vincenzo and Flavia—followed the biodynamic philosophy of Rudolf Steiner, who taught that agriculture could be radically transformed by spiritually communicating with nature. Because Steiner believed that the night is a time of renewal and healing, Vincenzo and Flavia did much of their work by the light of the moon. They sold their vegetables, fruits, grains, and cheese to a select clientele, but it was their magenta wine that really glowed. They never sold it and gave it only to friends or guests. It was coveted throughout the village and beyond.

After visiting the farm every day, driving from Gia's house only a couple of miles away, I was nursed back to health by the farmers' tender loving care and medicinal tea. The very first thing I was able to eat was a sweet peach that Flavia brought me. Sitting in the sun, the glorious juice dripped out the corners of my mouth, landing on my bare tan thighs. Flavia handed me a moistened rag and another peach as she smiled. I was able to eat a little more with each passing day, slept soundly, and soon began to feel better.

With our extra money, Dario repaid Gia for her loan, adding extra lire for her kindness. Of course, we also gave some money to Vincenzo and Flavia, who gifted us a bottle of their magnificent wine to take on our journey to London.

Before we left, I stopped at the internet café to make a long-distance call. Dario smoked cigarettes and joked with some childhood friends he had run into in the square while I called my mother.

"Hi, Mom! Guess what? I'm back in Italy."

She was silent for a moment.

"I have some bad news for you, Alika," she said.

I felt my heart swell and my throat close because I knew what she was about to say.

"Did Grandma die?"

"Yes."

"When?"

"A few weeks ago."

"I was sick and was thinking about her every night," I said as we cried together. "She was even in my dreams."

"She loved you Alika."

"When I was in Mexico, I wrote her a long letter. I just knew she was suffering. Did she get it?"

"She did. She was worried about you."

"It has been tough lately, Mom," I said barely keeping myself together. "I feel lost."

"Come home, Alika. Every night I'm sick with worry."

The timer was counting down the few seconds I had left.

"Sorry, my time on the phone is running out," I told her. "I love you, Mom. I'll call you from London."

As I wandered through the narrow cobblestone streets of Chieti, I thought of my beloved grandmother and the fact that we were both sick and dying at the same time. She was the one person from my early childhood who showered me with love, the one who created a sense of safety in my young life. She was the one who made me feel protected.

And now she was gone.

As Dario and I headed north on the train, we stopped briefly in Bologna before arriving in Venice for the night. As we walked through the city, looking for a place to sleep, the canals flowed from the sea like tendrils. I marveled at the grand palaces, elegant squares, and a full moon on the rise. As I stood on the Ponte dei Pugni bridge, sipping the last few drops of the magical magenta wine, the moon was reflected in the canal and created a rippling path. I imagined myself walking on the moonlit water and then floating above the city, drawing nearer to the glow.

Suddenly, a circle of light began to form around the moon, and I realized that it represented a zero—that number which had shifted the course of my life. At that moment, I understood that my grandmother was sending me a message from the other side. She wanted to let me know she had saved me from death. Communicating with me through the moon, she was letting me know that she had sent that miraculous zero which the bank could not understand.

I believe that certain moments in our lives are orchestrated from beyond our immediate understanding and I am convinced that my grandmother sent that zero through the wire that day when I was slowly wasting away. The message I received under the night sky in Venice was clear. My grandmother had saved my life. She loved me and would protect me from beyond the grave, no matter what.

After arriving in London, I finally had the courage to leave Dario. We were cruising down a busy sidewalk in Chinatown, looking for somewhere to eat lunch, when a dose of supernatural strength dissolved the twisted emotional glue that had bound us together. My grandma had handed me a miracle, and I was finally ready to break free from the cycle of abuse that haunted me. I turned and walked down the sidewalk in the opposite direction without saying a word, disappearing into the crowd before Dario even knew I was gone.

Bread, White, and Blue

Chapter 13

I had been awake for days wandering the streets of London when apparitions started coming out of the woodwork (or brick and mortar in this case), calling my name. Haunting echoes radiated around me saying, "Alika, Alika, come home."

"Home" was a distant concept. It was somewhere unfamiliar, somewhere mysterious. Lingering around the 24-hour French café, the night crawlers were stirring on the streets of Soho, and I was one of them.

Walking timidly on the sidewalk, careful not to step on any cracks, I looked up to see a giant eyeball staring at me, its gaze piercing. I began to hear loud footsteps approaching. The eye blinked before suddenly sinking into the socket of a scrawny man's face. He bumped into me and whispered "welcome" directly into my ear.

"You see them too?" said a woman sitting at a small round table at the side of the café.

"Where's home?" I asked her.

"As the saying goes, 'know thyself,' little lady. Home dwells within you."

I was suddenly very tired. I had been awake for days walking the streets and searching for somewhere to rest. Turning the corner, I listened to the faint voices continuing to say, "come home." I saw a small park inviting me in through the open wrought iron gate. The season had turned, and autumn beckoned the auburn leaves to fall onto the green grass. I bent over and gathered the leaves together, forming a large pile under a tree, and I lay down, sinking into the center. As the voices faded, I drifted off into a much-needed sleep. For now, this was home, though I felt I didn't know myself at all.

Victoria was a petite person with pink hair who, in 1994, lived on the dole while sharing her flat with street artists. When I saw her sipping coffee in the French café the next morning, I felt compelled to approach her while wearing my only dress, the gold lamé mini.

"Smashing piece you have on," she said with a bright tone gracing her refined English accent.

"Thank you," I said with a smile, admiring her dress in return. "This might seem a strange question, but would you like to trade dresses in the loo?"

"Definitely odd, but why not?" she said, surprising me.

We both had slender builds, and her dark blue, vintage, tight-waisted dress from the '50s fit perfectly. As we talked over coffee and cigarettes, Victoria learned that I had recently left my husband and had been on the streets. She kindly invited me to her flat, just south of downtown London.

It was comforting to finally stay in an apartment, and especially wonderful taking a bath with candles on either side of the tub. The musicians who crashed there and I often broke out into jam sessions and enjoyed each other's company over teatime—which took place whenever the electric tea kettle was steaming. Victoria and I became fast friends and sat next to each other while jamming with the group. I sang and she played the tambourine while others played bongos, guitars, and flutes. Sometimes we would dance together in the middle of the room and twirl then dip each other like a couple would. I tickled her funny bone, and we often laughed the night away.

One day, Victoria brought home various shades of blue paint, and asked if I would help her create a galactic mural on her living room wall. Mixing Palladium Blue with Jamaica Bay and Adriatic Sea with Bluebell, we invented additional hues and created fading depth and beauty. I did my best to emulate the swirling of the cosmos with clusters of stars by sponging off the paint to reveal small parts of the white wall underneath. It was a form of meditation to trust in the flow of the process and create art with an intuitive force that moved my hands across the wall. We filled the space from top to bottom with star-filled wonder by adding sparkle dust to the mix until the celestial mural was complete.

There was only one bedroom in the flat, where Victoria slept with her lover, so I slept with my fellow vagabonds sprawled out across the living room floor. The morning after we painted the mural, I rose with the notion of baking something scrumptious with the leftover bread I gathered from the local restaurants, saving it from being thrown in trash bins at the end of the night. Victoria and I would do whatever we could with the big bag of bread each day. We often lathered it with jam or peanut butter and honey when we had some in stock. Sometimes when the crust was too hard, I would take out the center of the bread and shape it into little balls, dampen them a bit, roll them in sugar, and fry them. Then we would indulge in sweet, crunchy goodness.

I wanted to surprise my new friends. We ate so little. Then it dawned on me. Bread pudding! Perfectly warm and filling, and oh so apropos—it was known as the "poor man's pudding" centuries ago in England, a humble dish that has stood the test of time.

This morning, I had the stuff I needed to make bread pudding, aside from raisins and vanilla extract. The cinnamon, sugar, butter, bread, and milk were the most important parts. Melting the butter and adding the milk felt so freeing. I relished the fact that I didn't have to eat vegan anymore. I didn't have to answer to Dario. The constraints of his control had been broken.

And there was a crowd to feed. They would wake up to the divine aroma of gluten, cinnamon, and sweetness in the air. I put the kettle on and waited for the others to shuffle into the kitchen for tea.

Tea in England, and many other places in the world, is for everyone. No matter how rich or poor an individual is, a cup of tea flows as naturally as water. It perpetuates the act of being polite and generous to kin and strangers alike. The bread in Victoria's apartment flowed too—we sliced, baked, fried, and toasted it for all. We gave what was so freely given to us, like smiles, air, and love.

Our friends leaned against the cosmic mural, eating their bread pudding, and sipping their tea. Suddenly, I had another idea.

"Hey," I said. "Isn't it a good day for a parade?

"What's the occasion, love?' Victoria inquired.

"Dunno," I said shrugging. "Let's *make* an occasion! We have all this leftover paint. Let's paint our bodies blue, play music, and start a parade! People are sure to follow."

"*Pazzo!*" Flavio said as he sipped his tea.

"Crazy or not," I replied, "let's do something fun today. It's beautiful outside! And in England, *that's* something to celebrate!" I was pumped. "Grab your instruments! Flavio, get your guitar. Johan, your saxophone. Guillaume, you'll have to bang a pot with a spoon. Oscar, sweet Oscar, get your flute. Dev, grab your tabla. Victoria, shake those maracas, and I've got the tambourine. We can sing the blues, painted blue!"

I had no idea at the time that in New York City, the Blue Man Group had already formed. Here in the red-light district in the heart of London, we were getting bluer by the minute. The boys painted their faces and arms, while Victoria and I painted our legs under our skirts. Then I got carried away and removed my dress, so I was braless as I painted my torso while Victoria painted my back. We covered every bit of me, from breasts to bottom, from head to toe—hair, underwear, and all.

After we dried a bit, and finished our tea, we headed outside and began to jam. As I led the way to Oxford Circus, we roamed the streets of the theater district looking like a blue Hare Krishna band. We often enjoyed the free and delicious vegetarian meals served at Krishna Consciousness Temple. However, we were not dressed in orange like they were. Today we were blue, jamming with our instruments while I sang my heart out.

As we continued our performance, passing the grand theaters of central London, from Piccadilly Circus to Covent Garden, we made merry all along the way. Onlookers smiled and cheered, laughed and gawked. Random buskers joined us, adding to the wild musical improvisation. Others marched alongside us or followed on our tails. I was triumphantly leading a band of misfits on the most splendid Sunday morning, when the police, also in blue, approached us in Trafalgar Square. They weren't hostile—they were laughing, actually—but they did halt the parade.

Because I was in the front and nearly naked, they approached me saying, "Okay, young lady, you'll have to stop this commotion and come with us. You can't be out on the streets like this."

They didn't handcuff me, but the crowd booed and jeered while the two cops led me to an old and tiny local police station. The older copper poked fun at me for reminding them of the pranksters from the Sixties. Fun was my intention for the band and the public. I never imagined that the fun would ripple into a police station as well. The officers caught the fun bug and enjoyed pretending that they were part of the parade as they led me to my cell.

Since I was the only female in the station, the policemen got a hoot and holler from the view of my skinny blue legs and thin torso covered in a thick layer of cracking paint. They didn't have any additional clothing to give me but shared their cigarettes and some of them asked me questions as we sipped on cups of tea. Victoria was on her way with some clothing but in the meantime, I told the cops stories of my travels abroad in Mexico, Asia, and Africa, entertaining them from behind bars.

"Now, that is all well and good, young lady," one of the coppers said, "but have you ever been arrested before?"

"No," I lied, and distracted them with another joke.

* * *

Two years before, I had been arrested in a humble neighborhood on the outskirts of London. It was at night, after the corner pub had closed, and I was hiding in the bushes because Dario had become angry and aggressive for no reason. As he searched for me, yelling my name in a rage, a neighborhood resident called the police.

The cops had no trouble finding him. He was sitting on the curb in front of the pub, slouched under a lamppost with his guitar by his side. I watched the scene from behind a bush as Dario shouted and an officer pulled his arms behind his back and shoved him to the ground.

Impulsively, feeling the police were going to hurt him, I rushed out into the street, pleading with them to leave him alone. Instead, they arrested me, too. I fought back, kicking and trying to wiggle loose because the alcohol was rushing through me, and stupidly, I thought that I could take them. As an officer's arm reached around my neck, I bit him hard on his wrist. I can only imagine how much that hurt. At that point, the other officers jumped me and tossed me into the paddy wagon next to Dario.

We were put in cells across from each other, where we slept off the alcohol over the weekend. Being locked up was not a bad thing for us because we had beds and stayed warm through the night, a far cry from the squat we were staying at over in Battersea. Because we were hungry and didn't eat meat, the beans on toast three times a day were scrumptious.

When Monday rolled around, we were sent to court. The officer I had bitten was present and showed his wrist to the lord justice who was adorned with a stark white wig. Not knowing what the consequences might be, I admitted that I had, in fact, bitten the officer.

"Where are you from?" asked the lord justice.

"Los Angeles," I said, looking up at him.

"And what are you doing in London?"

"After marrying Dario in California, we went to Italy to meet his family. Then we traveled to London to make music."

"Where are you staying?"

"Here and there. South London with friends, mostly."

"What do you do for money?"

"I'm a singer," I said, beaming. "We're gonna be big stars one day!"

"I see," he said, skeptically.

"We sing in the streets for now, and the tube, of course. The acoustics are so good down there. Dario and I have great songs and—"

"All right," the lord justice interjected. "Quite honestly, you look malnourished. You do know that biting a police officer is a serious offense, don't you?"

"I'm really sorry about that, judge."

"You will refer to me as lord justice young lady."

"Yes, lord justice sir, I apologize."

Looking at the officer, I said, "I'm so very, very sorry for biting you. I didn't know what I was doing!"

The officer looked annoyed.

"I should deport you," said the lord justice. "Do you have plans to leave England?"

Lying through my teeth I said, "We're going to back to Italy. Back to Dario's hometown."

"May I suggest that you stay there?" he sneered, striking his gavel. "Now get out of my courtroom and my country!"

I was shocked that he let me back out onto the streets, which by that time, was where I felt I belonged. Not knowing what would become of Dario, I looked for a spot to sit in the sun, wishing I had a coat to wear. I found a place to wait away from the cold shadows, thinking about how I had escaped trouble by the skin of my teeth, which was the culprit of my drunk and disorderly crime.

I waited about a half hour before Dario came out of the courthouse, holding his guitar high in the air, with a big smile on his face. I ran to him, and we kissed long and hard. He twirled me around, relieved, and said he needed a drink. It was time to find a street corner, make some dough, and hit the pub.

* * *

It didn't take long for Victoria to show up at the police station with a dress in hand, and charmingly ask the officers if I could come home. They pretended to be reluctant but handed me the dress through the bars.

"C'mon, love," Victoria said. "Since you aren't nicked, these nice coppas are setting you free."

"That's convenient, since I'm already free!" I said gleefully as I swung out of the cell. "Goodbye, officers. It's been a hoot."

Heading out into the sunny afternoon, Victoria and I giggled about the looks on the coppers' faces and the ruckus we caused that day. By this time, the paint had cracked hard on my skin and hurt something awful. When we got home, the gang was there, rolling spliffs and drinking more tea. After cheers, hugs, and a good washing, I asked if anyone wanted some French toast, minus the maple syrup.

Later that day, I checked in with my mother. She was shocked that I had finally left Dario, and I could hear that she was choked up. There was a convergence of emotion linking us and I could feel her relief to finally have her daughter released from the grip of an abusive asshole.

She informed me that my old high school friend Kari had been trying to reach me because she was having a baby. She gave me Kari's number and I called right away.

"Hi Kari! It's Alika!"

"Alika! Hi! Are you still in London?"

"Yes. My mom said you're pregnant!" I said with sheer excitement. "That's so wonderful!"

"I'm having a boy. I'm going to name him Zion, and I want to ask you something. Will you be his godmother?"

"Yes, of course," I said, tearing up, my heart glowing. "It would be my honor."

"Awesome! Are you planning on coming back to the States soon?"

"I will now!"

"You can stay with me," Kari said. "I moved to San Diego and teach social studies at a junior high school."

"Who is his father?"

"Charles, we met in Kenya. We got married!"

"Wow! Congratulations! My time on the phone is going to end soon. What's your address? I'll fly back to the States right away. Yayyyyyy! I'm so excited!"

"1249 Lincoln Avenue," replied Kari. "Yayyyyyy! I can't wait to hear about all your travels. We'll share stories!"

"Indeed, we will...goodbye hon! See you soon," I said as the line disconnected.

That was all the reason I needed to go back to the States. Zion, what a name! I loved him already. But I needed money for the plane ticket so I went back to the peep show to ask Oliver if I could work for about a week or so. I told Oliver that I left Dario and was going back to America.

"You should quit fucking around and get your life together," Oliver insisted. "But you can work. Jalissa will be here. I'm going to Jamaica tomorrow. Congrats on leaving that wanker. Take care of yourself, you promise?"

"Yes," I said, but I knew deep down I couldn't keep that promise. I didn't know how.

The Cult

Chapter 14

The heat in Los Angeles felt surreal as I stepped out of LAX and looked for the bus stop. I didn't want to go straight to the Valley to see my mom, not yet. Venice was a short bus ride away, and the ocean was calling. What would I be willing to tell my mom anyway?

On the Venice boardwalk, I found a resale shop where I donated my only garment and found an emerald-green dress that sparkled with gold flakes woven throughout the light fabric. This was a new start. I bought a Walkman and a Nirvana CD in tribute to Kurt Cobain. It was April 1994, and he had just passed on to the other side. Crossing the sand with my platform shoes in one hand and my bone-colored case in the other, I cried, listening to his raspy voice wrought with pain. The wind blowing from the west washed away the grit of my past adventures. *I am still alive* was all I could think while I mourned the sad end to a man who wore his heart on his sleeve.

I watched the waves crash as they waxed and waned on the wet sand inviting me closer. I had to take a dip. Not caring that people in America are uptight about exposed breasts, I removed my new dress and ran into the Pacific Ocean in my underwear. With my eyes closed, I felt the tingle of the cold salt water and listened to the seagulls flying all around with their high-pitched calls. I was home in a city that never felt quite right, but home nonetheless, ready to tell my mother nothing.

I decided to go straight to San Diego. I would call my mother from there. I just wasn't ready to face her, not yet. The Greyhound bus was cheap and easy. It was a relaxing ride as I relinquished control, trusting the driver to manage the traffic, allowing me to daydream while watching a flock of birds fly in the shape of an arrow. With intuition leading the way, the flock pointed to its destiny. I could find my way around a map but had no sense of direction.

Kari picked me up from the bus station, with a round torso and dreadlocks hanging from her head. It had been so long since I felt the warm embrace of a true friend. I wanted to sink into her soft brown arms and never come out. She was due in two months, right around my 25th birthday. What a present Zion would be! The first baby I could hold and love, hum lullabies to, and rock to sleep.

Kari's small, cute, Craftsman home was vibrant and cozy, with African masks and photos from many countries on the walls. We had both traveled the world and were joined by the experience that living abroad brings. Charles, her husband, was White and English, tall, thin, and blonde. He was sweet, attentive, and so excited for the arrival of their baby. They asked if I would be their doula. I had never heard that term before but learned that it meant caring for a mother before and after birth, while helping with the baby. I was honored to be trusted. They believed in me and that prompted me to believe in myself.

When the time came, Kari was a champion. I videotaped the birth, watching first-hand the primal struggle and then the miracle. Zion was perfect—gorgeous and perfect, glorious with his light brown skin and soft curly black hair. A newborn has a way of making the universe feel synchronized, when time and space align in a single precious moment. Holding his tiny body in my arms, he almost felt weightless, like gravity didn't exist for him yet.

We had a party celebrating Zion's birth with a drum circle, and ritually planted Kari's placenta at the foot of a tree in her back yard. By giving something raw and nutritious to the earth, we all felt a sense of completion as the rhythms of the drums pounded and the dirt was shoveled back into the hole, covering the tender mass that came from Kari's womb.

I took Zion on walks around the neighborhood in his stroller while Kari rested, singing him sweet songs like "You Are My Sunshine." I cooked, cleaned, and made tea for Kari while Charles was at work. Staring at Zion's sweet face, I prayed over him, thinking of my grandma in heaven and her love for children, asking for blessings and a fruitful life for his innocent soul, free from the kind of suffering that I knew all too well.

The following summer, I felt optimistic after a delicious Mexican lunch, walking around downtown San Diego, enjoying the ocean breeze. After a few blocks, I noticed a sandwich board advertising free yoga classes. Curious, I walked up the stairs under a sign that read, "The World Evolution Loft," breathing in the incense as I reached the second floor.

I entered a wide-open space and saw a group of people sitting cross-legged in the corner on a rug surrounded by plants and large windows. This was an old industrial building with exposed pipes and air ducts along the ceiling. When the group in the corner started chanting, the drone of the chant drew me closer. A redheaded woman with fine features and a peaceful smile waved for me to join them.

"Sit down, join us," she said with a twinkle in her eye as if she knew something I didn't. Sitting between other people my age, I found that deep place in my belly where sound flows, and the vibration relaxed me. We began stretching in all directions and the release of tension motivated me to push my body to its limits. Time ceased to exist. I followed along with the group, doing yoga, and caught glimpses of a serene kind of concentration on their faces, suggesting focus on the moment. Only this moment mattered, fleeting, yet continuous, breath by breath.

When we were finished, people introduced themselves with names like Shakti, Akasha, and Sati, and either bowed or hugged me. Then a large man, round in his center with a long red beard and a twisted bun on top of his head, approached us with a huge grin. He was wearing a white wrap around his hips that folded into shorts, a white tank top, and sandals. With his button nose, high cheekbones, and twinkling eyes, he would have made a convincing Santa Claus.

"Hi, I'm Murshid. Who are you?" he asked, with a shockingly thick southern accent.

"Alika. Hello…"

"How'd you like yoga?" he asked, sitting down on a decorative, round cushion.

"It's my first time and it felt great. Is this an ashram or something?"

The small crowd giggled a bit. I didn't really know what an ashram was.

With laughter that was larger than life Murshid said, "We are…a community. We call ourselves the Circle of Friends." He motioned to the redheaded yoga teacher to come by his side. "This is Khalifa. She can tell you all about it. I've got an appointment to go to. Bye y'all." He got up and sort of waddled away.

"Why does he dress like that?" I asked, puzzled.

Khalifa smiled, "Murshid is our spiritual guide. That is what his name means in Arabic. He studied Sufism overseas with numerous masters, and then started the Circle of Friends in America back in the '70s. We live together here in the loft and have built a center in the desert we call The Land. You can stay here if you like. We share chores and help each other by practicing the healing arts. We meditate and practice yoga daily. There is a kitchen upstairs and we host parties and concerts here in the loft and retreats in the desert. We bring peace to the world, one yogi at a time."

"I have space in my room," a pretty girl said. She had a perfect curve to her abdomen showing she was a few months pregnant. "I'm Uma. It's nice to meet you."

"Thank you," I said, sitting in the same spot cross-legged, planted, feeling as though I were part of a garden, growing roots. "It's nice to meet all of you."

Zion was already a year old by that time, and starting day care, so I moved in that day with my bone-colored case and a duffle bag full of thrift store clothes. Kari wished me well and said I could come by anytime. I was sure I would be visiting often to watch Zion grow up, but I was pulled into the routine at the loft like a riptide. I was constantly busy cooking in the kitchen for us yogis, intensely learning yoga, and assisting with the retreats in the desert. We were an active bunch of twentysomethings from all over the country, all seeking some kind of enlightenment. Murshid was revered as our mystical leader who would ritualistically meet with each member, rename them, and give them some kind of title or job to do.

"So, Alika, let's talk about your name," Murshid said. "Have you had any thoughts?"

"Nothing in particular," I said. "I don't know what I want to call myself."

"Let's figure it out. I was thinking Circe."

"Who's that?" I wondered.

"She is an enchantress."

"Why would you call me that?"

"Because you have an allure about you," Murshid said with a smile.

"But I want love in the name somehow. I feel so much love in my heart."

"That's it!" Murshid stood up, "Circe Lovefeeling!"

"Yeah! I like it!" I said with glee.

"Yeah! Actually, let's add "yeah." He said, "Circe Lovefeeling Yeah!"

Being a friend in the Circle gave me a sense of belonging to a family. We had so much fun at The Land preparing for retreats. We had a piping hot pool and an ice-cold bath on the deck, which also included a steam shower where we would sweat naked before roaming on the desert rocks to dry off. Refreshed and clean, we would then meditate in the sun. We also had sweat lodge rituals where we would hallucinate and during one of these spiritual journeys, I had a clear vision of the Virgin Mary blessing me. She was at least twelve feet tall, garbed in colorful robes and a crown that glowed with a radiance that enthralled me. This new community had given me a fresh chance at life and here was the Mother of God herself, blessing my rebirth.

Periodically, some of us yogis in training would fast to cleanse ourselves of the toxins from the substance abuse we indulged in from years past. To break our fast, we would chant while we cooked huge vats of Indian-inspired soups. We believed by chanting "OM" over the food, it would raise the positive vibrations and enrich the soup with our love. I was able to see the world in a new light, with mystical connections reaching out and touching everyone and everything. We were united through our love, our labor, and our goal of a new life.

Upstairs, we worker bees slept in a dorm-like space with thin mats on the floor in place of mattresses, while Murshid and his guests lived in luxury at the big house. We made any accommodations needed for his guests while they stayed at The Land and were taught that being of service to our spiritual leaders was a virtuous privilege. We were righteous in our servitude and blissful in our ignorance.

To be of service to each other, we learned the healing arts of Reiki and massage. In Japanese, Reiki means "universal life energy." We would channel this energy through the palms of our hands and tap into it to activate the natural healing processes, restoring physical and emotional well-being. It was a glorious feeling to release the trauma of my past through feeling this universal life force course through me. It seemed to burn away the synthetic toxins which I had relied upon to fill the empty hole in my heart left by Ricardo, Danny, and Dario. Now, with the heartbeat of the universe within me, that hole finally felt like it was filled with love instead of the superficial feelings of happiness brought on by alcohol and drugs. For the first time in a long time, I felt like a new and improved person, ready to go out and change the world.

At the end of the summer, there was a very special retreat when we hosted a guru from India. He was a tall thin man with a long grey beard, wearing a turban and a white robe that went down past his knees. He shared his wisdom and his favorite exercises with us. The Guru was different than Murshid, he was serene and poetic with his teachings in contrast to Murshid's sophomoric behavior.

When he wasn't teaching, the Guru kept to himself. One day, I asked him a burning question when he was walking toward his cabin.

"What is the most important thing I can learn from you?"

After looking up at the sky he responded with, "Your thoughts are very important," while tapping his finger on the side of his head. His eyes focused on mine, and it was clear to me that he was telling the truth. Our thoughts create our reality.

Murshid drove a Hummer and flitted around from his condo on the cliffs of Laguna, to The Loft, to The Land, and a mysterious additional home in Long Beach. Murshid always wore a grin, as if he had a bag of secrets that made him giddy. His big belly shook when he laughed, which was often. He seemed to be living his dream life and we all wanted to be as happy as he appeared to be.

I was cleaning the kitchen when Murshid approached me and said, "I'm taking you to meet some special people today, Circe. Come with me. We're going for a ride."

I felt special because I had never ridden in his Hummer before. He explained that these people were an exceptional group of ladies who had something very important to teach me. "You are being promoted, Circe," he said with a twinkle in his eye.

We arrived at a large house near the harbor, and when we entered, a group of women bowed and beamed at Murshid with reverence. He disappeared into a back room for a few minutes with the woman who seemed to be in charge. He returned, said his goodbyes, and drove away in his Hummer back to San Diego.

Lakshmi was the tall blonde woman Murshid had consulted in the back room.

"Circe, it's a pleasure to meet you," she said. "Murshid has told us a lot about you."

"Really?" I asked.

"Would you like some tea?" she asked and called for a housemate. "Kali, can you put on the kettle please?"

Laskshmi introduced me to Devi, Sita, Bhavani, Ishani, Deepa, and Parvati. These women ranged in age from 30 to 50 or so, and I was the youngest of the bunch. "How's the tea?"

"Delicious, I've never tasted anything like this before."

"It's a special blend of black tea from Russia," Kali said. "Have you ever been?"

"No, I haven't. I have done a lot of traveling though. I just returned to the States last year," I said, warmed by the tea and the comforting female energy in the room. "So, why haven't I met you before? Don't you ever come to The Loft or The Land?"

The women giggled a little.

"We have our own special purpose. Some of us were the first to start the Circle of Friends with Murshid, long before it became what it is now. We go way back. In fact, there would be no retreat center or loft without us," Laskshmi said with a smile. "You are very beautiful, Circe. Have you ever thought of how that could be useful?"

"What do you mean?"

"Well, we have a special focus to serve Divine forces. We practice peace and help to balance energy in the world. Men are the most imbalanced people on the planet, and we help them energetically to achieve a meditative state, which serves the world and generates peace on the planet." Lakshmi reached out her hand and touched my shoulder. "Murshid thinks you are a perfect fit to join us. It is a high honor to be chosen. We are the sacred fire that supports the entire Circle of Friends."

Kali tapped a crystal bowl with a small rubber mallet, generating a beautiful reverberating sound in the room, and the group of women began to OM. I closed my eyes and joined them. With deep breaths, we all carried the sound in layers and continued for several minutes.

Was their mission my purpose? I was chosen after all.

Suddenly, there was a knock at the front door. It was Khalifa. My roommate Uma was leaning against her, hunched over, and breathing heavily.

"Hurry, she's going into labor!" Khalifa said as some of the women helped carry Uma inside. "Run the bath now! We are having a water birth."

Lakshmi and Khalifa discussed the plan as the rest of us made Uma as comfortable as we could. Some of us undressed her, while others lit candles or arranged cushions around a large oval bathtub in the center of a room down the hall. Pictures of Hindu gods and goddesses lined the walls and plants filled the corners. When the bath was ready, we helped Uma into the water as she groaned from the pain. She was a petite young woman with a huge orb protruding from her abdomen. She wailed while the women started chanting.

I kept my cool. I had already been through this when Zion was born, so I knew I could help. I held Uma's hand as she squeezed my fingers with every ounce of strength she had until they hurt. Kali took her other hand on the opposite side of the tub, and Khalifa leaned over the tub's edge at Uma's feet, urging her to take deep, long breaths.

"You are doing great," I encouraged Uma. "You got this!"

Khalifa informed us that she had been in labor for a couple hours while they were stuck in traffic. Uma's breathing was rapid, and she pushed every minute or so. Kali put a smooth piece of wood between her teeth, so she had something to bite down on.

After about an hour, Khalifa said, "She's crowning!" The communal chant grew louder.

"Push, Uma, Push!"

My laboring friend was wrought with agony.

"I can't," she wept. "I can't do it."

"You got this, Uma," I urged her to keep going. "Ready, three big breaths and push out with everything you got!"

She forced every muscle in her body to push, and her loud guttural screams curled under my skin. Just then the entirety of the baby's head popped out as Khaifa held it in her hands.

"Keep going Uma. You are almost there. Your baby is here. Just one more big push."

Uma tightened her face and cried, ready to give up.

"You are so close. Uma, you got this, one more giant push," I said looking at her weary face. "Push!"

With a roar, and legs shaking from the strain, she heaved and pushed out a long and large baby boy, nearly fainting when she had finally released him from her petite body. Khalifa lifted the newborn up and out of the water and asked me to take him while she cut the cord.

"Suck the fluid out of his nose and mouth and spit it out."

I was stunned.

"Hurry!"

Holding the heavy, wet, slimy baby and sucking out the amniotic fluid, I had never felt so close to the force of life. Spitting the salty water into the tub, over Uma's exhausted body, I worked at it until the baby breathed his first breath and made a crying sound that riled all the other women up until they were squealing with joy.

Kali sat Uma up and I placed the new baby into her arms. This was the second baby boy I witnessed born into this world. Would I too have a baby one day?

"What will you call him?" I asked Uma, bringing her some water to drink.

Beyond tired, Uma smiled and said, "As in 'sweet like honey,' we will call him Madhav."

We tended to baby Madhav—who was a whopping ten pounds—and his young mother for a few weeks while at Long Beach. Kahlifa had gone back to the loft to carry on her duties running the yoga lessons and to make sure that things were in order. Lakshmi and Kali took me under their wings and taught me Tantric practices, particularly the mysticism behind the art of sensual pleasure. Without physically touching, I learned how to breathe to create orgasmic sensations. I learned massage techniques and energy work that stimulated the first chakra at the base of the spine and worked my way up to the seventh at the top of the cranium. I was taught that we could heal people and generate peace, more pointedly in men, through sensual practices.

When they felt I was ready, they invited me into a room downstairs where a man I didn't know was lying naked on a massage table. Soft meditation music played in the background as Lakshmi introduced me to Steve. He was a longtime client of the house and knew all the girls.

"Ah, who do we have here?" Steve asked.

"I'm Circe," I said, surprised at my nervousness despite all my training.

"I'm delighted to see a new face around here. What took you so long Lakshmi?"

"We are picky, Steve. Just relax." Lakshmi looked at me and nodded for me to begin.

Kali stood at his feet and laid her hands against his soles. I laid my hands on the crown of his head. Kali and I locked eyes and began deep breathing in unison. Lakshmi sat in the corner as Kali and I poured some oil onto our palms and began rubbing Steve's hairy middle-aged body. They had taught me that through my own focused breath, the orgasmic pleasure I generated in myself would enhance the orgasm of the client, connecting us all in a blissful experience that would vibrate throughout the world. With four hands massaging every part of him, Steve was euphoric. Kali began a low hum, I joined her, and together we moved like a wave with our hands and breasts rubbing the front of his body. We moved back and forth over the top of him. We pushed his negative energy out and filled him with positive vibrations. The hum became an OM and intensified as our massage picked up momentum. The OM became an AH as Kali fondled his genitals, and as the sound reached a higher pitch, he came in a flurry of ecstatic pleasure.

"Oh my God!" Steve heaved in between short breaths. "You ladies are unbelievable!"

As Kali and I wiped Steve down with steaming hot towels, we looked at each other, smiled, and winked. We had experienced our own sense of euphoria being together while spreading what we thought was world peace.

The weeks rolled into months living in Long Beach and I continued pleasuring men with Kali. I was convinced that I was doing something good for the world. I hadn't thought that this was sex work; it never crossed my mind. My brain was washed with this notion that there was a higher purpose, and I felt honored to be a part of it. Plus, I never saw any money exchanged, that was all happening behind the scenes. I cooked in the kitchen with Kali and the other ladies, cleaned the house, and met with male visitors in the room downstairs made up just for them. They never came through the main house. We ladies lived in peace with each other. Murshid rarely visited but called to speak to Lakshmi often, about business I presumed.

One sunny day, while I was watering the garden, Uma brought baby Mahdav to visit. He was so big! He had doubled in size, and she looked spent. I made some Russian tea and sat with them in the living room. The house was quiet because the other ladies were out shopping.

"I don't think I can do this, Circe," Uma said tearing up. "I don't think I'm cut out to be a mother."

"You have all of us, Uma. We are all here to help you."

"I want to go home to Chicago. I feel terrible, but I don't want this baby." Uma said as she broke down crying.

Shattered by her emotional breakdown, she fell into my arms. I just held her as baby Mahdav squirmed in his carrier.

"I must go, Circe. Please forgive me," she said as she squeezed me, before walking out the front door.

I stood there rigid, unable to move for a minute.

I stared at Madhav who was kicking his legs, aching to be released from the buckled straps that bound him. I picked him up and bounced him in my arms as he reached for my empty breasts searching for mother's milk. Uma left the diaper bag next to the carrier and I looked for toys or something to entertain him. I thought he might need a changing, so I laid him down on the rug and felt the pervasive sense of abandonment that he would certainly feel in his future. Here was this baby, beautiful, and full of promise, yet abandoned by his mother who should have cared for him. Who was his father anyway? When

Madhav grasped my finger and pulled me toward him, I kissed his belly and exhaled making a funny squeak that made him giggle. My heart warmed with the vibrant kind of love I had felt with Zion. I couldn't comprehend how someone could leave a precious child.

When the ladies returned, they were shocked to learn Uma had deserted baby Madhav.

"What happened?" Lakshmi said with panic creeping into her voice.

"She left. I don't think she's coming back."

I heard them call Murshid and then brainstorm on who might parent this big baby boy. They spoke of others who were connected to the Circle, living in the Northwest, who might raise him. As they talked, I tickled Madhav's belly and played peek-a-boo.

I had never seen Murshid angry before. He showed up to the house asking where Uma could have gone. I didn't say a word about Chicago, feeling instinctively that I should protect my friend. Baby Madhav kicked his strong, chubby legs and we played as I kissed his feet, avoiding the tension in the room. I loved this baby. After all, I had helped him to take his first breath.

"What about me? I could take care of him," I said hopefully.

Murshid and the women stopped and looked at me.

"Circe, we have other plans for you," Laskshmi said.

"Doesn't she know?" Murshid asked the ladies.

"Not yet," responded Kali.

Murshid crossed his arms, "Well, what are you waiting for?"

Laskshmi motioned for me to join her and Murshid in her office.

"We have some news for you. Have a seat," Lakshmi said as Murshid made himself comfortable in the chair behind the desk.

Murshid was serious.

"There is an important mission to Russia, and I want you to be a part of it," he said. "We are setting up a new school with friends of mine there. I want you to be the lead yoga and meditation teacher and in charge on my behalf. I believe in you Circe. It's very exciting that the Circle of Friends is expanding! I think you'll be great."

"Wow! Just like we've dreamed. Spread peace across the world!" I said, happy he believed in me. "When do we leave?"

"I booked your ticket for next week," Lakshmi said. "You'll be traveling with Khalifa, who will get you settled there and show you the ropes. You will basically be like Khalifa, but of your own school in Russia after she leaves. There are people we know quite well who are ready to receive you and make you quite comfortable."

Khalifa was Murshid's favorite, and I certainly wanted to be like her.

It was approaching Christmastime, and I was warned that I would need a very warm coat for the trip. Kali and I went shopping at the mall, which felt like an alien planet, so sterile and homogenized. We entered Macy's and I browsed through the winter coat section. There were fur coats, leather coats, and wool coats, all very new and expensive, it made me feel quite awkward.

"No worries about the prices, Circe," Kali said. "This is a gift from Murshid. Pick out any coat you want."

A long, heavy coat made of a steel gray suede stuck out to me. It was lined with soft wool and had a military style to it, which I thought suited the Russian motif. The tag read $2,300, but Kali said, "Don't worry about it. Try it on."

Laying the coat over my shoulders, I felt like royalty.

"I love it," I said looking at myself in the mirror.

"Done," Kali smiled and gave me a wink.

I had my bone-colored case packed with my passport, hygiene products, and my journal. I was instructed to starch my new coat and to bring a variety of clothes in my duffle bag. Kali and I traded some dresses, so I had what I needed. I was ready.

Murshid came to the house to pick me up in the Hummer. I was saying goodbye to Lakshmi and the ladies when I heard Madhav cry in his Pack and Play. I picked him up and gave him a loving embrace, gently handing him off to Kali.

"I think he's hungry," I said with tears welling in my eyes. What would become of him?

"Khalifa is meeting us at the condo. Let's go," said Murshid, hopping into his Hummer.

"I'm proud of you, Circe. You've come a long way."

I blushed, naively, as I settled into the front seat.

After an hour drive south on the freeway, listening to a classic rock station, Murshid sang "Sweet Home Alabama" with a huge smile on his face and informed me he was born there. He shook with laughter as he put his hand on my knee, looking at me with blue eyes glistening, and I wondered what was so funny.

I had never been to the condo in Laguna Beach before. It was right on the cliff and had stairs that led to the shoreline. "Grab your stuff. You'll be going in a taxi."

"I wish I had time for a swim!" I said, leaning over the rail on the balcony. "What a great view!"

Murshid went into a room down the hall while talking on the phone. I wandered around the living room and was struck by a huge statue of Ganesh, a supreme deity in the Hindu tradition. The prominent elephant head adorned with a crown and the big belly of a man sitting cross-legged reminded me of Murshid.

Still alone in the living room, sitting on the couch, I looked down and saw some Polaroid pictures on the coffee table poking out from under a magazine.

Curious, I noticed one of me on top of a pile with both of my names and the number 11 written on the white section at the bottom of the photograph. I shuffled through a dozen other Polaroids of young women in the Circle of Friends that also had their names with numbers written on them.

Emily-Sita #8.

Sara-Aashvi #9.

Josephine-Shyla #10.

It gave me the chills to think about what I had discovered. What did it mean?

I stiffened when I heard Murshid returning and slid the photographs back under the magazine.

"Kalifa is meeting us at the airport, she's running late. But before we go…" He stood in front of me, "Circe, I've been wanting to do this for a long time."

"What?" I said, squirming on the couch.

Murshid took off the wrap around his hips exposing his crotch, which was covered in red pubic hair.

"This," he said, holding his penis and pointing the tip at me as I sat on the couch.

My heart sank. It felt like a heavy blanket fell over my body. I didn't move. I just blinked rapidly trying to shield my eyes from the sight in front of me.

"What's wrong?" Murshid seemed impatient. "Do this for me."

I opened my mouth and began to move closer to him, but just before I touched it, I closed my lips. I couldn't bear the weight in my chest, and I pulled backward.

With a grunt and heavy exhale through his nose, Murshid stepped back. "After all I've done for you, you'd reject me now?" And he stormed off to the bathroom.

Motionless, I wasn't sure what to do. Then I thought of the photographs. My stomach, gripped by a powerful force, made me buckle over. It was painful and I thought I heard a faint, airy voice.

Don't go. Don't go to Russia.

Was this fear speaking?

Sometimes fear knows what's best and serves a purpose.

Or was it an angel from beyond?

Either way, when I heard Murshid flush the toilet, it shook off my stupor and I had an intense instinct to flee. I grabbed my coat and bone-colored case and jumped through the door, running out of the condo complex toward the street. I stuck my thumb out and tried to hitch a ride. Cars were swooping by fast on the Pacific Coast Highway, but one car slowed down and came to a stop.

"Where to?" asked the man in the car.

"San Diego."

"Sure thing, that's where I'm headed. Hop in."

About an hour later, and after making small talk all along the way, I was dropped off downtown. Thanking the driver, I asked him if he had a quarter to spare for the phone booth. "Yeah, no problem. Take care of yourself, Alika," he said, about to drive away.

That was the promise I made to Oliver back in London. The promise that I didn't keep.

"Sure thing," I said, wondering what taking care of myself looked like. "Hey, you're a lifesaver."

I found a phone booth and called Kari. I thanked God I remembered her number and was relieved when she answered.

"Kari, it's Alika. Can you meet me at the Greyhound bus station?"

"Hey, hon. What's going on? I haven't heard from you."

"I'll explain later. Can you bring me enough money for a ticket to L.A.?"

"Sure. But what's going on?"

"I need to get out of here. I'll explain when I see you. And Kari, thank you!"

When Kari arrived at the parking lot, she took Zion out of his car seat. He was a toddler already and so cute wearing his little denim overalls. She took his hand and he walked beside her with rapid little steps.

"What happened?"

I gave her the quick rundown about the yoga school, Long Beach, the pictures, Russia, and Murshid. She was flabbergasted.

"No wonder I haven't heard from you. You were brainwashed, sweetie!"

"I just need to get away from here. Now I feel paranoid that they will come looking for me. I love you. I'm so sorry I didn't come back to visit. Zion is so beautiful!" I knelt and looked him in the face. "You are a beautiful boy, and you have the best mama."

"Here's fifty bucks. I hope that helps, Alika."

"That's plenty. Thank you so much! I'll call you from my mom's house. There's a lot more to the story. They even named me Circe."

"Oh my God, Alika. Get away from that cult and call me!" She gave me a stern look before walking back to her car. "Nice coat by the way," she said over her shoulder.

Watching Zion patter away in his little sneakers made me think of Madhav. I ached wanting to take him with me, but I just walked into the bus station and bought a one-way ticket to Van Nuys, using the change to call my mother.

"Mom, I'm coming home."

"Where are you?"

"San Diego."

"I called Kari. She said you moved into a loft somewhere, I don't know. What have you been doing?"

"Yoga, Mom. I've been doing yoga."

Lament in Los Angeles

Chapter 15

Being home with Mom and her husband Ron felt bizarre. The house was all dressed up for Christmas with a manger on the coffee table and an artificial tree adorned with a random mixture of ornaments that didn't have a theme. Mom and Ron both worked at the same large grocery chain, so the house was quiet most of the time. I would sit alone on the sofa in the living room, which had been re-painted a canary yellow and was redecorated with new, but generic furniture. The Thomas Kincade paintings on the walls depicted charming cottage homes in lush countryside, which were quite a contrast to the plastic plants filling the corners of the room. The kitchen was remodeled and there was not a cockroach in sight. The additions of a primary bedroom and bath expanded the house into the back yard. The back porch had been enclosed and had two fat cushioned recliners in front of a large, flat-screen TV. Their yards were perfectly manicured. The past was still there, but the traumatic memories were shrouded beneath a coat of fresh paint. The dark closets, where the bogeyman used to live, had been cleaned out, and the floors were covered with plush beige carpets. Now this house was a safe place to be, but I wasn't used to the feeling of security. I felt on guard, believing that the other shoe was going to drop any second.

Tess was gone. My mother's life transformed when she met Ron and got married, and it seemed like getting my sister out of the house had been part of the remodel. Mom had finally got my sister on Social Security Disability for her paralyzing mental illness, and it was enough for her to afford a small apartment nearby where my mom could help her with groceries and check on her occasionally.

Tess grew to be a person who stayed up all night and slept all day. She was grouchy at best, and at times had rage-fueled outbursts. Tess had become a hoarder and recluse, accumulating mountains of recyclable materials, and she smoked cigarettes all day long while listening to classic rock on the radio. Tess had the uncanny ability to be the designated caller when the DJ announced the chance to see a rock band and frequently won concert tickets that she didn't use. It was a shame; those tickets lay hidden in the piles of magazines and newspapers strewn about her apartment.

My mother had gratitude in her eyes when she looked at me, but her undying love was expressed with minimal words. She finally had her daughter back in one piece. I wasn't dead. I wasn't missing in action any longer. And despite all the untold stories, she knew I had been through the wringer. She knew, the way a mother just knows, but wanted no details for fear it would hurt too much. She kept her questions to herself.

I asked my mom if she would take me shopping since all I had with me was my bone-colored case, the big coat, and the clothes on my back. I always had luck with thrift stores, finding exactly what I needed. With only $50, I found a dozen pieces to mix and match into stylish outfits. Mom always preferred large chain stores and loved to shop. She never bought anything for herself unless it was new, on sale, and had a coupon. It always amazed me how different children are from their parents. Were they ever the carbon copy parents hope for?

Boredom became the death of me, and constantly watching TV numbed my brain. It was nearing midnight, and I just couldn't sleep so I decided to surprise my mother during her night shift at the grocery store. But instead, I saw a person lying on the hood of his car, stargazing and smoking a cigarette in the parking lot. He was about my age, wearing a fake fur coat, and I was compelled to approach him.

"Hello. Sorry to bug you but could I bum a smoke?"

"Of course," he said, very animated. "I'm Paul." He pointed up at the stars and explained the method he used to make music inspired by the constellations. We stared at the heavens, and I laughed at Paul's jokes. Paul's wit was something out of this world. I told him some stories of my travels and we formed an instant bond. Cell phones were new on the scene but neither of us had one, so we exchanged landline numbers and said good night. As the stars would have it, I bumped into him at a convenience store the next night and he invited me to his home, which was around the corner from my mother's house.

On the outside, it looked typical for the neighborhood, with a mixture of cacti and rosebushes lining a small lawn. But on the inside, it looked like a museum of trinkets and collectables. Art, photographs, and niche sculptures surrounded numerous musical instruments throughout the house. Heavy blankets hanging over the curtain rods blocked out any glimmer of sunlight, and an old piano had ashtrays filled with butts on either side of the keys. There were a few chairs but no real sitting area—there was so much stuff that the pathway to the kitchen and further into the back yard was like a narrow winding road through a hoarder's wonderland. His attached garage had been converted into a music studio where he spent most of his time recording. Aside from the fact that it looked like a junky resale shop, the house was also filled with trash and smelled like dog crap.

The wall in his music studio had a huge handmade map of conspiracy theories, mainly political in nature, concerning the Bush dynasty. Paul played songs he had recently recorded and wowed me with his talent. His hyperactivity revealed he was certainly high on meth or some other hard drug, and then, of course, the pipes and bags of crystal in corners of the studio gave it away.

"Let me clean your house," I said. "It smells."

Paul paused and looked concerned. "You wanna do what?"

"Clean your house. It needs a good clearing out, Paul."

He then picked up a poster and unrolled it.

"It's Laurel and Hardy," he said. "This is a rare poster. I just don't have room on the walls to hang it because I have so many other amazing pieces. Look at this…"

I could tell Paul was a special person, lost to drugs, and in need of help. He was gifted, a kind of savant, maybe even an artistic genius. I was compelled by him, and my "fix other people" instinct ignited.

"I have an idea. Let's call it an incentive. How about you let me clean your house in a French maid's outfit?"

"Ummmmmm," he rapidly sputtered.

"Or better yet just undressed?" I said with a wink. "But you've got to lay off the drugs."

Paul tried to gulp down the nervousness creeping up.

"Um, yeah. I need to stop," he said with a big exhale. "I just don't know how."

"I'm going to help you. Are you ready for this? Because if I find any drugs, I'm going to flush them down the toilet."

"Can I ask you something?" Paul asked squeezing the back of his neck.

"Sure, what is it?" I said as I started to take off my dress.

"Why would you do this? And undressed?"

"One, I don't have a French maid's outfit. Two, I want you to agree because I have a feeling you are worth it." I smiled as my dress fell completely to the floor. "There's no time like the present. Let's get started," I said before turning around and bending over to pick up some crumpled paper off the floor, my lacey panties hugging my rear. I looked back at him with a knowing smile, "Do you have some trash bags?"

The project went from days to weeks as we filled dozens of black Hefty bags with trash. Paul's dog, Audrey, as in Hepburn, scurried around while we picked up her feces after buying a box of gloves and cleaning supplies. The back yard had a mass of broken furniture and random junk, and we soon realized that we needed a dumpster. I didn't encourage Paul to part with his beloved artifacts. Instead, we just dusted them off and rearranged them in an attractive fashion. I did find little baggies hidden in his collectables. Whenever I found a new one, we would ritually flush it down the toilet together. He was shaken, but excited to change. I held the space of healing that I had learned from the ladies in the Circle of Friends. I massaged him and used Reiki to clear away the negative energy that trapped him in his self-destructive ways.

It wasn't long before there was enough space for me to get on my knees and scrub the floors, clean the kitchen, and scour the scum off the bathtub. I took the blankets off the rods and washed the windows, dusted the surfaces, and washed his clothes. We created a sitting area around the piano, cleared off the dining room table, and organized his closets. I hand stitched homemade curtains with fabric I found at the Salvation Army. With all the tender loving care I could provide, the house became a charming home. Paul and I developed a sweet bond, enjoying each other's company free from drugs, and with creativity sparking, we had fun making music together. As I spent most of my time at his house, Paul asked me to move in with him.

I brought my bone-colored case, a new duffle with my thrift store outfits, and the big heavy coat I never wore and asked, "Can we buy some flowers? I wanna build the most beautiful garden you've ever seen in the back yard around the hammock."

Springtime was here, and after many trips to the nursery, I constructed a floral and succulent paradise. My parents had bought a new grill, so they gave us their old one, and Paul and I began having barbecue parties as he rekindled relationships with dear friends he had lost during his time as a junkie. We'd have jam sessions with wonderful musicians and made merry celebrating our burgeoning love and friendship. We dined in restaurants with his parents every week, and often joined mine at their home for dinner. Mom and Ron liked Paul. He was always good for a laugh.

I began attending community college by day and worked at the front desk of a small hotel by night, where I did my homework most of the time. Education became a revelation for me and soon I was on the Dean's list. Because of the verbal abuse from Ricardo as a child, I had always assumed I didn't have the brains for college. I had never thought of myself as intelligent and after so many bad choices I didn't seem to have common sense either. Now, because I was invigorated by passionate professors and the learning process, something clicked and everything from astronomy to art history to algebra fascinated me. Political science and philosophy were my favorite courses because of Professor Broslowski. He would often invite his inspired students to his home in the evenings for intense discussions while his wife served alcohol and snacks. I also became the TA for my professor,

Mr. Fishbourne, who was in a wheelchair and taught mathematics. I would write equations on the chalkboard as he lectured, and I taught classes for his struggling students during off hours to help them boost their grades. Light bulb moments were magical while I taught, and in turn I witnessed the same in my students. Dedicated teaching is like true love, a partnership both mutual and enlightening.

Paul's parents owned the house we lived in, and they gave him an allowance to live on, so Paul was fiercely recording music full-time without worries or bills to pay. I was thriving in school. Sex with Paul was fulfilling, conversation was exciting, and aside from occasional marijuana and cigarettes, we lived relatively healthy lives. Life was good and I felt like this relationship was one I could take to the grave.

As serendipity would have it, Kalani was also living in Los Angeles. She called my mother to check on my whereabouts and left her new number. I couldn't wait to give her a call.

Kalani said she had graduated college with a degree in psychology and was now enrolled in grad school at USC. I was so proud of her and invited her over to our house for a little reunion.

As Kalani entered through the door we gave each other a big embrace.

"Wow! It's so good to see you! What an interesting place," she said, then reached out her hand. "You must be Paul."

"Hello, Kalani," Paul looked happy. "I've heard so much about you."

I hugged Kalani again. "You look amazing! And grad school! I'm gonna cry. I am so happy for you."

Kalani looked me straight in the eyes.

"You look great by the way," she said with a smile. "No comparison from the last time I saw you. Paul, you must be good for her. Keep it up."

"Would you like some water or iced tea?" Paul asked.

"I made sun tea this morning," I said. "Want to see the backyard garden?"

"Sure, and yes, I would love some tea," Kalani said as she followed me through the kitchen and outside to see the garden. "Wow! It's beautiful! You did this?"

"Yes, I really got into it," I beamed, looking at the variety of flowering shrubs, pansies, daisies, lavender, and sage.

"How did you two meet?" Kalani asked.

As I began to tell her the story, Paul grabbed one of my legs and lifted my knee up. His other hand swooped around my hips, and he dipped me backwards, and planted a kiss on my neck.

"She drives me crazy," he growled.

Kalani looked away.

"Let's play some music," I said standing straight up. "I've got *Saturday Night Fever* on vinyl!"

I skipped into the house to spin the classic record Kalani and I had danced to as kids.

We were roaring with laughter as I imitated John Travolta's moves, gyrating my hips, and sliding across the floor. When the high-pitched harmonies faded, we looked for more records as the inevitable scratch from the needle sounded through the speakers. We ended up doing the Hustle together as the sweet air of nostalgia filled the room. Kalani and I caught up, filling each other in on the wild rides our lives had taken. She was astonished by the cult and appalled by my stories about Dario. It felt great to spend precious time with her, healthier and happier than I had ever been.

"I hate to go but have a ton of studying to do," Kalani said as she gathered up her purse. "I need to hear more though! We must get together again soon!"

"Let me walk you out," I replied as we headed out the door. "It's so amazing to see you. I am so happy for you! Wow, USC! You inspire me, Kalani."

"I'm happy for you too, Alika. You've come a long way. Stay in school, whatever you do. Trust me, it's the best thing for you." She walked past the rosebushes and looked back with a smile and a nod.

"We have to get together again soon," Kalani called from the car as we both waved goodbye until her car turned the corner and she was no longer in sight.

It was September 11, 2001. I was driving to school excited that a new semester was starting. The song playing on the radio was interrupted by a newsflash. A plane had just flown into one of the Twin Towers in NYC. My heart pounded as they described the scene when another plane crashed into the second tower and the confusion and horror on my face was echoed by other driver's faces as we waited for the red light to turn green. The radio announcer was in disbelief, as were the strangers beside me, and we looked at each other through our windows utterly terrified. Some of us were looking up at the sky wondering if more planes were coming down around us.

I turned the car around and went to my mother's house to watch the news. We saw people on the screen jumping out of windows, falling to their deaths, and could hardly process the tremendous horror we were witnessing. Then the towers fell. Just crumbled down into a pile of rubble as huge clouds of dust and smoke rose into the air. I recalled the sight of those buildings through the small cockpit window when I was returning to the States from Africa, and how they symbolized coming home. Now they were a pile of rubble and a graveyard. The United States was in turmoil. Fear flooded the world. Terror had struck and nothing would be as it was.

My emotions were already out of whack because of what was happening in the world, but I soon learned that it was also biological. I was pregnant. After taking three tests at home, I went to a women's clinic just to be certain. It was true.

I made a special dinner and planned to tell Paul that night. I served *salade niçoise* and potato leek soup by candlelight on the patio next to the garden.

"Paul, I have something incredible to tell you."

"What is it?" Paul said, slurping his soup.

"We're going to have a baby," I said brightly.

He nearly choked.

"What!" He sat upright, his body stiffening.

"I'm pregnant!"

Paul blinked his eyes and cleared his throat.

"I don't know what to say," he said slowly.

"I can tell you are shocked, but I am so happy. I think we'll be great parents. Of course, I'll have to quit smoking. You probably should too, with the secondhand smoke and all."

"Hold on. Are you certain you want to keep this baby? There are options you know."

"I'm not considering options, Paul."

"We must think about this. Can we even afford it? Babies are expensive," he said, scratching his head.

"Listen, we have all the support we need with our parents nearby. And we have a home. That's saying a lot."

"Right, but you are in school. I'm working on my music. We don't have time for a baby."

"Where there is a will, there is a way, Paul. We'll make time."

Silence filled the air. The hum of traffic in the distance had stopped. Then, with a deep inhale, the scent of the garden reminded me of the smell of a loving bouquet. A symbol of gratitude and joy that I wished Paul also felt.

That night, I visited my mother and told her about the baby, hoping for encouragement, but I could tell she was apprehensive.

"I'm happy if you are happy," she said. But her eyes told another story.

The people surrounding me seemed to think I was wrong for wanting this baby.

Jerry, Paul's father, came over the next day to talk to us. He walked in and sat down on the sofa and I sat across from him on the Queen Anne's chair.

"Alika, I know you are enthusiastic about this baby, but we don't think having it is the best decision at this point in your lives," he said to me. "You should establish careers first. Have some savings in the bank. You see what I'm getting at? I just don't think the two of you are prepared for this kind of responsibility."

I sat still as words failed me.

"I've arranged an appointment with a very good doctor who can perform the procedure safely and painlessly. I trust him and I'll take care of it. No need to worry about the cost."

Teetering from side to side, Paul bit his fingernails.

"Paul, do you have anything to add?" Jerry asked.

"I love you, Alika. I'm just not ready for this," Paul said, folding his arms as if to hug himself. "My father knows what's best. Please listen to him."

I felt an intense sadness that the baby inside me was unwanted. I felt alone in loving the boy or girl who was due to change my life forever. A baby who would provide me with the opportunity to love another with my whole heart.

"Leave me alone," I mumbled as I headed to the bedroom.

I cried into my pillow face down, imagining the fetus growing inside me. A baby I loved already. I had even been coming up with names and was imagining what he or she would look like, how they would smell, what color hair they would have. My pillow was wet when Paul entered.

"Get out! I said leave me alone!" I yelled.

"Okay, okay. My father is leaving. But he left a card with the appointment time and address."

I turned over.

"Get out!"

I went to my mother's house later that afternoon to tell her what happened.

"Maybe Jerry's right," she said in a soft voice. "You should get your feet on the ground and finish school first."

"Babies are a huge commitment," Ron added.

"But I love this baby," I said, my voice cracking.

My mom gave me a hug.

"There will be another opportunity down the road," she said. "Sometimes I wish I had waited and not had kids so young."

It was obvious that I was also unwanted.

I became frightened at the thought that I would be alone in raising this child. I wanted to surround this baby with love, the way Zion was, fully supported and celebrated. I went home and saw the doctor's appointment card. Putting it in my purse, I sat down and sank into the sofa crying a fountain of tears that sprang from a deep pain in my chest. I hugged my abdomen and began apologizing to the little life inside me for becoming such a coward.

The following Friday, Paul drove me to the doctor's office on Ventura Boulevard. I was distraught and on the verge of running away and raising my baby in a far-off land. I envisioned an African village where children were plentiful, played freely together, and bonded with the whole community.

I was shaking inside and cried silent tears when I was sedated. I wished that I were going into open heart surgery, because the pain in my chest was unbearable. My last thoughts before losing consciousness haunted me.

"Take my heart out! It hurts too much! This baby doesn't deserve this, and I don't deserve to live!"

When I woke up, a nurse walked in and asked how I was feeling. I turned my head in shame. I felt my face become distorted, like the Bloody Mary demon reflected in the mirror—the urban legend that haunted me as a child was back.

"Everything went well," the nurse said with a soft voice. "You just need a lot of rest when you get home."

"I feel hollow," I said as I began sobbing.

There was a knock on the door.

"She needs a minute," the nurse responded.

On the drive home, lying on the back seat, I stared at the fast-food wrappers Paul had thrown on the floor. I didn't want to move a muscle. I didn't want to do anything. I was stiffened with shock. Life seemed to have stopped.

I don't know how long I lay in bed, silent, not eating, and unable to sleep. The sun rose and fell, but it didn't matter. I was stinky and hadn't showered, but I didn't care. I had killed my baby, and I was dead inside because of it. It felt like the sacred connection I had with another soul had been severed with a machete, and it hurt like hell, as if a limb had been cut off. My tears might as well have been the blood flowing out of my body, signifying the separation of an integral part of myself. Though I was safe in bed, I felt lost at sea, ready to drown and be eaten by sharks.

Then, Paul came in and nudged me a little.

"Alika, you've got to get out of bed. Come on, take a bath, it'll make you feel better."

I didn't move or say anything.

"Let me make you something to eat. Hey, want some ice cream? I'll get us some Häagen Dazs. We can watch a movie and just relax."

Still silent, I pulled the covers over my head.

"I'm sure what you feel is devastating. I'm hurting too," Paul said.

At that point I threw the covers off me and jolted out of bed wearing an oversized T-shirt and underwear.

"Devastating? What do you know about devastating!? You didn't even want this baby!" I screamed at the top of my lungs, "Fuck you!"

I ran out of the house barefoot, speeding toward the busy avenue around the corner. Paul ran after me, but he couldn't keep up—the adrenaline was pumping through my body. My mind was firing with mania. I was senseless and out of control.

Cars swerved around me as I stood in the middle of the street and waved my arms, screaming, "Hit me!" With bloodshot and bulging eyes, I felt my heart racing as horns were honking, and people yelled out of the windows. Paul caught up to me, making his way toward the pile up on the street.

"Alika!" Paul yelled, trying to restrain me. Enraged, I fought back, pushing Paul to the ground.

"Fuck you!" I roared. "I just want to die!"

The scene caused someone to call the police. Sirens were blazing as two cop cars arrived and I began to run again. One car kept after me while two officers raced on foot. I turned a corner and tried to hide, crouched down behind some bushes. Hyperventilating, I was at a loss and didn't know what to do. The officers found me and slowly approached from the other side of the bush.

"It's okay, we are not going to hurt you. I need you to come out from behind there," a poised officer said. "Let's make this as easy as we can. Come on out. You will not get hurt. We are here to help you."

Paul approached, red-faced and weary.

"Who are you?" another officer asked.

Paul was shaken.

"I'm her boyfriend," he panted.

"What's her name?"

"Alika," Paul said. "She's been through a lot. She's…suicidal."

"Alika, I am Officer Maloney. No need to be afraid. I'm not going to hurt you."

As the energy drained from my body, my face was stiff with dried tears. I stood up, defeated, and walked toward Officer Maloney.

An ambulance had just pulled up and two paramedics came forward with a gurney.

Officer Maloney consoled me.

"We are going to take you to the hospital," he said. "Everything will be okay, Alika. These good people will take care of you."

Speechless, I just stood there and surrendered to the process. A female paramedic took me gently by the shoulders and walked me toward the gurney, laying me down.

"I'm Allison. I need to know if you have taken any drugs. Have you taken anything at all?"

"I wish I had a hundred sleeping pills, so I'd never wake up," I mumbled.

Allison turned to ask Paul.

"Has she taken anything?"

"No," Paul said, on the verge of tears. "She's just been in bed for days, no, weeks. I can't tell anymore."

"Okay, just relax," Allison said, with a genuine, caring look in her eyes. "We are going to secure you to the gurney and take some vitals."

The paramedics did their job after loading me into the back of the truck. As the driver started up the engine, Officer Maloney walked up to Paul.

"We are going to need a statement from you. What's your name and what happened?"

The siren started blaring and the ambulance rolled away as Paul began to tell the story.

"She hasn't been the same since..." His voice trailed off. Ill-equipped to handle intense emotions, Paul's mind was consumed with one thing: the moment he would be able to call his dealer.

Customarily, patients suffering from mental breakdowns aren't taken directly to a psych ward. They are processed through the ER for a medical evaluation to rule out intoxication and determine if any medical conditions are contributing to the symptoms. Then they are seen for a psychiatric evaluation to determine next steps. My mom and Ron were on vacation in Hawaii, and I was glad. I didn't want anyone to see me like this, including Kalani.

It was clear to the psychiatrist at the hospital that I required an intensive treatment plan. She told me that as soon as a bed opened, they would transfer me to Olive View, a county mental health hospital, which would accept my public health insurance. So I lay in bed and waited. My shame had thoroughly destroyed me. I felt embarrassed and so alone.

I didn't want to see Paul, but he came to the ER with flowers anyway.

"Hi, Alika. I brought you something to cheer you up."

"I don't want to see anybody. You should go Paul," I said looking away. "Thanks for the flowers."

"Kalani is in New York visiting family, she will be home the day after tomorrow," Paul was on edge, nervous, and fidgeting. "But she sends her love and said she will come to see you right after she lands in L.A."

"Thanks, Paul…I just want to be alone. Go home. I'm sorry."

Sterile and devoid of any hospitable attributes, Olive View was exactly what I needed to blend into nothingness. They put me on an anti-depressant and I started therapy. I spewed out the pains of my life, the crazy stories, and explained why I wanted to die. I didn't think I could forgive myself for what I had done. I felt like a murderer and a coward. The substance of my character had dissolved into a pool of acid, evaporating on the floor.

After talking to a therapist for a couple of weeks and numerous evaluations, my psychiatrist, Dr. Choi, met with me to explain my diagnosis. She was in her thirties, with black hair pulled back in a ponytail, and looked smart with thin gold frames that held her glasses on the bridge of her nose. She had petite gold earrings dangling from her ears and a massive diamond ring on her finger that looked like it had been carefully chosen by someone who loved and respected her. I watched the birds flutter outside the window around a bush that had spring leaves and small flowers in bloom.

"Hello Alika." Dr. Choi sat down beside me and bluntly said, "We have a plan to treat your suicidal thoughts and hopefully prevent an attempt in the future." The term suicidal had me stunned for a moment.

"I guess I am suicidal. I felt I wasn't worthy to live after what I had done."

"The abortion, you mean?"

"Yeah, I killed my baby. Not that I am against abortion. Women should have the freedom of choice. I just really loved and wanted this baby."

"Alika, we think you have bipolar disorder," she explained. "It is a condition that makes it difficult to regulate emotions and behaviors. It's associated with mood swings ranging from manic highs to depressive lows. You can experience high levels of risky behavior without any thought to the outcome, including suicide. Manic episodes may include high energy, reduced need for sleep, and a loss of touch with reality. The cause is unknown, but it could be a combination of genetics, your environment, and an altered brain structure. We can help you. With the right medication, you can live a normal life."

I had no idea what a normal life meant.

"There is no known cure," Dr. Choi continued. "But is it manageable if you commit to taking medication daily."

"Daily? Like I need to take pills forever?" I resisted the notion that I would have to be dependent on a drug every day. All the drugs I had taken in my life were by choice and temporary. Forever was a very long time. I looked at the hospital gown I was wearing and the applesauce stain on my chest. Applesauce was the only thing I could stomach in this place, that and saltine crackers. I was thin and looked as fragile as I felt.

"Essentially, yes. You would need to take pills every day for the rest of your life," Dr. Choi cleared her throat. "I suggest you think of it this way…in order to manage your life, you need your daily dose of stability."

The birds were chirping loudly, vying for something growing on the bush.

"There will be an adjustment period. I will have to find the right medication and monitor you over the coming weeks in the outpatient program. You will need to get a therapist. I suggest you see him or her at least twice a week. We'll start with lithium to stabilize you." Dr. Choi stood up. "There is hope you will live a fulfilling life."

Paul picked me up the next morning and wanted to bring me to his favorite Jewish deli for breakfast. It was a restaurant we frequented because his father had an account there. We always ordered whatever we wanted and never had to pay. I could almost taste their soothing matzo ball soup.

"I don't want to be in public, Paul. Just take me to the house," I said looking out the car window. Small post-WWII houses flashed by on the way home. The same boring scenery, the same stifling smoggy air. The Valley, where I was raised, depressed me even more.

When we arrived, Paul's house was dirty and disheveled. Dishes were piled up and the yard was covered in Audrey's waste. My plants had not been watered, and the flowers were dead. This did not feel like home anymore. This relationship was not what it was. It had died along with the flowers and our baby.

"I'm going back to my mom's," I said.

"I'm sorry Alika. I really am," Paul replied as his tears started to well up. "I was afraid."

I reached down to pet Audrey. "Sometimes fear has a way of fucking things up, doesn't it?"

Diana

Chapter 16

Moving back home was uncomfortable because Mom and Ron were walking on eggshells around me. I was unpredictable, healing from trauma, and adjusting to the fact that I had been diagnosed with a mental illness. They were constantly on guard having to remind me to take my medication, which I was incredibly resistant to. They were very kind, but I knew they just wanted to relax in each other's company. I took up space and disrupted their peace.

The lithium made me feel worse than I already felt. I became a couch potato, watching TV nightly with my parents and eating buckets of ice cream. Just being lazy, I lost interest in the things that I normally liked to do, like dance, paint, study, and write poetry. Eventually, I stopped taking my meds, trying to feel "normal" again.

Wanting to break up the monotony, I began to hang out at gay clubs and mixed with a group of lesbians who really liked to party. Sex was fun and erotic, but I also felt a sense of comfort knowing I couldn't get pregnant. I would stay up all night drinking and crash at any of their apartments to avoid going home. However, on one extraordinary night, I met Diana at The Abbey in West Hollywood.

She was beautiful. Tall and slender, she had black hair, porcelain skin, and irises that looked like fertile ground. When our eyes met, they formed an unbreakable bond, and I was drawn to her like a crashed wave gets sucked back into the sea. Wearing a black suit, she stood next to an empty barstool, leaning on the bar. It was a summer night, and I was wearing a slinky white shimmery dress and a dainty pair of high heels. Walking across the deck, under strings of lights that illuminated the patio filled with women laughing, flirting, and clinking their glasses in celebration, I felt sensuality in the air.

"Hello," I said, attracted to the unadulterated air about her. "I don't want to overstep if you are here with someone…" I let the sentence trail off.

She held out her graceful hand.

"I'm just here with friends. I'm Diana,"

"I'm Alika," I said with my eyes still locked on hers. "Nice suit. You carry it well."

"Thank you. I think you would look good wearing anything," Diana said. "You should be a model if you aren't already."

"You are going to make me blush, if I'm not already," I smiled.

"Are you copying me?"

"I wish I could make a copy of you and put you in my pocket."

I could tell Diana was a modest woman by the innocence in her eyes.

"Can I buy you a drink?" she said as she winked. Dimples formed when she smiled, and I thought they were adorable.

"Thanks, I'll have what you are having," and I hopped onto the barstool.

"Two Cosmopolitans please," she asked the bartender.

"Funny, that was my mom's favorite magazine growing up. She had so many, I used to line them up on the floor like tiles with my favorite model at the top wishing to be on the cover one day."

"Well, if you weren't, you should have been" and Diana handed me a martini glass filled to the brim with pink yumminess.

"What do you do? You look...professional," I said sitting up straight.

"I'm just a CPA. Let's drink. Cheers!"

"Cheers," I said lifting my glass. "To the moon, it's full tonight."

"To the moon," Diana winked again before she took a sip of her drink. I began to wonder if her wink was a sweet involuntary twitch.

We laughed up a storm for hours because we just had that chemistry that tickled each other's funny bones. The customary gay house music played in the background and women were kissing next to us at the bar. We paused, and a tender seduction pulled us together. Our lips met and the softness made me tingle. Her breath like manna from heaven, and we lingered there like a living marble statue—a masterpiece of pure love.

Diana was a very busy woman. She worked full-time at an elite accounting firm and was gathering all the necessary parts she needed to set up her own business. She was a workaholic, the first in her Latino family to graduate from college. At first, time with her was rare because she worked late into the night, but I managed to wiggle into her life. I'd come over and make her dinner at her condo, we'd laugh and make out, play music and dance. Each moment felt precious; the air was lush and caressed our skin with the hand of beauty.

Though I continued to pursue my associate degree, and Diana her own accounting firm, we both made a conscious effort to enjoy the pool and barbecue at her condo. We took walks in the park across the street and went to lesbian parties. I felt safe and valued. Plus, Diana had never used drugs, she didn't smoke, and she drank very little. She was good for me, and I was good for her. She grounded me, and I helped her to fly.

When I graduated from Los Angeles Valley College with honors, the gratification was overwhelming. Wearing a Lei from my mom and Ron, and an additional one from Kalani, I held a large bouquet of long-stemmed red roses from Diana, and my picture was taken wearing my cap and gown. That picture is forever ingrained in my mind because I was absolutely glowing. With a beaming smile and the glimmer of happy tears in my eyes, the moment was locked looking at the people that I loved most in the world. I was moved by the power of healthy pride, and I was happy. To me, that photo proved Ricardo wrong. I *was* intelligent, and I *could* accomplish my goals. I was finally beginning to wash away the lies Ricardo had programmed into my mind.

Because I hadn't seen a dentist since I was a kid, Diana's graduation present was the numerous appointments to do the extensive work I needed: a deep cleaning, many fillings, and the removal of my wisdom teeth. It all added up to a hefty bill, but Diana said I was worth it. She told me that my smile meant more to her than anything in the world.

Diana wasn't someone who needed fixing like Paul, and she wasn't a destructive person like Dario. Diana was perfection—kind, loyal, smart, and graceful. Her character ran deep like a well of water connecting to the undercurrent of the earth. I was the ocean atop, restless, crashing at the shoreline.

Diana was gay, through and through, and she had always known it. All her friends were gay, and I could sense that they were untrusting of me because I wasn't. Being bisexual and bipolar, I didn't trust myself either. I wanted to be a lesbian, for Diana, but I wasn't.

We were at a Super Bowl party when I got drunk. Kalani had invited Diana and me to her friend's house, and we were the only female couple there. I was proud to hold Diana's hand while people looked at us like we were aliens. I would kiss her cheek while catching glances from the straight crowd, feeding on the attention. The more I drank, the more my mind wandered, dreaming up sexy scenarios with attractive people swimming in the pool. I always felt promiscuous when I drank too much.

Lounging poolside during halftime, I watched a fit, handsome man I didn't know stand on the edge of a diving board, when I made a crude comment to Kalani.

"I must admit I miss a good dick."

I didn't know that Diana had just walked up behind us with two drinks in her hand.

"Here's your drink," she said, with all the life drained from her voice.

I felt my body become heavy with embarrassment. I could not muster anything redeeming to say and took my drink from her delicate hand.

"I think I'm gonna go," Diana said. "Kalani, can you give her a ride home?"

"Yes, of course," Kalani looked at my shamed face.

"I'm sorry Diana, don't go," I said as she walked away.

I felt a sadness that I had never felt before, a disappointment in myself for having betrayed Diana with my lustful mind. But I knew my comment was enough to break the trust between lovers, and I started to cry.

Kalani rolled her eyes, "Oh fuck."

I had been too much of a coward to face Diana after that day. Ashamed, I holed up at my parents' house. She didn't call, nor did I. She was worth fighting for, but I didn't think she would forgive me. Downward spirals of conflicting emotion began to consume me as I weighed my priorities of sex and love. I lost all courage to face Diana and wallowed in my depression. I wanted to commit to a life with her, but I couldn't at the time. Struggling with my sexual identity, I hadn't matured enough to nurture the love we shared.

I was at my mom's house when I got a call from my old friend Kent. I met him when we were on a modeling gig in the '80s. We kept in touch through my mother because he was diligent about holding on to the people in his life that he cared about, and I was one of them. A smart guy, he bought a house in Austin, Texas, after graduating with an MBA and now traveled on business as a consultant. He said he was building an extension onto his house at Lake Travis, but he needed someone to live there to keep tabs on the work being done while he traveled. He asked me if I would do it. He'd even pay me an allowance to paint it and oversee the job. In my misery, and with an instinct to make an escape, I accepted his offer.

He sent me a check for gas money and asked if I could be there within a week before he left for his next job on the east coast. I was manic and desperate to flee Los Angeles. Sitting on the sidewalk in front of my mom's house with my stuff scattered about, I frantically sorted through my belongings, wondering what to bring and what to leave behind. I piled things I didn't want any more like stacks of papers I should have filed, and clothes that I wore when I was pregnant. Memories of my recent failures haunted me, and my pulse raced. I supposed it was my mom who called Kalani and Diana to inform them I was leaving, because they drove up to the house one after the other.

"Alika, what are you doing?" Kalani asked, concerned.

"I've got to get outta here," I said, intensely packing the car.

Then I heard Diana get out of her BMW and the loud beep when she locked it. She walked up to me in her business attire, looking sharp but walking timidly.

"Alika, I want to say goodbye before you leave, and I brought this bag of things you left at my house. It's mostly clothes and make-up. Are you sure you want to do this?"

"Thanks," I said, taking the bag while shying away from her eyes. "I need a job, and this is a job."

"You could find a job *here*," Kalani said. "You need a support system now more than ever. Don't do this!"

"I've tried talking to her," my mom added. "She won't listen to me."

Putting in the trunk what I had resolved to take with me, and leaving a pile on the front lawn, I gave my mother a big hug.

"Will you throw this stuff away? I don't need it." Holding her shoulders, I looked into my mother's fretful face. "I love you. Thank you for everything. You are a great mom, more than I could have asked for." Then I hugged Kalani. "You are the best friend a girl can have," I said as my face burrowed into her soft blonde hair. I straightened up and looked into her eyes. I was so close, I could see the golden flecks in her irises. She had deep and wise eyes, kind and loving. "I wish I were a better friend to you. Forgive me. I love you."

With a heavy sigh, Kalani held me for a long moment.

"I love you too. Whatever you do, find a psychiatrist when you get there. Don't give up on yourself, Alika."

"Okay, okay. I will," I said looking at Diana over Kalani's shoulder.

"Well, I guess this is goodbye," Diana said softly. I passionately held her in my arms. I wanted to cry but took a deep breath to suppress the geyser inside.

"I am sorry. I never wanted to hurt you," I said with a tense throat. "I'll always love you, Diana. I'm just mixed up is all. I'm sorry."

"I'll always love you too Alika. Take care of yourself," and she stepped back, scuffling the sidewalk with her new black loafers.

I gave my mom one last big hug before getting into the car and starting the engine.

"She's gonna do what she's gonna do, Grace," Kalani said as she put her arm over my mom's shoulders, hoping to console her. "She always seems to pick herself up after a fall."

My mother's eyes welled up with tears, knowing too much time would pass before she saw me again.

As I drove away, I looked at the reflection of the three women in my rearview mirror. They stood on the corner, where I used to fold up my newspapers in the morning as a kid, and waved in unison. They were the three women I loved the most in the world but couldn't measure up to. Escaping again and letting self-sabotage win, I took a left on the busy street toward the highway. Reaching into my purse and throwing my bottle of pills out the window, I swerved into traffic and headed east toward the lone star state.

Lifted

Chapter 17

It had been fifteen years since I had traveled on Interstate 10 going east. I was flooded with memories of my honeymoon phase with Dario, then quickly remembered how I blamed him for making me feel worthless, which was how I felt in that moment, all on my own, so many years later.

This victim mentality would certainly be the death of me.

Driving along these long stretches of highway, I tried to listen to music through the static of the radio to distract me from how disgusted I was with myself. The two things in my life that were pure and good, my baby and then Diana, were gone and it was my fault.

After trekking through the wide stretches of barren land in Texas, which mirrored the emptiness I felt inside, I approached Lake Travis, on the outskirts of Austin. It seemed like an oasis, with rolling hills and trees surrounding a sparkling lake. I finally felt a glimmer of hope.

Kent invited me into his home, which was still under construction, and introduced me to the contractor. He said I had free rein to pick out paint colors for the new addition, because he had no idea what to choose. Kent had a sarcastic sense of humor and always made me laugh, not only at the world, but at myself. He accepted me for the flawed individual I was and hoped to help me by giving me a leg up in life. He had to get back to his business in New York, so I was left to find a way to fill up the hole inside my soul.

It wasn't long before I discovered lake life and the party scene and began drinking like there was no tomorrow. When the bars closed at 2 a.m., the boats docked at the pier filled up with drunks. We would recklessly whisk around the lake, flying over the water, howling at the night sky until the break of dawn. Midday on weekends, we would carry cases of beer and liquor on board and head out to the coves, anchor, and then tie the boats together in preparation for fun and frolicking in the sun. It was a *Girls Gone Wild* scene with topless dancing to loud music, skinny-dipping, and random sex in the cabins, sharing each other's lovers.

The painting and construction went on at the house while I was self-destructing. There were times when I was alone at the house and the haunting voices in my head would become so intrusive that I thought I could hear them taunting me. Hangovers were torture, but I would quickly start the cycle over again to avoid listening to the negative thoughts inhabiting my mind.

On good days, I would visit my new friend Maya, who lived across the cove from Kent's house, and we'd swim in the sunshine. We played a game where we would wave to each other to signal when to jump into the lake, and then we'd race to see who could get to the middle of the cove first. Maya always won. She grew up swimming on that lake. Maya had a canoe, and sometimes we would row to neighboring coves to smoke joints, watch the birds fly overhead, listen to the lapping water, and gossip about who was sleeping with whom. But on this day, she brought her Bible.

"Open it anywhere," Maya said. "And read the first thing that pops out at you."

I had never opened a Bible before and felt nervous flipping through the thin pages. I stopped on a page with the 23rd Psalm staring back at me.

"Read it Alika," Maya encouraged me.

Settling my nerves, I began.

"The Lord is my shepherd; I shall not want. He maketh me to lie down in green pastures: He leadeth me beside the still waters. He restoreth my soul…" As I continued reading, I felt something touch me inside, something like truth itself. I recalled my out of body experience from many years ago when I had a brush with death—or rather a peek into a life beyond what I had known. "Yea, though I walk through the valley of the shadow of death, I will fear no evil. For thou art with me…" I began to breathe rapidly, and my chest felt a kind of pressure, as if a great presence was touching my soul. "Thou preparest a table before me in the presence of mine enemies: thou anointest my head with oil; my cup runneth over. Surely goodness and mercy shall follow me all the days of my life: and I will dwell in the house of the Lord forever."

I closed the book realizing there was more to the story of life, and my mind opened with possibility.

"I have an extra Bible at home," Maya said with a serene smile. "You can have this one. Alika, read it, it'll do you some good."

It was a Sunday morning in June 2004 when I woke up to a knock at the door. Through the peephole, I saw a young woman named Polly, who I knew from the parties on the boats. She was dressed nicely, and I barely recognized her because I had only ever seen her naked or in a bathing suit.

"Hi Polly, what's up?" I said opening the door.

"Did I wake you? I'm sorry, but I had this hunch I couldn't shake. I had to come ask you if you'd like to join me at church today?" Polly paused. "It might sound crazy, but something told me to come pick you up."

I was taken aback and knew deep down this was a sign, but a touch of fear urged me to decline. However, I managed to push through and opened the door to let her in anyway.

"Yeah, okay. I'll get ready quickly. Hold on."

I rushed to brush my teeth and put on some deodorant and perfume. I put on my longest dress and tossed my hair.

"Let's go," I said, feeling the fear sink down my spine, to the root.

Looking out the window of Polly's truck as we rumbled down the road, I admired the cypress and sycamore trees and thought of the mycelium that connects them underground. Fascinating webs of fungi filaments in healthy trees transport nutrients to the ones that are suffering, so they can regain their strength. And here was Polly, extending her hand, just like the mycelia.

We reached the highway. "The church is close by. The music is about to start," she said blowing smoke out the window. The reek of her cigarette turned my stomach. I was nauseous from the alcohol still in my system. I had to close my eyes and focus on something else. Imagining roots extend deeper than the tree is tall, I longed for that kind of anchor.

We pulled into a huge parking lot. Families were briskly walking toward a large new building with wooden accents and shiny windows topped with a steel cross towering over us. People walking toward the main entrance looked so clean and happy. In comparison, I felt dirty through and through.

"It'll be alright," Polly looked at me. "The people here are really nice. Trust me."

A man extended his hand as we approached, "Welcome," he said as he gripped my hand. Could he tell I was trembling inside? Polly had to nudge me along. After we passed through a few more greeters, we entered a wide-open space with hundreds of people facing a stage. A band was fervently playing New Age Christian songs, with passionate lyrics about Jesus and love. The congregation was singing along, some were waving their arms in the air while others closed their eyes in prayer. Polly scooted us into some seats in the middle of the room. I was so nervous, I felt like I needed to pee.

As the band softened the music, a man in his mid-thirties dressed in a suit, tall and handsome, entered with a microphone and began a prayer.

"Lord, thank you for gathering us here today to worship you. May we bask in your glory and your grace. We know your mercy covers our sins. We are blessed by your sacrifice. Thank you, Jesus. Amen."

The music welled up and the band finished the song as the choir held up their hands and soaked in the spirit. This was nothing like the church Grandma took to me to. No candles, no robes, no chanting, no altar boys.

As the band left the stage, the preacher came back out and began his sermon.

"This morning I want to talk about shame. The Apostles Creed is the belief of the forgiveness of sins through Jesus Christ, and because of this, our shame is washed away. It is the foundation of our truth: there is more mercy in Christ than there is sin. But first, because all roads lead to Genesis, we need to recognize that there was a time when shame didn't exist. Shame tells us that our sins define us. We say, 'I'm no good' and 'I am not worth loving.' There was a time of complete safety in the perfect love of Eden. Adam and Eve were naked and exposed to God without fear. But it was through listening to the lies of the serpent that they hid from God. We teach shame in our society.

Babies aren't born feeling shame. We teach it to them. It is what we feel when we sin. We do things that afterwards we are not proud of, and we feel shame. Let's look at John 13."

Some people opened their Bibles, and some sat and listened to the gospel with contented looks on their faces. I felt my shame bubbling to the surface as the preacher continued.

"John talks about when Jesus knew his hour had come," he went on. "It was after the Passover meal and Jesus prepared to wash the Apostles' feet. Why would Jesus do this? Why would he humble himself so much to get on his knees and wash their dirty feet? It is symbolic, of course. In the moment Jesus cleaned the soles of the Apostles' feet, they were cleansed from shame, from guilt, from sin."

I couldn't stop thinking about the baby I lost, the baby I killed. It felt like shame consumed every cell in my body. I began to cry silent tears that flowed from the deepest trenches of my soul.

"Peter protested and said, 'You wash me? No, my Lord, I should be washing you.' Our faith-filled community is so wrapped up in serving God, but we must give up our pride and let Him serve us. Jesus says to Peter in John 13, 'Unless I wash you, you have no share with me.'"

I felt as though the preacher was speaking directly to me. The power of his delivery struck my heart. I wanted forgiveness. I wanted freedom from my pain.

"There is no danger in getting honest and confessing," the preacher continued. "There is only freedom from guilt and shame when you accept Jesus into your life. As God created a new skin for Adam and Eve to cover their shame and beckoned them to come out from hiding, you too are covered. If any of you feel compelled to receive the love of Christ and accept His forgiveness, come to the alter now. You may not know it yet, but Jesus said, 'You are already clean.'" The preacher walked to the edge of the stage, "Come." He waved his hand gently, beckoning people to step up. I shot out of my chair and joined at the back of the line.

Thinking of the time Danny wanted me to be "saved" over the telephone, I approached the preacher hoping this time it would really work. He laid his hand over my head. His gentle eyes appeared loving and not judgmental of the shame written all over my face.

"Do you accept Jesus Christ as your Lord and Savior?"

"I do," I said weak and crying.

A woman next to him wrapped her arm around my shoulders and escorted me off to the side.

"It's all right dear. You are forgiven," she said holding me as I let my sorrow pour out. I cried for a long time while she sat with me patiently and I felt the washing the preacher had talked about. A feeling of lightness overcame me as if God was cleansing my soul.

Baptized in the Colorado River that summer, I embarked on a new life. I committed myself to that church, attending every Sunday morning and Wednesday evenings. I joined the singles group at church and made new friends. Instead of going to the bars, we had barbecues together. Instead of wild boat parties, we went tubing in the river. Instead of selfish indulgence, we volunteered at Habitat for Humanity and at Bible studies for kids. We took our youth group of high school students to Mexican border towns and built homes for families living in cardboard shacks.

Joining Bible study wasn't enough to satisfy my desire to know all I could about my newfound faith, so I enrolled in the Austin Graduate School of Theology. It was located smack dab in the middle of the University of Texas in the center of town. Founded in 1917, it was a seminary where I could learn about the origins of the Bible, study Greek, dig into the history behind numerous translations of the text, and write about my spiritual discoveries.

I read and studied the Bible with passion, prayed often, and developed a profound God-consciousness that made me feel connected to the people and the world around me. I had no desire to drink or do anything destructive to my body. I curbed my desire for sex and wore a promise ring that reminded me to wait until I got married. Forgetting my diagnosis, I rode the wave of Christianity on a manic high and set my sights on becoming a missionary.

At the start of the fall semester, a professor at the college organized a trip for students to tour Israel during winter break. Professor Hailstrum, a fiercely passionate teacher of biblical history, would lecture while we visited ancient sites. We would tour the whole country and participate in a dig while living at Tel Tamar, where an active excavation was in progress.

After receiving a scholarship, I was all in! We would leave right after Christmas.

Soon after the semester started, Hurricane Katrina had just wiped out our neighboring state of Louisiana. Our church made great efforts to aid the people pouring into Texas seeking shelter, food, and supplies. I made trips back and forth to the New Orleans area with members of my church to help people get settled in temporary homes in Austin. I witnessed the U.S. military at work, bringing food and supplies and saving lives, being of service to a community that needed them. Watching emergency evacuations on the television inspired me to want to do something more with my life.

I helped to prepare meals in the church kitchen, participated in toy drives and delivered presents for displaced families during the holiday season. I was high on mania, unable to satisfy my deep urge to help the world when a thought occurred to me. *What better way to be of service than to be a nurse in the Army! And being a missionary at heart, I could save lives both physically and spiritually! That was it!*

I convinced myself to go to a recruiting office and stated that I wanted to join the Army. A man in uniform sitting behind a desk looked at me with all seriousness "How old are you?"

"Thirty-seven," I said, shocking myself.

"Have a seat," he said, shaking my hand. "I'm Sergeant Moore. What's your name?"

"Alika," I said, "Alika Jones."

"Well, Jones," Sergeant Moore said, and cleared his throat. "I appreciate you wanting to be of service to our great country, but I have to say that you'd better hurry up and join before it's too late.

Thirty-eight is the cut off. Of course, you will have to qualify and pass a physical exam. First, I have a few questions. Have you ever been arrested?"

"No," I said, hoping my bouts with the London police didn't count.

"Do you have a problem with substance abuse?" he asked while checking off boxes on a form.

"No," I said, burying my past.

"Do you have a mental illness?" Sergeant Moore looked me dead in the eyes.

"No," I said, only feeling like I was half-lying. I thought I had been washed clean by Jesus himself.

"Do you have a physical condition that would inhibit you from strenuous activity? Injuries of any kind?"

"No," I said thankful that my skirt covered the scar on my right knee which would reveal my bike accident.

"Lastly, are you a United States citizen?"

"Yes," I said with a smile, finally telling the whole truth.

"Are you a high school graduate?"

"Yes, I also have an associate degree with a 3.9 GPA," I said with pride.

"That's great. It will give you more options." Sergeant Moore leaned back from his checklist and stretched in his chair. "What kind of job are you hoping for?"

"I want to be a nurse," I said enthusiastically.

"You would have to pass basic training and combat medic school first, but nursing school is doable. Your education does help with additional pay, and you would start as a private first class. However, at your age you could only go into the reserves."

"I'm currently in seminary now and going on a class trip to Israel with my professor, so I won't be able to start until January or February," I said not knowing anything about Army protocol. "Is that okay?"

"Let's not get ahead of ourselves. We have some tests before we can accept you. But the short answer is yes. After processing, you can agree to a delayed entry program called DEP rather than a direct ship to basic. How would you describe the shape you are in? Do you run at all?"

"Can't say that I do."

"That'll be something you will have to get used to, Jones. I suggest you get started on that regularly, and right away." Sergeant Moore handed me a pamphlet. "Okay let's get you scheduled at MEPS. This is the first step. And there are a lot of acronyms you will have to learn, but this is the Military Entrance Processing Station. They will determine your mental aptitude, as well as physical and moral qualifications for enlistment. How about a week from now? Next Monday? You'll have to show up at 4 a.m., so prep yourself."

"Yes sir," I said, as though foreshadowing the near future.

"Here's the address. It's real close to here." Sergeant Moore stood up. "They will take care of everything. Prepare yourself for a long process and good luck."

"Awesome, thank you, Sarge!" I stood up with a salute and confidently walked out thinking about how great it would be to become a nurse, debt free, make money, and get in shape. This was a win-win-win.

Leading up to Monday, I jogged around the lake each morning after coffee and prayers and again in the evening. It had been two years since my last drop of alcohol, and I had already coughed up all the phlegm that congested my lungs from weed and cigarettes many months before. What I needed to work on was stamina and strength. I set goals to run farther and faster each day and had to work at regulating my breath. "Mind over matter" became my mantra as I did push-ups before and after each run and focused on the mental strength that was needed to overcome physical weakness.

On Monday before dawn, I arrived at the MEPS location to find a horde of young men and women awaiting entry. Even though I was nearly twenty years older than all of them, I did feel confident that I could keep up physically and even more so mentally. We met with our liaisons and the processing began.

Candidates were divided by branches of service, and we all received our morning briefing. Driven on pure instinct, I had chosen the Army and wondered in that moment why I hadn't looked at the other options. My cohort took the ASVAB test, which measures the potential to learn and qualifies a person for an occupation. I was dead set on being a nurse and I did my best on the test, which was long and tedious but not difficult. Next was the physical and medical testing. They separated the males from females and had us strip down to our underwear, bras, and bare feet. First, they inspected us for any inappropriate tattoos or piercings, but I had none. Then they measured joint health in wrists, ankles, hips, elbows, and knees. Next came the balance exercises. They inspected our foot arches and then we did the famous duck walk where we had to walk across the room with our butts on our heels while on our tip toes. I had no problems with any of it and I moved on to the medical testing. They did blood work, took a urine sample, tested for pregnancy and AIDS, and did a drug test. I was clean. They did a background check to see if there was substantial debt, criminal history, DUIs or incarcerations. I had none, so they moved me forward to meet with a career counselor.

"Hello, I am Sergeant Brady. You scored quite well on your tests and your educational background is helpful. I see you want to go into nursing."

"Yes sir!" I said enthusiastically.

"I don't see any problem with that. Of course, you will have to pass basic training, which is nine weeks long and then combat medic school for sixteen weeks, which is essentially EMT training. Then you'll be good to go. Are you prepared to start today?" Sergeant Brady placed a pen in front of me.

"No sir," I said. "I told the recruiter that I am going to Israel with fellow college students for three weeks. We leave this Friday. I won't be back until January 26th. Can I begin after that?"

"Let's see...we can set you up here to begin on February 1st," Sergeant Brady said. "Be sure to arrive back here by 4 a.m. and bring your contract. You can join the group of soldiers heading out on the bus to Fort Leonard Wood in Missouri. Just read this over and sign at the bottom."

The contract stated that I would start as a private first class, receive $1500 direct deposit each month, and was approved for nursing school as my career path. I nervously picked up the pen. My brain suddenly shifted into what felt like a slow, hazy, terrifying space of fear.

Sergeant Brady stared at me while I hesitated to sign the document.

What was I doing? Had I lost my mind?

"Come on soldier, hurry it up," Sergeant Brady said. "You need to line up to give your oath."

Contrary to what I was feeling inside, I signed the contract and got up to stand in a row with the other recruits. We each stood straight and waited. I felt a panic attack begin to overwhelm me. I was breathing heavily for fear of what I was doing, and a sense of clarity opened my eyes. I didn't believe in war. I didn't have confidence in government officials. I believed in peace and was a pacifist at heart.

My mind scrambled.

What if I get deployed to the Middle East and I write a story about what was really happening because of the Iraq War? Get the real scoop, like an undercover agent, and tell the world!

Major Thompson, a mild-mannered man, stepped onto a platform behind the podium. "Welcome to the United States Army, soldiers. It is an honor and privilege to serve our great nation. Now raise your right hand and repeat after me."

I stood with my right palm facing forward, feeling like an imposter, as we stated our oath of enlistment:

"I, Jones, do solemnly swear that I will support and defend the Constitution of the United States against all enemies, foreign and domestic. That I will bear true faith and allegiance to do the same, and that I will obey the orders of the President of the United States, and the officers appointed over me, according to regulations and the Uniform Code of Military Justice. So help me God."

The men in uniform standing all around us clapped and the group of recruits smiled and patted each other on the back. I stood there unable to move, stuck and speechless.

"Whatcha standing there for?" said a young man next to me as he patted me on the shoulder. "Put a smile on yer face. Yer a solider now!"

Holy, Wholly, Holey

Chapter 18

After a 15-hour flight, we landed in Tel Aviv on a beautiful sunny day, inhaling the fragrant salt air wafting from the Mediterranean Sea. Professor Hailstrum, a dozen of my classmates, and I all boarded a tour bus and drove along the coast. We eventually pulled over for a chance to soak in the scenery and buy refreshments from a stand set up at the lookout point.

The water was so inviting. I ran to the shore over the hot sand, skipping a step so I wouldn't burn my feet. I leaped into the water with all my clothes on and splashed into the small soft waves rippling toward me. Washing away the crustiness of the endless air travel, I felt invigorated being outside of the stale energy of the United States. There was adventure on the horizon, a new land and culture to discover, and new people to appreciate and adore. I was ready for it and whipped back up to the bus where my classmates were drinking *limonada* and ice café. I bought a black and tan tie-dyed wrap from a vendor and popped into the restroom to change out of my wet pants and tank top.

Boarding the bus and looking out the window onto a land that had been fought over for millennia, I thought what a blessing it was that I had received a scholarship which paid for the transportation, food, and lodging for what was bound to be an extraordinary experience.

When arriving at Tel Tamar in the Arava Desert, we were greeted by Rose Marie von Trapp, one of the children made famous by the movie *The Sound of Music*. She was a sweet and graceful woman who managed the guests at Tel Tamar and explained that it was an ancient mound that had been built up over several centuries of occupation.

"Welcome all of you. I will give you a bit of a history lesson about Tel Tamar and Israel in general after you all get settled, and we have a nice meal together. There are dorms for you to sleep in, women on the left of the hall, and men on the right. Pick a bed, it's dormitory style. It's wonderful having Professor Hailstrum back and all of you here. Dinner is at six o'clock."

I had never traveled in such an organized manner. Everything was already taken care of, and all I had to do was relax and enjoy the trip. Dinner was delicious and consisted of falafel, an Israeli salad made with finely diced tomato, onion, cucumber, bell pepper, and lemon juice, accompanied by the best pita bread I had ever eaten. Afterwards, we were served tea and powdered cookies while we listened to Rose Marie's lesson.

"All over Israel, remains have been found dating back to the Stone Age, Bronze Age, and the Iron Age. According to the Bible, the Israelites evolved into a kingdom which after a few decades split in two—the Kingdom of Israel in the north, and the Kingdom of

Judah in the south. The southern monarchy was small, isolated, and ruled by the House of David. The northern kingdom was stronger and more prosperous. It had developed extensive commercial ties with the countries surrounding it. However, the Assyrian empire brought an end to the northern Kingdom of Israel in 722 BC. And then, 130 years later, the more rebellious southern Kingdom of Judah was conquered by the Babylonian King Nebuchadnezzar. Try saying that ten times fast!" Rose Marie continued. "The people of Judah were exiled to Babylon, but fifty years later returned to their homeland to rebuild the temple. Yet again, the land was conquered in 332 BC by Alexander the Great along with much of the east. The Greeks ruled until the Roman conquest of Israel and beyond. In 63 BC the Romans appointed King Herod as King of Judah and he built many important projects including the Temple Mount in Jerusalem. The Romans ruled for 400 years despite the Jewish uprisings and the teachings of Jesus of Nazareth giving birth to Christianity.

"The Byzantine Empire conquered the land of Israel in the fourth century, and then the Muslim Empire in the seventh century. It was then that the Muslims built the Dome of the Rock in Jerusalem. Eventually, the Crusaders occupied Jerusalem and for 200 years built major infrastructure and architecture projects. In 1291, the Muslims expelled the Crusaders and built mosques on top of their churches. Ottoman Turks then conquered the land of Israel and built the walls that still surround Jerusalem today. All in all, you can imagine the multitude of artifacts that have been uncovered and the knowledge we acquire the more we excavate. Israel is a treasure trove of archeology, and we will learn more about our dig here on the Tel tomorrow after breakfast," finished Rose Marie.

Professor Hailstrum piped in.

"And after our introduction on how to dig by our friend Yigal Levy, an experienced Israeli archeologist in charge of the expedition here, we will head to Masada, which is the site of the last Jewish stronghold opposing the Romans. A fascinating story that I will tell you on the way there. Those of you who prefer the cable car are welcome to avoid a rather strenuous hike up the mountain. But I will be hiking, and I suggest you do the same for the full experience. It's been a long day, let's get some sleep. Tomorrow, adventure awaits!"

Lying in my cot, I was amazed by the country that I came to discover. I had three weeks to soak in the experience of a lifetime before diving into the scariest commitment I had ever made—beginning boot camp back in America. Having ridden the pendulum to its extremity most of my life, would I ever be able to rest in the middle?

After breakfast the next morning, Yigal Levy, a sturdy and strong man in his fifties, spoke passionately as he told us about his excavation on Tel Tamar over the last decade. He had charisma and a rough, genuine nature which I found attractive. He informed us that the next day we would dig with small hoes or rakes, gently brushing the artifacts we'd uncover by removing the dirt. If something significant was found, it would be handed over to The Israel Museum in Jerusalem, but if we found small shards of pottery, likely Roman in this case, we could take it home as a souvenir. Yigal planted his eyes on me, and it gave me the tingles. It had been two years since I had had sex with anyone. My promiscuous nature ignited, and I knew I would not be able to resist him. I slid off my chastity ring and put it in my pocket.

The journey to Masada took about an hour as I looked out the window and watched the desert pass by under the blue sky. I imagined people migrating on foot across this land and the turmoil that had taken place. The road signs read in three languages—Hebrew, Arabic, and English, demonstrating the fact that today, this was a multicultural land where the people within its borders lived together in peace. It was on the edges where the problems lay.

On our way up the trail, Professor Hailstrum explained that Masada was the first great fortress built by King Herod in 35 BC. The city lay atop a mountain nearly 1,000 feet in elevation and overlooked the Dead Sea. During the Great Revolt, a group of Jewish rebels, called the Sicarii, overtook the Roman garrison and inhabited the fortress for nearly a decade. When the Romans succeeded in building a huge ramp to the top, despite the defender's fight to keep them back, they arrived to find the city ablaze and all the inhabitants dead, except for a single woman and a few children. Legend has it that the rebels performed a mass suicide so as not to be taken prisoner.

Reaching the top, we took in the view. I marveled at how an entire elaborate city could be built so high up on this mountain almost 2,000 years ago, all on foot, with more muscle and perseverance than I could imagine. Roaming around the ruins, I thought about the horror the lone woman and the children faced as the dead fell all around them, and how terrified they must have been when the Roman soldiers arrived. I often thought about the true losers of wartime—the innocent bystanders who were captured, killed, raped, and imprisoned. My imagination moved me to tears as I empathized with the pain and fear of that woman and those children. As usual, I let my emotions wash over me and dissipate. The highs and lows came and went like the wind.

As the temperature rose, the Dead Sea in the distance looked so inviting. Later that day, we floated in its warm, thick body of water which was far from refreshing. It was difficult to avoid getting the incredibly salty water in our eyes, which stung something awful as it was nine and a half times as salty as the ocean.

Looking at Jordan on the shore to the east, I felt connected to a vast history, wondering how many people floated in this water over the course of time. Down the trail from Masada, The Dead Sea had been a health resort for King Herod, and today the mud masks sold at the souvenir shop were a treat to take home.

Arriving back at the Tel and being greeted by Rose Marie warmed my heart, and I felt compelled to crochet her a hat. I always carried a crochet hook in my purse, and I had packed some dusty blue, soft pink, gold, and white yarn in my suitcase, ready to relax at night crocheting with my nimble fingers. I got busy making the hat while our group talked about our day on the mountain, and we laughed about our adventure floating in the salty sea.

Professor Hailstrum stood up.

"Tomorrow we will dig first thing in the morning, and then I have a treat for you," he said. "We will go to the Ein Gedi Nature Reserve. It is an oasis in the desert, a lush mineral spring with a waterfall and a delightful place to swim where the ibex roam."

"What's an ibex?" a fellow student asked.

"They are wild goats that climb the rocky terrain and come to Ein Gedi for food and water. The males have very large, curved horns. They're magnificent creatures." Professor Hailstrum gathered his thoughts. "And the following day, we will visit Tel Hazor, a national treasure, as well as the ancient city of Megiddo. I've also arranged a lovely dinner in Tiberias at night."

Then Yigal, the archeologist, entered the room.

"Hello my helpers," he said with his big voice. "Ready for tomorrow morning?"

"Yes!" the crowd replied in unison.

"We will start at 6:30 a.m. while it is still cool and there is enough light to get started," said Yigal with his delightful Israeli accent. He was addressing the room, but when he looked at me, I could feel his eyes undressing me and his desire roused a warm, forgotten well of sensuality whirling between my thighs. Yigal tilted his head toward the back door before he said, "Good night one and all. Rest well."

Putting down my hook and yarn, I nonchalantly scooted out the front door and met him around the back. Under the light of the moon, Yigal grabbed each of my shoulders and pulled me close to him and I felt his teeth gently bite my neck. I felt weak in the knees, but he held me up as our lips met and my pent-up passion was unleashed. I felt the first drops of an orgasm trickle when he pulled me by the hand, and we swiftly jogged over to his trailer.

Yigal tore off my tank top and kissed my breasts as I arched my back. His arms held me up and then lifted me, so I felt weightless and ready to be devoured. I was turned on by his thick hands and strong arms, his rustic face and seasoned, rough demeanor. We both unzipped our jeans, peeled them off, and then struggled to remove our boots. Finally free from all clothing, we ripped into what felt like a sex dream without words, fully heated in our hungry bodies. Our eyes met in an ecstatic embrace. Intercourse, hidden, and even forbidden, felt like a secret only the lucky ones could keep. Experiencing the intensity of the perfect fit of our bodies, made to coalesce, and with a pleasure that consumed every cell, I became a dam breaking open and let the flood flow out onto the sheets below us.

After lying together for a couple of hours and repeating our sexual escapade again and again, I strolled alone back to the dorms. Under the light of a bright moon, I gazed at the ruins all around me. With my legs still a bit weak, I balanced on top of what was once a thick wall to an ancient Roman bathhouse. Professor Hailstrum explained earlier that the hypocaust system was very effective at heating the stone floors from underneath, generating a steam bath. I still felt steamy myself—I was revived and relaxed. I decided to lay flat on an ancient wall and watch the bright stars twinkle above the desert.

After a quick breakfast the next morning, we set out to excavate the area south of the 10th century fortress. Many people found pottery shards and my friend Julie found a slingshot. As we continued scraping and brushing away the dirt, Yigal, looking grounded, sipped his coffee. I looked up at him, raising something that looked interesting and didn't seem like a typical rock. I wiped it clean as Yigal walked over to me.

"Good God," he exclaimed. "It looks like you found a signet ring!"

He explained that these rings were a form of identity and often used to seal documents after pressing them into hot wax, like a signature. I wondered about who had worn this ring and mused over how much things had changed yet remained the same. No matter the era, people make their mark.

Yigal kept the ring to give to The Israel Museum, and after another couple hours of digging, we all got ready for our trip to the Ein Gedi. Yigal did not join us, and I found that I missed his formidable presence. The cool mineral water felt glorious under the hot desert sun. The ibex poked their horned heads out through the bushes. Swimming to the waterfall and feeling the rush of the water above my head had me in awe of the power of gravity. Life is composed of so many fascinating elements, I just had to laugh at the enormity of it all.

Before heading back to Tel Tamar, we went to eat and drink at a large Bedouin tent standing alone in the desert, a distinctive dining experience to say the least. The Bedouins of the Negev Desert are an indigenous Arabic nomadic tribe, and for decades have been citizens of Israel. Sitting low in a big misshapen circle on beautiful carpets and decorative cushions, we ordered food and hot tea. Much to my surprise, Yigal joined us for dinner. He sat next to professor Hailstrum and winked at me now and again.

We all delighted in the communal meal of *mansaf*—tender meat layered with paper-thin flatbread on a pile of aromatic rice, topped with toasted nuts and accompanied by a tangy yogurt sauce. We ate a superb meal with our hands and drank a unique blend of hot black tea. There were three pots flowing—one with mint, one with cardamom, and one plain with black tea and sugar. Afterwards many of us drank local beer and made merry sliding off the pillows and loving life as we lounged on the floor.

When I got up to find the restroom, Yigal followed me outside.

"I can't stop thinking about you," he said with intensity as he looked at me.

"You've got me hooked too, Yigal," I said coming closer to his face.

We were so close to a kiss when Julie, my bunkmate, approached from the tent.

"Hey guys! What a meal, right?"

"Yes, delicious," we said as she passed. "I could eat you up all night," we both said under our breath, and laughed at our synchronicity.

"Meet me in my trailer tonight, and every night before you leave," Yigal said squeezing my hand, and then he turned to walk back inside.

And so, I did. I would meet him at night and soak in the ecstasy after long days touring ancient ruins with the group. During the day, the group of us ate lunch in cities like Nazareth, Tiberias, and Be'er Sheva. We also visited the Golan Heights with its wineries, and then

Caesarea National Park filled with well-preserved Roman ruins, like a big amphitheater where we all laughed at our operatic renditions. Visiting Capernaum along the sea of Galilee was special because of all the Biblical references to the teachings of Jesus and the miracles he performed there. I took a private walk, in silence, along the grounds and communed with the peaceful energy, appreciating the purpose of this trip, which was to deepen our spiritual experience. But I couldn't help but think of Yigal and the sexual bliss we experienced together. I was no saint and didn't want to be.

Our excursion in Israel was ending too soon, but first, we would stay in Jerusalem for the weekend. When I said goodbye to Rose Marie, I teared up as we held each other in a warm hug. She had such a calm and peaceful energy, reminding me of Virginia, my sweet grandmother, so reverent and kind. Yigal was shaking hands with professor Hailstrum and fellow students when he signaled for me to meet him outside the kitchen.

I was waiting there between two trees when he appeared from around the corner and pressed me flat against the wall. He kissed me right on the lips and opened his mouth. Then he reached his hand down in between my legs over my jeans, lifted, and squeezed me. I burned up as his strong hand pressed on the most delicate part of my body, and I became limp in his arms. I extended my arm down and stroked him over his pants and we both felt a rush overcome us. Just then we heard voices coming closer and we scrambled out toward the clearing. We quickly engaged in conversation about the dig and pretended to give each other a casual embrace.

"Goodbye Yigal," I said. "You've made this trip unforgettable."

He hugged me once more and whispered in my ear.

"Take care of yourself, Alika. You are beautiful, don't ever forget that."

I found the old city of Jerusalem fascinating, with the Jewish quarter, alongside the Christian, Muslim, and Armenian quarters existing in harmony side by side. The Jewish section was filled with men and boys wearing black suits and hats with white shirts, each walking with a purpose. The first place we went to was the Western Wall, on top of Mount Zion.

As we approached the most sacred wall in the world, professor Hailstrum explained that the large blocks at the bottom were built by King Herod around 19 BC. It was a project to extend the smaller area where the First Temple stood, built by the House of David, and transformed the Temple Mount into the almost rectangular wide expanse it is today. Jerusalem has a long and complicated history, and professor Hailstrum loved to talk on and on about the Temple Mount specifically.

I decided to approach the volunteer table and was handed a note card to write a prayer on and place it in the crevices of the stones. My first thought was of the baby I lost. Moved to tears, I wrote a prayer asking God for another opportunity to become a mother. I wanted to love someone with my whole heart and not just a fragment of it. Complete, whole, unlimited love—giving the gift of my best self to a child for eternity. As I folded the card, I thought of baby Zion and how perfect he was when he was born into this world. The significance of being here and recalling being godmother to Zion, at Mount Zion, made me feel like all was well as I tucked my prayer for a baby of my own into the crevice of the stone.

The group continued our tour by walking to the Christian quarter and the Church of the Holy Sepulchre. Professor Hailstrum talked about the two holy sites—the place Jesus was crucified and the empty tomb where he was buried and resurrected—and have remained the focus of this church after numerous takeovers through the centuries. As a group, we walked through the four stations of the cross, the Via Dolorosa.

It wasn't difficult imagining how gruesome the experience of crucifixion was after seeing the film, *The Passion of the Christ*, in 2004—the same year I walked into that church in Austin. Walking on the stone slabs, I couldn't help but envision scenes from the film in all its horror. I had to break away from the crowd and cry. It was overwhelming to think of the torture that Jesus had endured right where I was standing—the angry mobs mocking him and those who loved him crying out in anguish as the blood dripped from his body. After so many years living in fear, the magnetic force of Jesus pulled me into God-consciousness. Feeling a love beyond my understanding, I felt valued and accepted, loved by the Holy Spirit.

Walking around Jerusalem watching all the people of different faiths bustling about, I was convinced that Jesus was not the only path to communion with God. I respected all faiths and thought that God had limitless expressions of divinity. God is everything, the great weaver, the brilliant ether that binds us all together, life-giving energy—the power needed to exist in this world and beyond. I began to feel a peace I had never known before as I strolled through the quarters of the ancient city while sublime mania, infused with spiritual enlightenment, fulfilled me. I felt as though I was rising, like a balloon gently floating into the air, puffed up beyond my normal limits. I lingered in that experience as long as I could until someone spoke to me and broke the magical spell of euphoria. The balloon around me silently deflated, and mania would slowly fade away as normal life came back into focus.

Staying at the Rosary Sisters Hostel on the edge of Old Jerusalem, built in 1884 and managed by Sister Agatha, was relaxing. It had always been a place of service, whether initiating newly consecrated nuns, housing an orphanage, or most recently, hosting pilgrims in Israel. With high ceilings and numerous arches, Catholic artwork, and countless crosses, our group enjoyed the peace and quiet within its walls. Homemade bread and jam in the morning, served by graceful nuns, was delightful. And as we sat in the garden, complete with old, twisted olive trees, we planned our last hours in this fascinating city. We were certain we would visit the museum and view the Dead Sea Scrolls. We'd also explore more holy sites within and around the walls of the Old City, people watching, which was my favorite, before the weekend was over.

Throughout Israel, there were young soldiers standing about, holding guns, and wearing camouflage. Service is mandatory, with exemptions and varying service positions, and requires the commitment of every citizen to protect their country. Little did I know that nearly 20 years later, horror would penetrate this region of the world once again. Would it ever stop?

As I boarded the plane back to Austin, I thought of my next steps in life. The U.S. didn't need me to protect it. It already had an abundance of protection, more than was necessary, overcompensating for its lack of maturity as a country. Yet soon, I would be waking up before dawn and running for miles, absorbing harsh criticism, and having orders yelled in my face. After this uplifting trip, I was ready. I'd just have to stay quiet, get strong, and "suck it up."

Arms

Chapter 19

On the first of February, six years into the new millennia, I arrived at the station at 4 a.m. as I had promised. There was a knot in my stomach as I boarded the bus, and it continued to twist my gut as I crossed the highways through Texas, Louisiana, and Arkansas. It was hard to digest what I was doing on this bus headed for what would essentially be a lockdown—an intensely controlled environment, and in freezing weather to boot. I felt half-crazy, and half-excited, but on an adventure and taking a risk, which was my familiar. I sat in the window seat next to a young girl of about 18, who eventually dozed off with her head tilted onto my shoulder. I looked around at this busload of young recruits and thought about how we were all in this together. "Battle buddies" was the term we would soon call each other, and our first battle was to survive boot camp.

Eleven hours later, we entered Missouri, and rolled into Fort Leonard Wood, mid-winter, and nearing midnight. Those of us who had fallen asleep were woken up by Drill Sergeant Miller. He entered the bus, and with a deep bellied voice ordered us to gather our stuff and get out on the lawn.

"Now!" he yelled from the front of the bus, wearing his stiff round hat. "Get your lazy asses up pronto!"

We all gathered our bags and hurried out of the bus where Drill Sergeant Parker was ordering us to form straight lines on the grass. "Hurry up! Move!" he hollered louder than would be expected from his thin frame. I rushed into a spot in the middle of the pack.

Drill Sergeant Callow was screaming at the top of his lungs for us to line up and stand straight while randomly aiming insults at people in the front. I thought about what great actors they were, so committed to their roles with punishing attitudes, deep harsh voices, and eyes that cut like razors. Did they laugh with each other in the break room at how nervous they made us?

"Is that a smirk on your face?" Drill Sergeant Callow snarled at me. He had a southern accent and was short and stocky.

"Sorry Sergeant," I said, confused about what to say.

"You will address us as Drill Sergeant!" he yelled. He was steaming. "What's your name?"

"Alika Jones, Drill Sergeant!" I said loudly, shivering from the freezing cold air.

"Congratulations, Jones. You just earned push-ups for the whole group," he said with a sinister smile. "All of you drop and give me twenty! When you are done, stand at attention. Move!"

Some of us struggled after ten or so, and some whipped them out, standing up quickly. I got to about sixteen before they became difficult, and I had to push with all my might.

"Those of you still on the ground are sorry excuses for soldiers," Sergeant Parker said with a perpetual scowl. "Hurry up!"

Drill Sergeant Miller, who was a calm and reserved man with dark skin and a muscular build, seemed to be the highest ranked and in charge. He stood front and center with his arms crossed in front of him.

"All of you will now form one long line as you proceed to enter the building behind me. This is where we will inspect your bags, cut your hair if necessary, and supply your uniforms. You will get medical clearance and then receive your dog tags. You will then put on your uniform and take a mug shot before we assign you to your bunks. I would not expect to sleep tonight. Now, first row, move out."

"Move with a purpose! Second row, follow quickly," Drill Sergeant Parker shouted. "Third row, hurry up!"

Hours passed and dawn came and went while we were processed. We cleared inspection, were issued uniforms, and took the worst pictures of our lives for our military ID card. The day dragged on as we stood in line after line. Anytime someone yawned or nodded off, a drill sergeant would scream in their face, "Wake up!"

Finally, we were assigned bunks in the dormitories, told to take showers, and to be outside in formation in fifteen minutes. Scrambling and dragging from exhaustion, we females hurried to clean ourselves in one large communal shower. Most were between 18 and 21 years old, but one woman looked to be about my age. Later, I learned she was Lucia Rivera from Puerto Rico, and she would become my closest ally. I wondered about her story. Why was she here? All of us naked and lathered up, I noticed that Lucia was in great shape, learning later that day that she was a surfer and loved beach volleyball.

We put on our brand-new desert tan camouflage uniforms as quickly as possible. We had to tuck a beige T-shirt into our cargo pants and use a beige nylon belt to keep the pants secure. Then we put on the desert camo jackets, attached our names with a Velcro patch, and laced up our tan boots. We left our recycled winter coats, which were still made of the old jungle green camouflage and had our last names sewn into the top left corner, in our lockers. Most of us had long hair, and we struggled to form a bun at the nape of our necks that would fit under the back rim of our hats, which were like soft baseball caps.

As we ran out to the quad to get in line with the rest of the company, we saw the guys already doing push-ups and our drill sergeants screaming in their faces for being late.

"Oh, the females have finally graced us with their presence! Drop where you are and give me 20!" Drill Sergeant Callow shouted.

Push-ups became jumping jacks, which became sit-ups, which became planks, then more push-ups. These were randomly demanded in between everything we did throughout the day every day. We were rushed through the mess hall, we were taught how to march, how to respond to orders, and quickly learned how to hurry up and wait. After no sleep the night before, it was finally time to turn in for the night.

Thrilled that I got a bottom bunk in the same room as Rivera, I lay with my hair luxuriously loosened and fiddled with my dog tags. We were issued two because if a soldier died in battle, one would stay with the body and the other one would be taken for record-keeping purposes. The two metallic labels clanged together, marked with my first and last name, my military ID number, religious affiliation, and my blood type, which I learned was O negative. The nurse told me that by having a universal blood type I would be sought after in medical emergencies because I could donate blood to anybody who needed it. I lay on my bunk thinking about the serendipitous circles in my life, O in my blood, the zero that saved my life, and the full moon that guided me. I slowed my breath and fell into a deep, well-deserved slumber.

Our alarm clocks were the loud voices of drill sergeants while they banged rods on our bed frames at 4:30 a.m. We were told to put on our physical training uniform—black gym shorts, a grey T-shirt that had ARMY in bold stamped across the chest, and sneakers. We then had to get in formation for our morning run. We would run five miles every morning in the dark, in the dead of winter, while pushing through the cramps in the side of our guts.

Over time, fighting the weakness in my body, I built up my stamina until it had me running in the middle of the pack. There was always a drill sergeant at the tail end torturing the stragglers with loud insults. Accepting the customary motivational tactics, we picked up the pace as a group. I learned to develop the mental strength necessary to overcome physical challenges. It was truly a case of mind over matter, whether I was running in the morning, racing through obstacle courses, carrying a person across a field over my shoulders, or just holding my M4 assault rifle parallel in front of me until my arms felt like they would fall off.

We were responsible for our M4s twenty-four hours a day. We would march, lay on our bellies, shoot targets, or do endless drills with them. We learned to throw grenades, wrestle, and march for miles carrying heavy backpacks, but it was the gas chamber that was the most extreme. The masks we were given couldn't keep out the toxic gas, and we all endured the torment of choking while our eyes burned, our nasal passages ran like rivers, and it felt like our ears were bleeding. After being let out of that chamber I cried, not for my few minutes of suffering, but for the innocent millions who died during the Holocaust because the door never opened and fresh air never came to save them.

We did not have permission to go to the store on base, so all sweet treats, chips, cigarettes, and alcohol were forbidden. We consumed nothing beyond the bland food in the mess hall, but when the mail was given out, I could look forward to the candy and homemade cookies my mom would smuggle onto base in large tampon boxes.

There was one soldier who seemed to have a mean streak and disliked me from the start, shooting me dirty looks. McGrady was short, not very athletic, and never got any mail, so I assumed she was sad and angry. I prayed for her. I shared my secret candy and cookies with my new friends and at times would offer her clique of girls something sweet to eat. McGrady always refused. When I informed my mother in a letter about McGrady's attitude, she had the idea of becoming McGrady's anonymous pen pal, sending her words of encouragement in a letter each day. I would watch as she opened these letters. McGrady was confused every time, but touched, and I kept my mother's identity a secret.

I stood by Rivera, who had a hard time carrying heavy backpacks on long marches, and I wouldn't let her fail. I would pray by her side, out loud and boldly, summoning the courage she needed to complete tasks and tests. We became close comrades and enjoyed telling each other stories in our downtime before lights out. I practiced my Spanish and we laughed at my oddball sentence structure and the slang words I knew. She had a teenage daughter whom she adored and was hoping for grandchildren in the future. That idea hit me square in the face. I also could have a teenage daughter at my age.

When it came time to fight, something fierce kicked in; I was unbeatable when it came to wrestling the other females in my platoon. I earned respect from the younger soldiers as the "tough old lady" after squirming out of their grip, and quickly putting my opponent in a headlock that would have killed them if the match hadn't ended. For someone who didn't like fighting, I sure was good at it.

Basic training was physically empowering and provided us the understanding of the word camaraderie. Our drill sergeants started shedding their mean façade as we progressed, and they began to demonstrate their pride in us. There were a few who had to drop out due to injury or mental incapacity, but most of us grew stronger than we would have ever imagined when we began the process. Apparently, the excessive physical activity kept my mania at bay as the testosterone pumped through my body. I was able to focus because the structure proved to be a cure for my usual impulsive behavior. Boot camp was exhilarating, and I felt powerful, grounded, and accomplished. Graduation was in sight.

McGrady had been softening day by day, but it wasn't until the whole platoon was socializing with their families after our graduation that my mother revealed she was McGrady's secret pen pal. McGrady teared up and hugged my mother and then turned to me.

"Congratulations, Jones. Sorry I was so hard on you."

I smiled as I saw the chip fall from her shoulder.

My mother had that proud look in her eyes, so moved to see me wearing the deep green formal Army uniform complete with a traditional beret. The fact that I was doing something constructive made her hopeful. We embraced and I felt her love for me. The fact that she and Ron flew out to Missouri to witness this moment in time made me grateful I had family to back me up. I wasn't alone in the world. Having a nice meal off base, while Ron told us stories of his service in the Army, allowed us to form a bond like never before. I felt more like them than I thought I was, kind of normal, and maybe, just maybe I could live satisfied with my life like they were. But the next day, I would be shipped out to San Antonio, Texas, bright and early, for combat medic training and forced to "suck it up" on a whole other level.

Advanced Individual Training, or AIT, was the track each of us would take toward a career path in the army. It was time to part ways, and we all boarded different buses with our heavy olive-green canvas duffle bags. I was sad to say goodbye to the girls in my company whom I had grown so close with, especially Rivera who was going off to become a truck driver. With tears in our eyes, we hugged each other, and I promised to visit her in Puerto Rico someday. How sweet it would be to lounge in bathing suits on the sand after a game of volleyball and a dip in the ocean, sip cocktails, and reminisce about boot camp.

"Mama, you stay strong," Rivera said with her Puerto Rican twang. "And keep those prayers coming for me. I'll miss you, Jones."

"I'll miss you too," I said choked up. "Kiss that future grandbaby for me."

"Don't worry Jones, you will have kids too. Keep the faith," Rivera said and walked toward her bus.

Arriving at Fort Sam Houston wasn't nearly as scary because we had been broken in as soldiers. We had already developed the resilience and the readiness required to follow orders and perform the physical feats necessary to satisfy the drill sergeants' demands. We already knew the chants we would shout while marching on campus. We already knew how to rush through the showers and the mess hall to get back in formation on time. We already knew the drill sergeants in charge would be even harder on us. And we knew we would have academic classes in addition to our physical training. The challenge of becoming a nurse had just begun.

I was placed in Charlie Company. The whole platoon was in combat medic training and a smaller portion of us would move on to nursing school. I had grown accustomed to our previous drill sergeants. The new ones seemed genuinely angry and not apt to putting on a show.

Eyes forward, standing straight, lips closed with controlled breathing through the nose, I was as still and serious as I could be, but I couldn't help but think that it was all so silly, the way the drill sergeants were looking us up and down like tigers ready to pounce.

I spotted a beautiful female drill sergeant, fierce with dark skin, in the dead of the night. She was stunning with chiseled bone structure, glistening eyes, full lips, and she looked like she could kick anybody's ass. She saw me looking at her and walked directly toward me, even though I was in the middle of the squad. Her gorgeous face was so close to mine I could smell her natural scent combined with the soap she used.

"What are you looking at?"

"Nothing in particular, Drill Sergeant!" I said loudly with my chest puffed.

"Nothing in particular, eh? You sound like a smarty pants Jones. Are you a smarty pants?" she asked me as I looked at her name tag which read Pierce.

"No, Drill Sergeant!" I said in my most formal soldier voice.

"Why are you here Jones?" Pierce said, her eyes filled with suspicion.

"To become a nurse, Drill Sergeant," I said getting the sense that she just knew I was not very patriotic.

Drill Sergeant Pierce leaned so close to me that she was breathing in my ear and whispered in a deep resonating tone.

"I've got my eye on you, Jones."

The classroom setting was strange after spending all our training time outside. Civilian teachers taught us EMT techniques, anatomy, and basic biology. We were tested weekly, and it was difficult sitting through the lessons with so little sleep. The unlucky soldiers were the ones who stood watch all night at the door of the barracks, causing them to nod off during class. Drill sergeants were not in the classroom to scream at us, so we would rely on each other to stay awake.

Eventually, we started intense training by camping out on government land, performing mock battles, and practicing survival techniques. We erected huge, green canvas tents and set up stoves for heat so we wouldn't freeze at night. We ate MREs (meals ready to eat), which were flexible bags of rations containing things like spaghetti or beef stew, with side dishes like mashed potatoes or corn in separate bags. I especially liked it when I got spreads like peanut butter and jelly because the main courses never tasted quite right. As we hungrily sat on the floor waiting like dogs, the stiff, plastic bags were thrown at us and we'd eat everything after ripping them apart, sometimes trading with a fellow solider to get what we wanted.

During mock battles we would "save each other's lives" after simulated bombs were dropped, and we had to rescue each other from "bleeding out" from our fake wounds. We worked together when we'd charge forward to attack or escape from "enemy fire" and had to retreat. The whole operation was complete with sound effects and mock villages built in fields. In these "villages," we would get out our syringes and inject saline into each other's arms behind cover, protecting us from "enemy fire."

Near the end of combat medic training, we were assigned specific duties, and I volunteered to work at Brooks Army Medical Center near the base. My new orders were to report to the Soldier Recovery Unit on the third floor after breakfast. I learned how to clean wounds and apply soft bandages to the arms and legs of young soldiers who had been severely burned and were in critical care. The smell of pus and blood turned my stomach but the heartbreak of seeing these young men puffed up like balloons and suffering unimaginable pain gave me a purpose. Yet I was angry at the military for sacrificing these boys, some not even 21, who were so badly injured that they might not live another day. I always wanted to believe that war was avoidable, but history has proven me wrong. I witnessed horrible suffering and death, and I cried every time a soul in the burn unit would leave this earth. Jesse was only 20 years old, and he loved to talk about his childhood in Kentucky fishing with his father. He didn't make it, and eventually I couldn't take it. I have always maintained that humanity, flawed as it is, will one day come to its senses and give up warring with one another. It has been a pipe dream for as long as I can remember. But true peace isn't for the masses; I would have to find it on my own.

As the weeks mounted, I couldn't stand going to the hospital anymore and generally started to become weary of Army life. I was accumulating money in the bank each month and I grew antsy to spend it. Deciding that I couldn't take the food, nor live in a barracks any longer, I rented a secret apartment off-base. I was four weeks away from graduation, but I couldn't wait. On leave one weekend, I retrieved my car from Kent's house in Austin and drove it to San Antonio with some personal items like my art supplies, cookware, CDs, and civilian clothes. I bought a twin mattress and some furniture from Goodwill and set myself up in an apartment with a pool that I could see from my balcony.

Each weekend I would go to my sweet haven to swim, play music, dance, and cook for myself. During the week, I dreamed about being there and sometimes would sneak out just as we were all heading back to the barracks after dinner to retire for the night. I'd creep toward my car on a real-life mission and drive to my retreat, sneaking back onto base before early PT roll call. It was thrilling to break the rules, and I never got caught—it was easy to fool the soldiers at the gates, because I was older than most recruits. I came off as a "lifer," as if I had been in the Army for many years.

When it came time for graduation, we were encouraged to go out in our civilian clothes the night before the ceremony. We were all so excited to hit the bars off base after making it through such strenuous training. One requirement was that we stick with a battle buddy, so I asked Roberts, and we decided to hit the town. She was the one girl who could do more pushups than I could and ran faster than every other female, including the drill sergeants.

It was so liberating to drink freely with my fellow soldiers in a bar blasting music as we took turns singing karaoke, dancing, and laughing the night away. The fact that I had not had a drop of alcohol for the last three years had changed my constitution. Old habits kicked in and two drinks became six, which then became eight, and I ultimately lost track of Roberts. I was flying high and flirting with the soldiers who were more advanced in their training and didn't have a curfew to keep. I didn't stop drinking or dancing until the bar was shutting down. It was then that I finally realized I had to rush back to base. I jumped into my car, blasting Madonna's latest electronica CD, and sang "Nothing Really Matters" at the top of my lungs. Speeding and swerving down the road leading to the gate, I didn't imagine in my drunken mind there would be a problem passing by the MPs when I flashed my military ID.

"Pull over and step out of the car," one of the soldiers ordered me.

"Hey, I'm graduating this morning. I need to go get ready."

"Step out of the car," he repeated.

Stumbling in my high heels and form-fitting lavender dress, I mustered the balance required to stand straight and saluted the soldier as I started to lean sideways.

"What is your company and who is your superior officer?" he said as the other soldier picked up the CB radio.

"Charlie Company. Captain Moore," I slurred.

It wasn't long before a jeep pulled up and two more MPs got out and walked toward me.

"What do we have here?" one of them asked.

"She's inebriated and driving."

"Please let me go. I've got to get ready. I'm gonna graduate this morning," I pleaded.

"I seriously doubt that," the MP said with a soulless tone as he got out some handcuffs.

"No. Please. No!" I began to breath rapidly and panic.

Without mercy, I was handcuffed and brought to the back of the jeep.

Crying and enraged at the same time, I began cursing them out as they proceeded to drive to a holding cell on base. Ignoring my pleas, I was put behind bars with nothing but a cold cement floor to sit on. Self-pity consumed me as I imagined all my comrades suiting up for graduation when Captain Moore walked in.

"Jones, Jones, Jones. What in the hell were you thinking?"

"Please Captain Moore, let me graduate. Please!" My voice curled in desperation.

"That's not going to happen, Jones. You really messed up," he said with disdain in his voice. "I'm beyond disappointed in you. We had high hopes for your career, Private. Get up."

They took the handcuffs off, and Captain Moore drove me back to the barracks. The sun had risen, and the company was in formation about to march to the ceremony. I had to walk past all of them in shame while they stood in parade rest.

Roberts and I caught each other's eyes, and she looked down knowing it was wrong to leave me at the bar. Humiliated, still in my high heels and lavender dress, I was brought to the office in front of the whole company. Being stared at by everyone wearing their suits and berets, hung-over, and with my eyes smudged with fallen mascara, I felt like the world was spinning out of control when Sergeant Pierce walked into the office.

"Jones! I knew you didn't have it in ya," she said with a gratifying look on her face. "You are the loser I always thought you were."

A female MP was called to stand guard while the drill sergeants convened outside. I sat there stewing in my shame before Sergeant Pierce came back and ordered me to go to the barracks and change back into my uniform.

"You don't even deserve to wear a uniform, Jones," she said, disgusted. "Wash up and be back here in ten minutes, you maggot." Pierce looked like a panther that had caught her prey. She beamed with a predator's glee as if natural order had been restored.

The MP followed me to the empty barracks. Rows of beds were made tight with the scratchy deep green blanket tucked sharply in at the corners. My two-minute shower washed away the crusty smear of tears on my face. I quickly wrapped my hair in a bun and brushed the vodka off my teeth, dressed, and rushed downstairs.

When I returned to the office, I was stunned to see Major Cook sitting at the desk. He was an older man, weathered, with a dignified air about him. He was looking over papers and ignoring my presence for a few minutes before looking up at me standing at attention with my arm in the salute position.

"At ease Jones," he stated calmly. "A DUI is a serious offense."

I conjured a deep belly breath.

"Yes sir."

"We have discussed the issue and because your record is good, and this is your first offence, I've decided to give you an Article 15 in lieu of a court martial. You are lucky that most of the drill sergeants vouched for you."

"Thank you, sir," I said in my best soldier voice.

"You will stay with Charlie Company and be recycled into the next group of soldiers and report to Sergeant Burns for extra duty, every day for forty-five days. You will be fined a thousand dollars, your rank has been reduced from E-3 to E-1, and you will be restricted to the base without leave," he said with a monotone voice. "You got off lucky, Jones. We could have sent you to court, and who knows what they would have decided. You wouldn't want to be in a military prison, that's for certain."

"Thank you, sir! I am sorry for my actions, sir."

"Stay out of trouble, Jones. The next time we won't be so lenient. You are dismissed."

The MP walked me to a building where Sergeant Burns was expecting me. A roomful of soldiers sat silently in rows of chairs.

"Jones, come here," Sergeant Burns ordered. "DUI huh?"

"Yes, sir," I cowered.

"You should be sent to court, Private. Don't know how you wiggled your way out of that one."

"I'm grateful, Sergeant."

"I don't know how grateful you'll be when I'm done with you. Sit down, Jones," he said as he stood up to address the group. "All right, fuck ups, we are on a mission to sweep up the entire base starting with the mess hall. You will make this base so shiny that I will get promoted and get away from you losers. I hate this job, you all make me sick! So, unless you want me to make your lives a living hell, you will clean like your life depends on it. Move out and form a line by the closet for your brooms. I said move!"

For the next forty-five days, I thought about the houseplants dying in my apartment. I swept the barracks and the quad, cleaned toilets and showers, all the while watching the new soldiers in our company go through the training I had already completed. I longed for the pool, my home cooking, and my CDs that were collecting dust. I was late on the rent and needed to call the apartment manager's office to explain. I was still hopeful that things would take a turn and I could enjoy living off base and finally attend nursing school.

Sergeant Pierce often mocked me when she saw me, and it was getting under my skin. She seemed to relish embarrassing me every chance she could when I passed by her squad carrying a broom in hand.

"Look at this loser with her broom. Don't end up like this sorry excuse for a soldier and become the base maid," she'd shout. "I think you missed a spot, Jones," and she'd laugh along with the squad in formation.

During physical training one morning, a soldier I knew from boot camp, who was held back for medical reasons and was new to the squad, told me some devastating news. He leaned over and whispered that my friend Rivera had been deployed to Afghanistan and was killed in an explosion. The shock paralyzed me. I couldn't move. I stood there while everyone else did jumping jacks and I broke down heaving with grief. I wrapped my arms around myself and curled up on the ground against a pole. Rivera dead? What of her daughter? Her grandbabies? I pictured her face and sparkling dark eyes happy on the beach in front of her home she talked so much about. She was so proud to be Puerto Rican and loved the people of her country, the ocean, the food, and the music. A sweet soul, funny, with a warm heart, I could never visit her like I intended to or ever hug her again.

Sergeant Pierce hurried over and began ordering me to get back in formation. She got in my face and wouldn't stop yelling when I turned to her and screamed, "Leave me alone, you bitch!"

Sergeant Pierce stormed off to the office and returned with Captain Moore, who barreled toward me and grabbed me by the arm. He dragged me closer to the rest of the soldiers and began jerking around.

"You WILL do PT like everyone else, Jones!" he commanded.

"Stop!" was all I managed to say, but he continued to throw me around like a rag doll as I remained limp in his grip.

"You WILL show respect to your superiors Jones!" he growled as he clutched his hands on my neck. I felt the air sucked out of me as he forced my body back and forth, up and down, simulating the pushups everyone else was doing.

That's when several other drill sergeants approached and pulled him off me. The whole company was in shock while Sergeant Pierce grinned. Finally able to catch my breath, I sat up and was consumed with thoughts of Rivera, a senseless death of a good woman, who made me laugh and brought joy to the world, had me thinking about the magnitude of grief brought on by war. So many people had lost their loved ones for what? I was cracking in half, split with rage at the chain of command whose orders had caused so much pain. The MPs arrived and ordered me to get up. They brought me to the hospital to clear me of any injuries. I had none but the one in my heart. Rivera was gone.

I was given some papers by a soldier from the inspector general's office and was told to make a statement. As I wrote down what happened, emotional torment had my brain swirling and my anger at everything military had me steaming inside. I wanted out. Out of this uniform, out of this company, out of the military. When I was cleared to leave, I was brought back to the barracks and told to pack up my things. Due to the incident, I moved to Echo Company because I couldn't be on the same premises as Captain Moore. I was given a new bunk and became an extended holdover.

I didn't train. I wasn't doing extra duty. I was in limbo. I visited the inspector general's office, made a complaint, and asked how I could get out of the military. I was given a phone number for a GI's rights attorney, and when I called the number on the card, a man named Allen answered the phone. I explained to him what had happened.

"Can you get statements from any witnesses who saw the incident?" Allen asked. "It will help in the process of pressing charges."

"I don't care about pressing charges. I just want out," I said with desperation in my voice.

"Well, you are tied to Charlie Company. They practically own you," he said as a matter of fact.

"What can I do?"

"To be released from Charlie Company, you'd have to go AWOL for 30 days. They would have to release you for desertion at that point. Then you could turn yourself in at any fort in the country and take your chances at either repercussions, or because of your situation, be assigned a new company with a fresh start. With the incident you've just been through, you'd have some leverage as to your reasons, and you could request to be discharged. However, if you had eyewitness accounts of what happened, it could go a long way."

"Thank you, Allen. You've been very helpful," I said, dreaming of driving away and never coming back.

As I made my plans to sneak off base, I pulled soldiers aside who had witnessed the attack. I was able to gather twenty-one statements, packed my bag with essentials, and left most of the Army stuff behind. Getting in my car and driving away from Fort Sam Houston felt like a freedom comparable to leaving Dario on that liberating day, though this time I was breaking the law. As I drove up to the gate, the soldier standing guard motioned me to pass through with a nod of his head. I drove to my apartment ready to pack up what I could fit in my black RAV4 mini-SUV.

The plants had died and the furniture was dusty. I grabbed my clothes, boombox, CDs, my big coat, hygiene products, passport, and the bone-colored case, leaving everything else behind, and headed east toward Austin. I didn't know what to do for 30 days or where to go. I didn't want to visit friends or go back to my mom's house for fear that they could be implicated in my crime by harboring me while on the run. I thought, why not take a cruise, and lay low? With mania in control, I fled and drove to Florida to catch a cheap cruise to the Mexican coast.

Jackson

Chapter 20

I was able to secure a cabin and boarded the Carnival cruise ship, the most inexpensive cruise line in America. Breathing in the salty air, I felt awkward not having to answer to orders. Elderly folks leisurely walked about and sipped their cocktails. No one knew my story. I was just another passenger taking time off from the hectic life on land.

After settling in and grabbing a bite, I decided to take a dip in the pool and dry off in the sun. My eyes were closed, and I felt the heatwaves through my eyelids when a drawing of a rose was placed on my lap. I looked up and blocking the glare of sunlight stood a man with tattooed arms from wrists to shoulders.

"Hello, beautiful," he said boldly with a deep voice and a Cajun drawl.

I could feel a tingle welling up underneath my bathing suit bottom, magnified by the warmth of the sun. An instant sexual chemistry erupted in my body.

"Hello, handsome," I said. "Have a seat. I'm Alika."

"Jackson." He took my hand and pressed his lips to my fingers. "I've been watching you, and it seems you are traveling alone. Or is someone seasick in your cabin?" he said with his piercing pale blue eyes looking straight into mine. His brown hair was long, past his shoulders, and he was lean, with inviting lips.

"I'm not traveling with anyone. What about you?"

"My ex bailed on me before the trip. Turns out she hooked up with my best friend."

"Ouch," I said sipping the last of my margarita on the rocks.

"Can I get you another drink?" he offered standing up.

"Yeah, thanks," I smiled.

He was sexy and funny, and we laughed, telling stories over a few more drinks before we couldn't help ourselves and we kissed. His lips felt soft yet firm, and excitement caressed my whole body. The heat of our breath expanded my senses, condensing the air between us as if we were already touching each other head to toe.

"Wow," I whispered in his ear. My heart was pounding.

"You are so hot," he said putting his hand on my thigh.

"I feel like I'm already cumming."

"Your cabin or mine?"

"Mine."

Grabbing my key card and towel, he followed me down the long hallway until we reached room 128, and he softly held my ass in his hands as I opened the door. Without hesitation, he pressed my strong slim body against the wall, and we kissed passionately, feeling each other's bare skin as I clutched his back. He lifted me up and my legs wrapped around his hips as our centers rubbed against each other and his erection pressed onto me, thrilling me beyond control. He slid the bottom of my bathing suit to the side and placed his perfectly formed penis into me, satisfying my anticipation of his manhood. Ecstasy exploded with every motion, and he swung me onto the bed, entering the deepest part of me. We lay there breathing each other's air, the heat of his breath intoxicating, and we paused, as I laid under him soaking in the perfect fit of our parts. The satisfaction of the last piece completing life's complicated puzzle clicked and everything felt like it should. Jackson pulled out and tore off our bathing suits. We looked at each other's naked bodies, propped on our knees in the middle of the bed, vulnerable and ready to be merged with abandon. He pushed me down onto my back and we ripped into each other, fucking with a fury. As beads of sweat secreted, the wetness on our stomachs became slippery, and the mirror fogged up while he slid in and out of me for hours upon hours. The exhilaration had no end in sight. I wanted it to last forever.

With no window in the room, it was impossible to know what time it was when we woke up. We made love again with a tenderness that made me feel wanted and admired, stimulating every inch of my body and mind. We tickled each other, laughing and playing, realizing we had met our erotic match when we started to tell each other about our histories. He was from Louisiana, a tattoo artist, and had a 5-year-old daughter.

"What's her name?" I asked, intrigued.

"Katrina. I call her Kitty. She was born before the hurricane, so she needed a nickname after that bitch ripped the state apart. But Kitty changed my world. You need to meet her. Come to Louisiana with me."

"Honestly, I don't have anywhere to go after this. Um…I need to tell you something."

"What is it beautiful?"

"Well, I'm AWOL right now."

"What? You're in the military. AWOL? What the fuck happened?"

"Long story. But I need to turn myself in after 30 days. I'm headed to Fort Sill in Oklahoma, but before that I need somewhere to crash for a couple of weeks."

"I'm staying with my friend Mack in Baton Rouge right now. My fucking ex and her new asshole boyfriend are living in my trailer, motherfuckers. But of course, you can come with me anywhere."

"Thanks, there is nowhere I'd rather be than with you," I said blushing. I just met this guy but couldn't imagine not lying in bed with him every night.

"It's settled then. I've got a few tattoos lined up in Mack's shop, and you can meet Kitty. You still gotta tell me what happened. AWOL? Fuck, girl!"

We went to have coffee and I explained everything, but then it was time for an excursion in Mexico. Time for the beach and authentic food without having to sing for my supper like I did years ago in this vibrant country. Jackson shopped for some souvenirs for Kitty while I haggled in my broken Spanish. We had all day to drink margaritas and eat tacos, swim, and lie on the sand before retiring for the night on the ship. More lovemaking, stories, and showers together made the time fly by. We had one more day in Cancún before the ship cruised back to Florida, so we took a tour on an ATV, having a blast splashing through the mud and roaming in jungles. We washed off in crystal clear pools in the mouth of a cave, and then we saw the ruins in Tulum. We even had a professional guide to lead the way. It was relaxing and enjoyable to be a tourist in this country without the desperation, drugs, or the dire need to make a buck along the way.

The ride back to the U.S. was fun. In between all the amazing sex, we won at blackjack, caught a stand-up comedy show, and danced to cheesy music playing on the deck. For a time, I forgot that I was trying to lay low, but as we docked, I remembered just how uncertain my life was.

Hitting the highway on I-10 west through the Florida panhandle, I followed his dented and faded rust-colored car. The port of Jacksonville to Baton Rouge was a straight shot of nine hours. Whether it was a coincidence or fate, I had just met a man named Jackson near Jacksonville and the chemistry was electric. We couldn't wait to make love again. Halfway there, and somewhere in southern Alabama, we pulled over and found a deserted country road. Pressed against the back of my car, he held me up as I stared at the moon, full and bright. Kissing passionately, with our eyes locked, he came deep inside me. With my legs still wrapped around his hips, I linked my arms around his torso and laid my head in the nook of his shoulder, somehow knowing I had just conceived. The stars had aligned, and I just knew that the miracle of a new life was inside me, ready to grow.

He held me up with his arms wrapped under me as I lingered weightless, clinging to his body. He was still inside me, and with my arms clutched behind his back, I didn't ever want to let go. The full moon spoke to me once again. I felt the spiritual lineage continue. I knew in this moment I was going to have a baby.

Sweet Destiny

Chapter 21

When we went to pick up Kitty, the look on her mother's face alarmed me. Jeanie was a woman scorned, standing on the porch of her rundown home in the trailer park in a small town outside of Baton Rouge. I waited in the car as Jackson argued with Jeanie and Kitty ran out and grabbed him around his legs. It was clear she loved her daddy and was overjoyed to see him. Jackson's ex-best friend Garth stepped outside and put his arm around Jeanie's shoulders.

"You better have Kitty back here in two hours," she said.

The family drama was boiling.

Jackson was flushed with anger but held it inside so not to scare Kitty as we drove away and went to a local park. Running to the swing set, Kitty called, "Daddy! Daddy, push me!" She was adorable and sweet as can be with black hair, pale skin, and crystal blue eyes. She was missing her front two teeth, causing her to lisp. I witnessed the bond they shared, wondering if I would have a boy or a girl. My warm secret gave me comfort. I hadn't told Jackson that I felt pregnant, fearing that I might sound crazy since it was only last night that the seed was planted. I just knew at 38 years of age that I would finally have the same connection with my own child that Jackson felt with his daughter. I jumped on the swing next to Kitty as she giggled from him tickling the sides of her ribs. Stretching my legs and building momentum, I swung high to the limits of the pendulum and recalled how I would jump off as a child when the swing was at its peak.

Kitty asked for pizza, so we drove to an Italian restaurant that had booths lined with tall red cushions reminding me of Grandma's kitchen breakfast nook. Jackson gave Kitty a few quarters for the old-fashioned candy machines that used a crank to release cheap toys and candy down a little ramp. Kitty caught the gumballs with her tiny hands and skipped back to us when the pizza arrived.

"So, Kitty, are you in kindergarten?" I asked her.

"I'm in kindergarten and I can sing my ABCs," she said proudly.

"I taught you your ABCs, right Kitty?" Jackson needed the recognition. "And your numbers too."

Jackson's phone rang. Jeanie wanted Kitty to come home.

"We are just now eating some pizza. Can't you wait another hour? You aren't the boss of me, woman!"

Tensions between them were high. Rightly so, as the drama behind it all was deeper than I realized at the time. A tangled web of infidelity on both sides weaved their pasts together since they met in high school and opened a tattoo shop after graduating. The stress of running a business is enough to strain a relationship, but also being young parents amid the tattoo scene in a very small town had taken its toll.

Jackson was thirteen years younger than me, despite us looking the same age. I was in the best shape of my life after the rigorous training in the Army. Jackson was great with Kitty, which inspired my hopes that he would be a good father to my baby as well. Though I barely knew him, I clung to the faith that he would love the baby nestled inside me as much as he loved Kitty.

Crying when we dropped her off, Kitty held Jackson tight. He took deep breaths to summon the strength he needed to part ways with her as he pressed her on his chest. While Jackson held his daughter, Jeanie looked at me sideways as if I was just another woman in a long line of ladies by Jackson's side.

After we left for Mack's tattoo shop, Jackson was fuming about Jeanie and Garth, and his car followed suit shortly after, starting to smoke from under the hood. As I followed him in my car, a 'pop' and a 'bang' startled me as he pulled over to the side of the road.

"Fuck! Damn it! Fucking car!" Jackson screamed as his fist pounded the roof of his dying vehicle.

The hood was too hot to touch, and the smoke was getting thicker.

"Step back, Jackson!" I shouted, sensing that it was going to blow up. As Jackson came jogging toward me, we sat together inside my car watching his old Pontiac burn up.

"At least we can get around in my car," I said trying to be optimistic.

"Fuck that car. My brother gave me a junker he didn't want. No wonder!" Jackson lit a cigarette. "Let's just go to the shop and see Mack. He's got some tattoos lined up for me." The foul stench of the burning tobacco repulsed me. "Want one?"

"No, thanks."

Mack was a tall, thin man with dark, silky hair past his shoulders and tattoos all over his body. "Jackson, my man! How was the cruise?"

"Fucking awesome! But man, my damn car just blew up. This is Alika. I met her on the boat. Sexiest woman alive."

"Hello Mack."

"She looks clean," he said looking at my arms and legs. "Don't you have any tattoos? I've never seen Jackson with a girl who didn't have tattoos."

"No, I don't."

"I'll ink you up if he won't," Mack said.

"No, thank you." I felt put on the spot. "Never had any interest."

"Suit yourself," Mack turned to Jackson. "Hey man, there's a chick coming over in a half hour that wants some wings on her hips. Wanna do it?"

"Hell ya! I need the money, bro." Jackson went to wash his hands and draw a mock-up.

I sat in front and looked at dozens of examples of designs on the walls—dragons and hearts, horror figures and cartoon characters— when a pretty teenager, about 18, walked in wearing jean short-shorts and a cut-off T-shirt exposing her torso. Jackson asked her to lie on the massage table face down and pulled her shorts down mid-ass. He sat down by her side with the tattoo machine in hand and proceeded to ink her with wings starting from the middle of her lower back and out toward her hips, as if her ass could take off in flight. Her T-shirt was so short that her lacey bra peeked out as her head rested on her hands. The expression on her face was a combination of pleasure and pain. Jackson was concentrating on the tattoo, but I felt a deep insecurity creep up and I wondered if he desired her. It seemed so sensual the way he leaned on the hump of her rear and had his face so close to her body, drawing with ink and wiping the excess off with a cloth. This was a world I knew nothing about and as the buzz from the tattoo machine sounded, I felt my nerves tense up with insecurity, wondering as the hours passed if Jackson would be faithful to me.

When he was done, the girl got up and twisted her body to look in the mirror. She lifted herself up onto her tippy toes and kissed Jackson on the cheek, thanking him for her new fresh wings, and flew out the door high on adrenalin. Jackson looked proud of his work and counted the $350 dollars in cash, turning to ask Mack, "Hey you got any weed?"

"Yeah," Mack said. "It's back at the house. We're done for the night, let's go."

Mack also lived in a trailer park. His home was neat but had glass terrariums filled with snakes lining the walls which gave me the creeps. I was so tired that I curled up on a La-Z-Boy chair and dozed off while listening to them talk about plans for a new tattoo shop. Mack was opening it up with his buddy in Philadelphia, and they spoke together about Jackson managing the shop. I was half-awake, thinking of "the city of brotherly love" as Mack's fluffy cat purred next to me, easing me off to sleep.

The remaining couple of weeks flew by as I counted down the thirty days that had to pass before I needed to go to Oklahoma and turn myself in. I had the paperwork ready to make my case, eyewitness accounts and inspector general reports that would hopefully release me from my ties to the Army. I prayed that the attorney was right about going AWOL and that I wouldn't end up in court, or even worse, jail. When it was time for me to leave, Jackson said he would stay in Baton Rouge and work in Mack's shop making the money he would need to set us up in Philly.

"Everything will be okay. We can start a new life, in a new city. Call me as soon as you hear something. I'll wait for you," Jackson hugged me tightly and we both said, "I love you."

A nine-hour drive was too long to do alone, so I stopped halfway at a roadside motel somewhere between Dallas and Fort Worth. I still had my military ID and was able to get a discount on the room. Jackson's warm body wasn't there to spoon with me. I felt half empty. Fear of the impending future clouded my mind, and I reached for the Bible on the nightstand, flipping the pages to John 4:18. "There is no fear in love; but perfect love casteth out fear: because fear hath torment. He that feareth is not made perfect in love." I needed to trust that I was loved and protected and that things would go smoothly when I arrived at the base. As the guru had said in San Diego some years ago, "Your thoughts are very important."

Pulling up to Fort Sill, completely in uniform, I was frank with the MPs about turning myself in. With deep breaths, I waited for an escort to lead me to a holding room. I didn't have to wait long before Sergeant Conklin walked in. I stood up and saluted him.

"At ease soldier," he said. "So…I've been informed that you've been AWOL, Jones."

"Yes, sir. I have paperwork to explain everything."

"Hand it over. But first, can you summarize what this is all about?"

"I was assaulted by Captain Moore and then became a never-ending holdover. I was advised by a GI rights lawyer to go AWOL and turn myself in after 30 days so that I could be released from my company."

"Lawyer huh?" he said beginning to shuffle through my papers. "What are these? Witness accounts?"

"Yes sir, it happened during PT in front of the whole company after I learned that my best friend from basic was killed overseas."

"My condolences. I'm going to read through this. We have a bunk for you with the other holdovers. It's time for chow. I'm going to investigate and will call for you when I'm ready."

"Yes, Sergeant. Thank you, Sergeant!"

It was so strange being on base again after being immersed in civilian life. Now, the routine and the discipline needed to fall in line were an internal struggle. My uniform was just a shell covering a vulnerable human being, swirling with emotions. I continually talked to the spirit of my baby under my breath with assurance that everything was going to be okay.

I was called out at morning formation, after about a week of moving from physical training to the mess hall and doing all the mundane chores they could throw at me.

"Private Jones, report to the medical clinic for evaluation," Sergeant Conklin ordered. "Then report to my office."

"Yes Sergeant!" I said, happy that things were moving along.

The clinic had me on the roster and I entered a private examination room, undressed, and put on a hospital gown. When the doctor arrived, he said he needed to check to see if I had any injuries. I told him I had none but did have a burning question.

"Can I get a pregnancy test?"

"Have you missed a period?"

"Yes. I think I am three weeks pregnant, or is it too early to tell?"

"No, we can do a test. That would be a significant development in your case. Is the father in the military?"

"No sir," I said.

"Okay, I'll send a nurse in, and then I'll be back with the results."

This was it. I was finally going to find out whether my hunch was right. The nurse came in with a cup for a urine sample, and I thought to myself that she was a mirror of who I would have been if I had lasted in the Army. I certainly would have never met Jackson. It was all because I had gotten drunk that night. One night of excess tipped my destiny over into this moment.

"The test is positive," the doctor said when he stepped back into the room.

"I knew it, I just knew it!" I smiled brimming from ear to ear.

"You are free to get dressed and report back to Sergeant Conklin. Bring this report with you. It may change everything."

"Thank you, sir." I could think of nothing else other than my tiny little baby.

After handing over the paperwork to a soldier outside Sergeant Conklin's office, I waited while listening to muffled voices talking from beyond the wall.

"Jones, you can come on in," Sergeant Conklin said, opening the door. "Have a seat." He settled down behind his desk, next to two other men in uniform and asked, "First, do you have any plans to press charges against Captain Moore?"

"No, Sergeant. I don't. I think what he did was wrong, but I wasn't injured. I just feel I was treated unfairly, and I lost my zest to be a soldier."

"Well, what you did was wrong too. Going AWOL is a serious offense, but with your medical developments, we are prepared to discharge you from the military in lieu of trial by court-martial."

"I promise I won't press charges, Sergeant. I just want out."

"Sign here, Jones. We'll give you a general discharge, but I don't want to hear from you again."

"Thank you, Sergeant Conklin, thank you," I said, feeling a surge of freedom.

"Pack your stuff," he said as he handed me my discharge papers and the stack of paperwork that I had given him when I arrived. "You are free to go."

I stood up, saluted the three men behind the desk, and walked out of the office. Squealing with joy, I tore off my hat and threw it into the air. It was over! I rushed to my bunk and packed. Apart from my civilian clothes and the thick green camouflage coat with my name sewn on it that I was told I could keep, I left the uniforms folded neatly on my bunk. I wouldn't be deployed to the Middle East to care for the injured and dying after all. Instead, I would care for a brand-new life. This was a shot at getting it right, to love and be loved.

I called Jackson after leaving the base to tell him the news.

"I'm out! It's official, I'm free!"

"Awesome sauce! I can't wait for you to come back, sugar. I miss you."

"I'll be in Baton Rouge tomorrow afternoon. Should I meet you at the shop?"

"Yeah, I'll be there all day. I have a good stash to go to Philly with at this point. We just need to say goodbye to Kitty…that's gonna tear me up."

"I know. She's so special, Jackson. And I have more news but I'm gonna wait until I see you."

"What is it? You've got me on pins and needles."

"I really want to tell you in person. You'll just have to wait with a pin in your ass. I love you."

"I love you too. Gotta go, my client is here. Bye sugar," he said as he hung up.

I was horny and couldn't wait to see him. When I finally got to the shop, after sleeping at rest stops in my car along the way, I ran in. "There she is!" he said swooping me in his arms. We kissed so passionately that heat flushed through our bodies. He carried me to the break room and shut the door. Lifting me onto the table, he ripped off my pants, kissing me everywhere before entering me.

"Hey, quiet down in there," Mack said as he knocked on the door.

Jackson put his hand over my mouth, and we made love until we came simultaneously, both out of breath and tingling all over.

"I missed you baby," Jackson said collapsing on top of my chest.

"I missed you too," I whispered stroking his hair.

"So, what's this news?" he asked zipping up his jeans.

I looked him in the eyes and smiled, "We are having a baby."

"What? You're pregnant?" Excitedly, he planted a long kiss on my lips. "That's wonderful!" he opened the door and announced to the whole shop, "I'm going to be a father! Again!"

He was happy and that made all the difference. We were happy about our baby *together*. I started to cry tears of joy as he took my hand, and we walked around the room receiving congratulations from everyone in the shop.

"You baby-making fool," Mack said as he slapped Jackson on the back.

Time is Never Late

Chapter 22

Philly bound, I started to think about names, but first we had to stop and say goodbye to Kitty. The news had spread through the grapevine and Jeanie started to rip into Jackson, standing on her porch, arms crossed and angry that he was having another baby.

"You didn't want another one, and you know I want a boy to carry on my name," Jackson stated as his fury rose.

"*And* you are going to Philadelphia! What about Kitty?!"

"I'll come back and visit. You hardly let me see her as it is! What's the difference where I am?"

"Good luck with this asshole," Jeanie shouted staring straight at me sitting in the car.

Jackson hugged Kitty tightly. "Daddy's gonna miss you Kitty Cat. I will be back for your birthday. There is no way I'll miss it."

My heart broke for Kitty. At least she had a father who loved her even if her life wasn't perfect. Jeanie took Kitty by the shoulders and stood behind her while Jackson walked back to the car. Kitty broke down crying when Jeanie lifted her up and carried her through the door flipping Jackson the bird on her way in. With one last "Fuck you!" she slammed the door.

"Bitch!" Jackson retaliated as he started the ignition.

Rattled, we drove away in silence. I had to break the tension and turned on the radio. It was still on the '70s pop station I was listening to while driving through Texas. Crystal Gayle sang "Don't It Make My Brown Eyes Blue," but Jackson popped in a metal rock CD, which disturbed me. A stunning woman with the longest hair in show business was singing a ballad, but he found comfort in the screaming voices and rapid guitar licks that met him at the boiling point of his anger. I couldn't stand it but tolerated the noise and realized that the culture he was immersed in, tattoos, metal rock, and horror films was the opposite of my preferred interests. What did we have in common beyond sexual chemistry? What would we talk about on quiet mornings over coffee, or lying in bed under the covers on cold nights?

The trip got easier the further we got from Louisiana. We held hands and were hopeful about our new beginning. Jackson had enough money to secure an apartment and get us settled in. I had enough to pay for gas, food, and motel rooms until we found somewhere to live. The shop was on the outskirts of Philly in Germantown, so we looked for a two bedroom nearby and found a quaint little apartment in a 100-year-old ornate brick building in Mount Airy. It had laundry facilities in the basement, old fashioned arches, and a grassy courtyard in front. I thought I could lay with my baby on a clean, soft blanket in the summer months under the shade of the trees and watch him or her sleep after a good feeding. We thought about names again. Cora if she was a girl and Max if he was a boy. I didn't have a preference, but Jackson desperately wished for a boy. I couldn't relate to his need to carry on his family name. He hadn't proposed to me yet, so I mulled over if I even wanted his name. It didn't make sense to me why Jackson Wilson, a man who had a distant and neglectful father and a mother he hated, would even care about such a thing. He often ranted about how mean and crazy his mother was. A selfish woman who took advantage of vulnerable people, especially her children, and concocted scheme after scheme to get by in life. Jackson's resentment toward her was intense and it hurt my ears when he would rant and go down that spiral. He hated his ex-wife as well. None of this was a good sign. Resenting the important women in his life made me reflect on the resentment I had for the men in mine.

While our baby grew, so did the tattoo shop Jackson was managing. He would be away for long hours and sometimes would not come home for dinner, even when I made his favorite dishes. I learned how to make étouffée, a Cajun rice dish with shrimp and vegetables in a kind of gravy, homemade fried chicken tenders, and meatloaf with mashed potatoes. I was playing the housewife role, keeping a beautiful home clean with furniture from thrift stores and décor from yard sales. I made curtains and crocheted winter hats for all three of us and was starting on a baby blanket with soft greens, cream colors, and golds.

After applying for and then receiving state health insurance, I found a midwife who accepted it. I wanted a natural birth free from the environment of a hospital. When I was in my second trimester, I had an ultrasound, and we learned that we were having a girl. Jackson begrudgingly accepted that he wouldn't be having his boy but still would often kiss my belly and sing made-up songs to baby Cora, whose name was Greek in origin and meant "core" or "heart." She would become the center of my life.

I talked to my mother often. She was thrilled about the baby. "When am I going to meet Jackson?" she asked. "Is he taking good care of you?"

"Well, I hope you visit us when the baby is born. She's due in October. And we're doing good, though Jackson's mostly at the shop. He takes the car, so I walk a lot, which is good for me. I take the stroller to a neighborhood coffee shop to meet friends for tea and scones. I also do prenatal yoga with other pregnant women due around the same time. I'm happier than I've ever been, Mom."

"I'm glad to hear it Alika. And I like the name Cora. It's pretty."

"I like being a housewife. It's relaxing."

"Speaking of...aren't you two getting married?"

"Not sure about that. He has a complicated relationship with women."

"That doesn't matter," my mom insisted. "You should be getting married."

"We'll see what happens."

"Sometimes I don't understand you, Alika."

I knew that was an understatement.

"I love you. I still don't understand what happened with the Army, but I'm glad everything worked out. See you in a couple of months, sweetheart."

"See you then, Mom. I love you too."

As my body went through drastic changes, so did my mind. I felt a superhuman quality, full of energy and optimism. I was ready to give birth and be a mother. I was strong and limber. All my weight gain was right around the womb—every other body part was my normal trim self. Jackson and I kept a robust sex life and enjoyed laughing together. Once a week, we cuddled up and watched the hit show *Breaking Bad* when he was home. But more and more often, it was already dawn when he opened the door, and I believed him when he said he was working all night.

I was high on estrogen and progesterone and spent time painting old furniture for the baby's room. I collected toys, stuffed animals, books, and baby clothes, rejoicing in creating a gentle paradise for baby Cora. I was in a world all my own, content, excited, and at peace, ready to be the mother I always dreamed of.

July became August, and then came September. I was counting down the weeks. Cora was due the last week of October, but it was the first of the month when I started to feel something unusual stirring. It was a sunny day in the park with blue skies, and I was watching the autumn leaves fall into the river when my water broke. I called Jackson to pick me up and then called Bonnie, my midwife. The internal pressures in the beginning stages of labor had me focused on my baby girl. Breathing deeply, I meditated on the process and laid my hands on my abdomen, tapping into the harmony of the universe. I was one with the creative force of life, on the river's edge, when the pressure started to mount. Jackson pulled up and rushed over to me in a panic. By that time, I was buckled over leaning on a tree and breathing in a rapid pattern.

"Let's get you to the car, sugar," he said as he slowly guided me up.

"Have you talked to Bonnie?" I asked waddling toward the car.

"Yes, she's waiting for us."

I leaned, face down, over the passenger seat with my knees on the car floor. My tailbone was banging against the glove compartment every time we hit a bump in the road. I was collecting bruises that I wouldn't feel until later, and the tip of my spine would be tweaked and painful when I sat down for months afterward. All I could do was count my breaths like I was taught. When we arrived at the birthing center, Bonnie was waiting outside and came to help me out of the cramped space in the car.

"The baby's coming," I said with a big breath.

"You got this. I'm all ready for you. You are doing great," Bonnie encouraged.

Jackson escorted me up the steps and into the birthing room. Bonnie took off my dress and underwear that were soaked with embryonic fluid, wiped me down with a cool cloth, and wrapped a robe over my shoulders.

"I don't need that," I groaned and swung the robe off. Naked, I let out a loud moan. Cora was pushing my hips apart, making way for her arrival. The pain was manageable. I didn't need drugs; I didn't need anything. This was happening and nothing was stopping my baby from entering this world. For a few hours I dug deeper within, taking deep breaths, and imagining my birth canal widening while Cora inched her way through it. She felt huge but I knew she was tiny. Extending my arms over a big pink plastic exercise ball, I hugged it tightly with my knees on the floor.

"She's crowning!" Bonnie announced. "Come here on the bed and lie back. The baby is coming!"

As I lay there, legs spread wide, Jackson held my hand and Bonnie watched Cora's progress, her hands ready to catch Cora's head.

"Push, Alika, push with everything you've got!"

I roared and pushed and pushed and pushed until her head squeezed out.

"She's here! Your baby is here! Keep pushing, you're almost done Alika. One more big push!"

With every ounce of strength, I pushed with every muscle in my body, and Cora slid out onto Bonnie's hands. After suctioning the tiny nostrils, Bonnie placed Cora on my chest. Our spirits synchronized, we were one being and individuals simultaneously. Rooted, relieved, and rejoicing in life, happy tears fell from my eyes. My baby was born. She was slimy and beautiful. Bonnie gave me a soft cloth to wipe Cora clean, and her little lips started to move. She was hungry. I gave my newborn my breast and she managed, after a short time, to suckle the nutrients she longed for. I cried with joy.

My sweet baby was healthy, and she was perfect.

"You did good, Alika," Jackson said, kissing my forehead. He then reached down to do the same to Cora. "She's gorgeous, just like you."

Cora slept peacefully and often. Nursing her was the most natural connection I had ever felt with another human being. Jackson enjoyed bathing her, rocking her, and changing her diapers, at least for the first month or so. He began "working" late at night again, not coming home until daybreak. I listened to his excuses, half believing them. Cora was my whole world. She slept in the middle of the bed, and I cuddled with her, trusting that my intuition would keep her safe. I had a crib, but after she cried like hell alone in it at night, I couldn't stand to leave her like that. I fed her in the middle of the night without having to get up, and we slept in peace.

I bounced back quickly and was wearing my normal clothes after a few weeks. The autumn weather was still quite pleasant, and Cora and I would stroll to the park after stopping by Sam's Coffee, Tea, and Eatery, the busiest coffee shop in the neighborhood. We went there every day before winter settled in. A few of the women I had been doing yoga with also had their babies and we would often get together on "playdates," but we really just wanted to talk. I felt so fortunate that my baby wasn't colicky and didn't have trouble latching onto my nipples. Some of the women had long, excruciating labor experiences or C-sections. Cora was only 6 ½ pounds when she was born, unlike the 11-pound baby my friend had given birth to. Listening to their frustrations made me so grateful for the ease I had experienced. How did I get so lucky?

Jackson wanted to have sex far sooner than I was ready for, but I gave in even though my sex drive had substantially diminished. Sometimes I would go through the motions just to please him, at other times I was sincerely excited. As fate would have it, I knew, like I had known the first time, that I was pregnant again. Cora was only three months old when I felt that second spark within me. I waited to say anything until I took the test and sure enough another baby was on the way. We came to find out later that the baby would be another girl. By this time, Jackson was often taking road trips to Louisiana to see Kitty and check in with Mack, leaving me home with Cora, my fish tank, and houseplants. My belly grew, as did Cora, who began crawling, then standing, plopping on her rear on the floor when she attempted to walk. Her teeth were growing in, and I would make her homemade baby food with sweet potatoes, giving her the center of a corncob for teething after biting off the kernels. Watching her take her first steps out on the grass in the courtyard was so heartwarming, but it saddened me that Jackson missed these special moments. What could be better than watching our baby grow?

Time is something that doesn't wait for anyone. It goes on its merry way, without considering the pace of individual humans. With billions of people marching to their own drum, it is a wonder how the constant forward motion of the future unfolding continues regardless of the beats each of us keep. When patience aligns with time, as in meditation, it feels like time ceases to exist. Caring for Cora, nursing her, and connecting with the new baby inside me felt like pure harmony.

Collecting Keys

Chapter 23

December in Philadelphia had closed in fast.

The delightful days of autumn shifted to the callous chill of winter, and even my big wool coat couldn't protect me from the freezing cold. However, I needed to be outside on the sidewalk. Jackson was still in Louisiana and hadn't been home for months. The neglect had forced the girls and me into a homeless shelter, but it was a week ago that everything went awry.

"The posters are five dollars each," I said. "Both the Manet and Monet are in perfect condition."

"I'll take them both," said Richard.

Richard was a nice guy who also frequented Sam's Coffee Shop and made an effort to come by my sidewalk sale with a coffee in hand for me each day. He flipped houses for a living, and he was generous enough to offer to let us stay at one of the row houses he was remodeling on Upsal Street since we were desperate for a roof over our heads. Because of the harsh winter, construction had been put on hold, and I set up a little camp on the second floor for us to sleep at night.

Over the last week, I spent my days across the street from the coffee shop with our belongings spread out on the sidewalk.

"Oh, those? No, my mistake. I can't sell those. I'm sorry. The Rumi and Rilke are not for sale. But those cookbooks are two dollars each."

I would watch my playdate friends gather inside with their tea, pastries, and babies, everyone half-awake after another sleepless night, and talk about how motherhood had changed their identities.

Their partners hadn't withdrawn their love the way Jackson had.

As I sold my wares, I watched them go in and out of the coffee shop, and hoped they would buy something from my sale on their way home.

Conjuring the salesperson in me, I persuaded a spectator. "Those chairs are fabulous, aren't they? Only 50 bucks for the pair."

My baby girls took long naps and stayed warm in the van I had gratefully purchased with our tax refund after Jane was born. I hustled my goods, fueled with mania, in a hurry to settle into the Upsal Street camp before sunset.

The darkness of the winter skies was overbearing, but luckily there was a street lamp directly outside the old row house, beaming light onto the toppled furniture, tools, tangled extension cords, dust, and more dust that surrounded us. Cold, sharp air seeped in through the gaps in the window frames. My daughters snuggled so close to me that we breathed as one body, intermingling beneath layers of blankets, topped off by my long wool coat.

As we lay between the past and the uncertain future, I mentally prepared to leave. Southward bound, we would soon go somewhere warm and far away.

My children each suckled their designated breast—Cora on the right, and Jane on the left. It was my daughters' ritual while falling asleep, their bellies filled, and energy expired after having to work for the warm milk they loved. The girls were fifteen months apart, nestled into the hollows of my shoulders, oblivious to the precarious situation we were in. When they dropped their heads and were sleeping like stones, I carefully slipped out from between them and stood up, wrapping my floor-length coat around my back. Stretching my spine, I checked on my minivan, which was parked a floor below on the street.

A fresh layer of snow had covered the dark green roof that protected the only belongings we had left. Experiencing the brittle fact of homelessness, I gave away everything that I couldn't sell. Watching the snowflakes, my mind wandered. Nothing else is as white, I thought, perhaps they signify a new start. A strange concoction of loss and liberation stirred within my mind. Everything was gone—everything, including Jackson and any hope of reassembling the future I had imagined.

Before falling asleep, I reminisced about the first warm day of spring when I had taken Cora out for her initial stroll in the mild weather. I recalled being a joyful new mother, pregnant with Jane, pushing the carriage, still hopeful that my young family would thrive. The sun caressed my chest that day as I cruised along, wearing a halter top that I had just crocheted to match Cora's hat. I loved to expose the perfect curve of my abdomen, certain that the baby could feel the same soft sun as I did while walking to mommy-and-me yoga class. I remember arriving at the cottage where other women coddled their babies as we assembled in a circle and began our deep breathing. As I tickled Cora, who rolled between my legs, I imagined the new baby girl inside me, at peace, growing all her parts, letting her know that she was already thoroughly loved.

Just after dawn, we hit the highway. I envisioned an imaginary banner across the rear of the van reading *Florida or bust*. After some traffic through Jersey and Washington D.C., we managed to drive quickly through Virginia and the Carolinas. I began to picture the beach, eager for the sun and shaking off the frost.

The monotony of highway travel always made my babies sleep. Left to my own thoughts, a cluster of recent memories invaded my mind as I drove.

January

It was approaching noon after Jane was born and we were set to go home—but Jackson hadn't come back to the birthing center after leaving the night before. Our new baby was perfect and ate well, falling asleep on my supple stomach, which grumbled as she twitched.

I picked up the phone to call Jackson again, then decided not to. Instead, I ordered a Philly cheesesteak to be delivered from the local sandwich shop.

Jane had a full head of blonde hair, which was a surprise. But her face looked just like Jackson, and my resentment of his absence diminished as I admired this miniature miracle in my arms, so peaceful, as if she were recalling what it was like in heaven. She then let out a wide and heavy exhalation, larger than her tiny frame would be expected to carry—as if to say, "Hey, Mama, don't forget you have me."

Kari had come to visit two weeks after Jane was born. Barack Obama had just been elected President. We had made plans to go to the historic inauguration together with our children—something we'd imagined back in high school, the two of us dreaming of a better world. Zion was a teenager, handsome and smart, and Kari now had a cute, spunky five-year-old girl, Zola. The owners of Sam's Coffee Shop were ecstatic about the turn of events and arranged a tour bus to take their excited patrons to Washington, D.C., early in the morning for a reasonable fee. After congregating over hot drinks and baked goods, we headed off to witness the swearing-in of the first Black president of the United States. A passionate and charismatic person, he inspired us with his impressive speeches and transparent humanity.

It was a freezing day, and with nearly two million people in attendance, it was so crowded that we struggled to find a comfortable place to stand and watch. Layers of blankets, hats, and mittens protected my babies as I pushed them around the National Mall in their double stroller. Finally, we settled in front of the Washington Monument since we couldn't get close enough to see the event very well, but Kari and I listened to Obama's speech and watched the large screens, brimming with emotion as he spoke, his voice magnified tenfold through the speakers.

"We, the people, declare today that the most evident of truths—that all of us are created equal—is the star that guides us still; just as it guided our forebears through Seneca Falls and Selma and Stonewall; just as it guided all those men and women, sung and unsung, who left footprints along this great Mall, to hear a preacher say that we cannot walk alone; to hear a King proclaim that our individual freedom is inextricably bound to the freedom of every soul on earth."

Our noses were frozen, but our hearts burned bright as Obama's words filled our spirits with hope and promise. This milestone made us think that America was finally evolving, and we would bask in the inspiration of a brilliant, caring, and beautiful first family. Our world had taken a turn for the better, but my world was turning upside down.

October

When Jane was only nine months old, the lease to our apartment expired and the building was scheduled to be demolished. We had to move. Meanwhile, Jackson had not returned from Louisiana after being summoned for yet another beguiling family drama. His stories of medical fraud, a burning house, bloody fights, insurance scams, shots fired, his ex-wife demanding money, slander in need of squelching, and always another funeral, created a tangle of tales that I couldn't keep straight.

Jackson called to apologize that he couldn't send me any money because he was broke after the tattoo shop in Philly had closed and he was in debt to Mack. It was the same old rubbish, and I was sick of it. But I didn't have time to be sad about our empty bank account and failed love story. I went into survival mode.

With no family in town, I was forced to pack up the entire houseful of stuff, find somewhere to store it, and appeal to a local shelter. As weeks became months, Jane had started walking and Cora started talking. While I watched my children play among the tombstones on the side of the church where we were staying, I read a letter from the housing authority stating that I was still on the waiting list for an affordable apartment.

Each evening, we were due inside for curfew by 7 p.m. We ate dinner, I let the kids run around, and then went to our cots by 9 p.m. I would lie down, a horizontal pillar of comfort, my babies' well-being my only purpose, before we all had to vacate at 7 a.m.—rain or shine.

I often sat alone at a table with my babies in a church basement. After I put on my shawl and gave my breast to Jane, I was shot the same offended looks I got every night from some of the other moms I roomed with. I was the crazy white girl who breastfed her baby, while the other mothers used formula in bottles provided by the church we stayed at. I was an outcast—in the shelter and in society. As my baby suckled, I felt her fondling my other nipple. I'm not alone, I reminded myself. Millions of other women across the globe unashamedly give their breasts to their babies.

Every evening, I was destined to have the same conversation with the volunteers who served us at the shelter, and to answer the same questions:

"How old are your children?"

"Cora just turned two, and Jane will be one in January."

"Where's your husband?"

"Well…he abandoned us."

"Have you found a job yet?"

One night, a middle-aged woman in a floral dress sat down across from me with a pinched smile and a tray of baked goods.

"Would you girls like a brownie?" she asked us.

Cora reached for one.

My key ring fell to the floor, which still had the key to my apartment dangling from it. There was no need to give the key back. The old door with the old lock would be gone by now. The key became a symbol of security, privacy, safety, and a home. It was a reminder to keep my hope alive.

November

Our time in the shelter was almost up—but it was the stomach flu that ended our stay there. We were vomiting all night long, both girls were inconsolable, and the exhaustion was killing me. It was pouring rain outside. Jane was crying on the floor, and Cora was pulling at my nightgown. I was bug-eyed and bloodshot after a sleepless night stuffing a garbage bag with sickening sheets.

Then a nosy volunteer picked Jane up and said, "It appears that you need help, and I mean serious help." She had a do-gooder attitude and a savior complex that scared me. "I'm going to see to it that these children are safe and receive the care they need."

As she started dialing a number on her cell phone, never had such a cold fear consumed me. Paranoid at the thought of having my children taken away, I reached for Jane, who dived out of the woman's arms into mine.

"I have a sack of filthy, wet sheets that I need to take to the laundromat," I told the volunteer, struggling to stay calm despite my panic and nausea. Balancing Jane on my hip, I stuffed a duffel bag with toys and blankets, certain not to miss the diapers, wipes, towels, toothbrushes, coats, sippy cups, soap, and snacks. Weak, in a fury, and knowing I looked feral, I took Cora's hand and headed for our van. Standing in the rain, fastening the girls in their car seats, I thought of that nice guy Richard, from the coffee shop, and his offer to crash at the old row house he was remodeling. The house on Upsal Street.

December

After a full day of driving south along the east coast, we stopped in Savannah, Georgia, for the night at a cheap motel on a mossy, tree-lined street. The room had a musty smell, but the bed's slope, the petite coffee maker, and the thin, hard, dry soap, wrapped like a package, were vast improvements from where we had been sleeping for the last five days. We could jump, tickle, and play on the springy mattress. Cora's soft hair had finally grown in. It was a light brown and curled on the edges just as mine had done as a child. Jane's thick blonde hair fell into her eyes and needed a trim. Wearing the much-loved matching dresses that I had saved from the sidewalk sale, with a print of purple blooms and yellow butterflies, Cora and Jane threw pillows at each other, then at me.

Forgetting all else, we began to laugh. Sometimes laughter begets itself, stretching time, pushing the past back and the future forward as if it were its own form of creation where silliness reigns supreme and we wonder why we ever cried.

When joy is so fulfilling, its expanse pushes out the excess fluid from our bodies, and we must pee...or weep...or both. We weep that we have wept before, and we cry still because we have finally stopped weeping. That makes only more laughter, and we look at each other, realizing that we are each laughing for a different reason. That makes the moment even funnier.

Then the laughter sounds funnier because one of us heaves, another snorts, and then we can't catch our breath. It is wild and free and has no one to answer to, and that makes us laugh and cry simultaneously until we taste the salt of our own tears dripping from the gutter above our upper lips. Descending notes of laughter and several sheets of tissues signified the beginning of the end, but the TV filled the room with the musical theme for the show *Twilight Zone*.

"Doo, doo, doo, doo, doo, doo, doo, doo. There is a fifth dimension…"

Again, the imminent tsunami called Hilarity draws near and begins to suck us in. These elongated happy moments, these images and sounds, have been a long time coming. Afterward, we ached in our bellies, and even in our jaws.

After a good night's rest and a late check-out, we headed to a diner for some breakfast. I finished the pancakes my girls left on their plates after eating my own large veggie omelet, ordered a side of fruit to go, and slid the little packets of jelly into my pockets.

Admiring Florida's east coast as I drove further south, I slipped in my favorite West African CD. A smile spread across my face when the female choruses came in—so smooth, so joyful. Music was my companion on this sunny day, and my girls traveled well. Stopping at the occasional beach, we played in the sand, digging holes and making piles. Amazed by the warmth, we could have lounged all day, but I was determined to find a camping spot. Eventually needing to rest, I pulled into a nearly empty parking lot in a generic mall off the highway in the city of Melbourne. The half moon was already visible as the sun was setting, and we were far enough south that it was warm even at seven o'clock at night. After I set the girls free from their cramped car seats, Cora ran around the van, ecstatic that she was allowed to move as she pleased. Jane gathered her balance and gripped my fingers, walking steadily. Silhouettes in the neon glare of the Walmart sign, we stretched our bones, then slept until dawn.

Facing the rising sun, I thought about how far we had come. There were only 174 miles until we reached Miami. Before traveling any further, I decided to shop at Walmart for the essentials we would need for camping by the beach. I had raised nearly $500 from my sidewalk sales. We would live on that for as long as I could make it last. I had plenty of blankets and a cooler I had saved. I also had some cookware and utensils, a rope and towels, a bucket, soap, flashlights, clothes, and a small plastic potty. I decided to buy a kerosene grill, a tent, a lantern, and food.

Passing through Miami, we rolled down the Seven Mile Highway in the Florida Keys, which was as far south as we could get. The state parks were booked solid. As we crossed bridge after bridge connecting the small islands, we passed stores that sold key lime pie and conch. We found a vacancy at the Big Pine Key Fishing Lodge, which was packed with gigantic RVs and dozens of snowbirds from the north. This merry crew of retirees was busy decorating the social hall for the approaching Christmas Party. Christmas Eve was only a day away.

After entering this tropical wonderland and reading the list of activities posted on a bulletin board, I decided to book a campsite. There were crafts for the kids, Mr. and Mrs. Claus would arrive on a fishing boat, and there'd be a New Year's dance featuring contests in the jitterbug, the two-step, and the twist. The cashier handed over a shiny new key to the main entrance.

Wow, I thought. People are happy here, happy to be warm, happy to treat each other like family, happy to see the children. We've made it!

The ladies assured me that more youngsters would be arriving from up north—they came every year at Christmastime—and there was a playground next to the showers. I was in no hurry to set up the campsite, so I let the girls loose on the dance floor while holiday songs played, and someone gave me a cup of heavily spiked eggnog. I let out a huge sigh—it was the bourbon *and* brandy that tasted so good—feeling as though I was exhaling the stress built up from months past.

Strings of lights were wrapped like candy cane stripes on every pole and palm on the lot. A picnic table stood under the large butterfly bush on our campsite, providing a strong elevated surface for Cora to stand on while I handed her some ornaments I saved from the sale. With Jane on my hip, we hung snowmen and stars, shiny bulbs, and strings of imitation pearls. Then a neighbor appeared from around the bush and introduced herself with some tinsel to share.

"Hello," she said. "Welcome to the fishing lodge. I'm Rose. My husband, Harold, is just coming back from the boat. He's been growing his beard out all year to play Santa Claus, and it's nearly Christmas Eve!" Rose gave Cora and Jane two tiny stuffed elves. "You girls made it just in time," she said smiling.

"A fish!" Cora called out. "Mommy! A fish!"

"Fish!" Jane mimicked.

The wet scales coating the big and beautiful fish Harold was carrying had the sheen of a shiny spoon.

"Well, helloooooooooo!" sang Harold. "I hope you girls are hungry. We sure have a lot of fish to go around!"

The white of his long beard stunned me with its beauty. I had been wrong about the snow. There is something as white.

As Harold looked me over, I thought he was admiring my vintage polka-dot dress.

"I would bet a million bucks," he said confidently, "that you're a dancer."

"You're right," I said, flattered.

"Well, my sweet Rose injured her hip not long ago, though she's been the reigning jitterbug champion for a few years running, and I'm looking for a partner. I'd be tickled if you'd accompany me."

"I'm in," I said, shaking his hand. "Hi, my name's Alika."

It had been too long since I felt that unmistakable *click* of being in the right place at the right time.

"Mommy!" Cora shouted. "Look!"

A small deer was stepping onto our site, approaching us completely without fear.

Rose approached with some lettuce and handed it to the girls.

"Don't be frightened, children," she said. "You can feed them. They're very gentle."

"Mommy! He's eating!" Cora was elated as the lettuce crunched in the deer's mouth.

"Have you seen the beach yet?" Rose asked. "It's just around the bend there."

I took the girls and walked slowly hand-in-hand down the path that led to the shore. Once we passed the mangroves, Cora took off running toward the shallow, waveless water. For a long way, the cove appeared as if the ocean were just one huge puddle, and I felt secure that my toddler was safe. It was so quiet that the pitter-patter of Cora's footsteps splashing, and her giddy laughter, sounded as if they were out of a utopian dream.

The heat penetrated my sundress, warming my pale skin beneath. I finally relaxed by sitting on a rock, with Jane at my feet, playing in the sand. Looking at the sea always had a way of opening my mind up to an array of possibilities.

Maybe we could settle in this slice of paradise.

Soon Cora fell into my lap, beaming after her jog. Hugging my daughters, I looked up and over the calm, vast ocean, admiring the bluest of skies, and I smiled. I finally felt peace again, expanding my soul. Silent tears of joy welled in the pockets under my eyes. As I rubbed Jane's soft blonde hair below me, the teardrops moistened her scalp as they fell. An enormous wave of relief washed away the struggle. This would be our home until four walls and a roof sheltered us once again.

Night noises inhabited the tropical air, and the rhythmic sounds of frogs and insects mixed with the random snaps of the fire I fed. With fresh fish in my belly and the sun soaked in my skin, I felt restored. As my babes slept in the tent, I watched the smoke drift straight up until it disappeared. With each stick tossed into the heart of the flames, I considered what to do next.

I could drive across the country and park in front of the beige stucco house where I grew up. Surely, I would stub my big toe on the crack in the slanted walkway, as I had always done as a child. My knock on the metallic screen door would beckon my mother to greet us. She would hug me and be joyous to see the girls, but I would look like a failure. My ex reminded me too much of my biological father, who also couldn't grow accustomed to family life. The fatherless cycle continued.

When Jane grumbled a request for a midnight feeding, I went into the tent, kissed the crown of her head, and placed a breast within her reach. Swaying between being awake and dozing off, I became absorbed in the beats of the night. As the sounds grew louder and the rhythms became increasingly intricate, exhaustion overtook me. Half dreaming, I recalled a summer evening at the shelter. Fireflies had lit up the field next to the church. After we were told to come inside by the pastor, he scolded Cora for running indoors. She stopped and turned around, looking at me as if to say, "But, Mama, they don't know that I'm free!"

Family First

Chapter 24

Cora climbed trees like a monkey, Jane had her first birthday party, and I got very tan while running out of money. Almost two months had passed while the kids played with other children, and I blended in with happy people on vacation. We enjoyed trips to Key West, gatherings at the social club, and daily walks on the beach. Talking on the phone with Jackson was torture because he was pissed that we wouldn't go to Louisiana to live with him, and he couldn't admit it was *him* that left *us* in the dust. I didn't trust him, and I didn't want to move into a trailer park surrounded by his family's drama. The blossoming love we once shared had turned to rot.

The girls and I were on our own without a game plan. When speaking with my mother on the phone, she pleaded with me to come back to Los Angeles and stay with her and Ron until we got back on our feet. I agreed it was our best option and sold my camping equipment to raise enough gas money to travel across the country. Placing my ribbon for winning The Twist contest on the dashboard, we checked out in the office handing back the shiny key, and set out on a road trip crossing through eight southern states. We did not stop to see Jackson in Louisiana or visit my friends in Austin. I just kept on pushing forward, due west, while sleeping in the van at rest stops along the way.

My mother and Ron set up a small bedroom for the three of us with a queen-sized bed covered in fresh sheets that smelled like a flowering field. Sleeping with the girls on a clean, new bed was marvelous after a year of cots, a tent, and my van. We arrived at the house around midnight. I slept for a good nine or ten hours. Quietly slipping out from between the girls late on a Monday morning, I hoped they would sleep a bit longer. My parents had already finished their breakfast and were reading the newspaper when I walked into the dining room.

"Good morning sleepy head," my mother said as she got up to hug me.

"Good morning. Is there any coffee left?" I asked rubbing my eyes.

"How do you take it?" Ron replied walking to the kitchen.

"Black with honey please," I said sitting at the dining table.

"Really? All right, to each their own."

"Isn't that weird, Alika?" my mom said.

"I guess I'm weird," I said as a matter of fact.

"How was the drive?" Ron asked setting the mug in front of me.

"Thank you. The drive was long and excruciating."

I felt awkward to be in such a vulnerable position at my age.

"Jackson's been calling. He sounds angry," Mom revealed.

"He's always angry," I said sipping my coffee, which lacked the satisfaction of a good dark roast.

"Do you have any plans?" Ron asked.

"I was thinking about finishing college. I'm so close to getting a bachelor's degree," I said, hopeful for support.

"That's a good idea Alika. You should finish," my mom said as she took my hand. "You and the girls can stay here as long as it takes."

"Thank you. Both of you. This means a lot. It's been rough," I started to tear up.

"You've been through a lot, and I probably don't know the half of it," my mom said as Ron handed me a tissue. "We love you and the girls. We're glad you came home."

When the girls woke up and came out to the living room, my mom scooped them up into her arms showering them with kisses. They each wanted some mother's milk which made my parents uncomfortable.

"I'm in the process of weaning them. At least Jane is potty training, thank goodness."

"They eat food, don't they?" my mom asked.

"Yes, of course. Can we make them some scrambled eggs? Maybe cut up some fruit?" I began walking to the kitchen.

"Sit down, I'll make it," Ron said. "You can relax."

"You should go to the welfare department today and get medical insurance for the girls. Maybe some food stamps. I'll watch them. Take a shower, you need one," my mom instructed as she bounced Jane on her knee. "I'll bathe the girls."

"Okay. You're right. I should also go to the DMV and get a California driver's license," I thought out loud, more pragmatic than I had been in a long time.

"And you should think about therapy, Alika. It would do you some good. Here is an extra key to the house. Don't lose it."

I was still being treated as a child. But I had to agree, I certainly hadn't proven otherwise.

I stood in line at the DMV for a couple hours, took the written test, and got a new picture. My hair was still long and brown, and I thought I needed a new hairdo. I needed to reinvent myself, maybe cut it and dye it blonde, red, purple? With my temporary license in hand, I headed to the Department of Health and Human Services. I waited again for a couple of hours thinking about how things had turned out. Here I was, so happy to have my beautiful babies, but I came home broke, without a leg to stand on. When my number was called, I felt the sting of being just that, a number without a name or place in the world.

The eligibility worker wanted paperwork. I showed her the birth certificates and explained that I had two kids and didn't have any money, but I planned to finish my college degree. She said I qualified for around $300 in food benefits, $200 in cash benefits, and medical insurance for all three of us after turning in the paperwork they needed once I enrolled in college. I felt grateful and thanked her profusely. I walked away rationalizing that it was okay, I needed the help. This time I couldn't run away, dance for a living, or sing in the street. This time I had babies to support and no addiction to feed. It was time to get my life together. I wanted to become a college graduate.

That summer, I spent my mornings strolling the girls to the park and my afternoons taking them to children's museums and play centers where they could be stimulated by new experiences. Kalani was still in L.A., and we would often go to the beach together. Jane could play in the sand for hours and Cora loved to run along the shore. Sand toys, snacks, sun, and seagulls defined our weekends when Kalani had time off from work.

She was adamant that I should begin therapy.

"After all, you've been through a lot Alika," she said, worried that if I didn't receive some help, I could do something else to derail my life. "You should seriously reconsider medication."

"I don't want to take drugs. I'm fine. But you're right, I should talk to somebody. I feel like such a failure."

"These are the feelings you need to talk about with a professional. I will always be your friend, but I can't be your therapist."

Kalani suggested I check out a clinic where graduate students offered therapy on a sliding scale. I began to see Lauren, a woman who was about my age, forties. She was smart, kind, pretty, and compassionate, and I admired her. She had a beautiful ring on her finger given to her by a loving husband, lived by the beach in Santa Monica, and was embarking on a respectable career. I had to get over comparing my life to hers and begin to dig into a well of emotions I had buried deep. We met every week and talked about my abortion and the desire to end my life. We talked about Danny, Ricardo, Dario, the rape, and my sister. I revealed my drug and alcohol use over the years and began to accept that I had trauma. I tried to make sense of my crazy life, the sleepless nights wandering the streets for days, my impulsive behavior, the risks I took without any thought of consequences, and the depressive demons that swirled in my head. The only answer was that something was skewed in my brain. I told her that deep down I never accepted my bipolar diagnosis.

"The lithium made me feel worse."

"New medications are available now," said Lauren. "Consider trying a modern solution. Coming to terms with your manic-depressive diagnosis is the first step." Lauren cleared her throat. "Bipolar disorder requires medication to live a stable life, both mentally and emotionally. Think of it like a diabetic who needs insulin, or someone who needs medication for high blood pressure. Your children deserve the best mother you can be, and it requires taking responsibility for your mental health."

I was able to receive daycare benefits after enrolling at California State University Northridge and began classes that fall. Transferring my community college credits, as well as the credits from the seminary, I chose to pursue an English degree with a minor in religious studies.

I adapted to life at home and had a harmonious routine: dropping the girls off at preschool in the morning, going to the university, and then picking them up in the late afternoon.

Since Lauren and Kalani persisted in telling me that I should try medication, I discovered a psychiatric program with UCLA on campus and made an appointment. After many long discussions, I was given a new prescription, abilify and lamictal. Simply put, one pill for the highs and one for the lows. I didn't show any sign of side effects like rashes or itching, so I continued taking the pills every day before bed.

The girls had been weaned, so I felt confident I could put medication in my body without harming them. I did begin to experience mental and emotional stability, and it felt like I was finally able to focus. My college courses were the perfect antidote. I was finally able to experience a smidgen of autonomy.

My mother helped with the girls when I had late classes because I had gone full throttle and took a ton of courses. It felt good to think, to converse with intelligence, to write essays and have a point of view. I became creative again, writing plays and poetry. It was a joy discussing the philosophy of world religions and dissecting novels. I qualified for grants and won scholarships, to supplement my student loans.

Christmas was approaching and I decided to hire a photographer to take those classic pictures of the girls and me on the beach all wearing white. He took shots of the girls playing in the sand and all of us dipping our toes in the ocean and chasing each other along the shoreline. He captured our smiles and joy with a professional camera on a clear sunny day against bright blue sky as I carried both girls on my hips, confident and poised as if life were perfect. These photos became my first custom Christmas card. It was time to reconnect with friends and family; after all, I wasn't living on the fringe of society anymore. I was part of it, and it felt good.

Paul still lived around the corner from my mom's house, and when I itched for company, I started visiting him now and again after the girls fell asleep. He was still making music and always had people in and out of his house sleeping on his couch and in his garage. He was starting to lose his hair and it was turning prematurely grey. He looked like a wreck, but he was still as funny and witty as ever. Sometimes I would pop over when I felt a fire under my ass and would bum a cigarette. Though I was medicated and feeling stable, it wasn't a cure for my addictive nature, and I would often indulge in hanging out, bringing a couple of six packs of beer to share.

I continued to progress with my courses and earned straight As. I took Pilates, tennis, and ballroom dancing classes to balance out the headiness of my program and graduated with honors in two years. I couldn't get enough of academia, so I enrolled in graduate school. I became a TA in the English department and had a job on campus teaching credit recovery courses to struggling freshmen. But when I felt antsy and needed a break from home life, I would head to Paul's house.

I befriended one woman named Sahira, who was homeless and staying at Paul's among a bunch of guys who were doing plenty of drugs. She smoked weed and began sharing her joints with me. She explained that she was once sexually harassed by Paul's friend when she was sleeping at night and asked if she could crash at my house for the weekend. When I introduced her to my mother, she offered to clean our house and take care of the chores in exchange for temporary housing until she could get back on her feet. My mom had always been soft-hearted and over the years had often shared her home with people who needed help. She agreed, and Sahira moved into the spare room that night.

Sahira shared stories of her background with me as we walked around the block smoking joints in the evenings. She was originally from Turkey but was adopted by a German family as a baby. She came to the U.S. when she was thirty on a temporary visa and wanted to become a citizen. She tirelessly spoke about how much she loved the United States and how she had once worked for the military, role-playing a Middle Eastern civilian during training sessions for soldiers. It seemed suspect, but we believed her. She had dark hair and eyes, and a strong German accent that could make anyone feel uneasy. I related to her because she didn't have a place in the world and felt sorry for her because it seemed no one cared. My mother and I took her under our wings and helped her fill out the forms for citizenship.

Sahira and I loved to play with the girls at home with all their toys. My mother had given Cora and Jane every My Little Pony figure, a slew of Barbie dolls, and a play kitchenette that kept them in their world of make believe for hours on end. Sahira continued to clean the house and help my mother with things like sewing, which she seemed to be a master at, and would also join my girls in their toy kitchen while they made pretend meals for her. We had disco parties by rapidly flicking the light switch on and off, dancing to current pop music that the girls liked. It was summer and hot, and we taught the girls to swim in my parents' new, raised pool, each of us with a child on our hips, bouncing and splashing in the water. We put together elaborate birthday parties for them with bouncy houses on the front lawn, blew up dozens of balloons, and dressed up like Disney princesses to surprise them in the middle of the party. Sahira made beautiful dresses for the girls which spun out when they twirled. Sahira became a part of our family.

One day she offered to cut my hair, insisting that she had been a hairdresser back in Germany. We set up a chair in the grass in the back yard and I leaned my head back as she sprayed it with a water bottle. Her fingernails combed my scalp, and I kept my eyes closed, listening to the birds in the trees. As my hair fell onto the grass with each snip of the scissors, I wondered if birds would snap up my locks to soften their nests for their hatchlings. I trusted Sahira as the sun warmed my face, and the slicing sound of scissors cut my hair too close to my eardrums.

It wasn't long after she had moved in that Sahira became part of my routine. We would drop the girls off at preschool in the mornings, and then she'd come to campus with me. She would go to the library to use the computers and read publications while I was in classes.

Sometimes, we would meet in my car to smoke a joint on my breaks. I started going to theory class high, then linguistics class, losing my zest for my courses. I began slacking on my homework.

Sahira started to show some concerning signs when she began talking about a boyfriend, someone she had never mentioned before. He turned out to be an actor she followed on the internet. But it was after Sahira started pointing to the sky, claiming that helicopters were after her, that my parents and I convened. We weren't sure what to do. Suddenly, Sahira insisted that my box of yarn was evil and threw it into the back yard, looking at the sky, screaming, "Leave me alone!"

Ron and my mother were talking about calling the police because Sahira couldn't be reasoned with. I thought to call Kalani. But then Sahira had a crazed look in her eye, ran to the girls' room, picked up a teddy bear, and stormed out of the house.

It was an hour later, and the sun had set. We were stunned when the police knocked on the door. They asked to enter our home and stated that I was accused of child abuse. One cop looked in the refrigerator and the kitchen cabinets, the other inspected the girls' arms and legs to see if there were any bruises. After finding nothing, they said they needed to ask the girls some questions in private. Cora and Jane were distracted watching *Curious George* on TV, but the officer turned off the television and told me to wait in the living room.

Sahira was sitting outside on the curb with the white teddy on her lap next to the police car. I stared her down through the window and felt rage welling up within me. How could she accuse me of abuse?

What in the world would happen to my kids? Would I be arrested? My mother hugged my stiffened body and assured me it would be okay despite my racing thoughts.

The female officer waited with my kids while the male officer returned to the living room.

"Who is the woman who made this accusation?"

"She was homeless, and we took her in" I said, desperate to explain how we befriended her, fed her, and gave her a bed. "She has been acting psychotic lately, paranoid that helicopters are looking for her."

"Well, we don't see any signs of abuse or neglect. Normally, I would have to call child welfare right away, but I don't see a need for that. You seem like good people. Generally, we discourage taking in strangers because it is very hard to get them out. Legally our hands are tied."

"I've already packed up her stuff," Ron said as he carried a suitcase outside and put it on the curb. "You aren't welcome here anymore," he shouted so Sahira could hear him.

"Can I see my kids?" I asked. "They have got to be scared."

"Go ahead. I have a couple more questions for your parents."

When I walked into our bedroom the girls were jumping on the bed. The female officer was smiling. "They're cute," she said with her hands relaxed on her heavily laden black belt as she walked into the living room.

"Mommy!" they said in unison as they fell on me.

"Sahira said she was gonna kill you," Cora told me as she put her arms around my neck.

"What?"

"She said she was gonna kill you and keep us." Cora continued.

"No one is going to kill me, honey. Don't you worry about a thing. I got you," I consoled my babies with my arms folded around them.

My blood was boiling, but I decided not to make a huge scene. I didn't want to traumatize my kids any more than they already were. This bitch was messing with my children.

I carried both girls on my hips and walked into the living room as the officers were leaving.

"Like I said, I wouldn't bring people you don't know into your home," the male officer warned again, as he walked down the stairs of the porch.

The lights were flashing on the police cars in the darkness of the night and the neighbors were standing on their lawns wondering what was going on. The police officers said something quietly to Sahira that I couldn't hear. She grabbed her suitcase and began walking in the direction of Paul's house.

I couldn't sleep that night. I imagined her slashing my tires. I imagined her waiting for me behind a tree with a knife ready to pounce. I imagined her going to the girls' school to steal them away. What was she be capable of?

I wanted to release that bottled up rage by kicking Sahira's ass. So, the next morning I went to Paul's house to confront her. He said Sahira had stopped by but left late last night and he hadn't seen her since. She had disappeared.

It wasn't long before Jane started to throw tantrums. She would cling to my leg as I was leaving the house, crying, and not able to let me go. Sahira had made her mark and scarred my youngest daughter, while Cora seemed to brush off the whole incident. But Jane was terrified and would have attachment issues for years to come. It seemed like that witchy woman had put a curse on me too. I found myself unable to focus on my studies and was envisioning Sahira jumping out from behind every tree as I would leave or return to the house.

Was she watching us?

Smoking weed became my escape from the anxiety and the stress, but only added to my paranoia. I found a dealer through Paul and began smoking joints several times a day. I liked them rolled with tobacco, European style, and hid my habit from my parents. I smoked at the baseball fields I used to walk through as a tween on the way to middle school. There was no flasher, no gang of misfits, just me smoking alone.

Sahira seemed to have vanished. There were no sightings of her at the daycare or my college campus, and eventually she started to fade from my thoughts. I was smoking so much weed that it made me restless. Everyone seemed to be dating online, so I built a profile and started looking for dates as a distraction. After sorting through numerous men, I connected with one named Darrell who had a Harley Davidson motorcycle and a shiny new Tesla. On our first date, we rode on his bike along the coast while my parents watched the girls. Darrell and I developed the perfect superficial relationship. We would wine and dine, and I'd stay at his high-rise apartment in Beverly Hills and have sex until the late hours of the night high on cocaine. He was a producer in show business, which gave us all kinds of access to fancy underground clubs. A wildfire had been ignited.

Eventually, he introduced me to swinger parties. I had so much pent-up sexual energy that I exploded on the scene. We went to fancy houses in the Hollywood Hills where we wouldn't know what we'd find when opening a bedroom door—someone blindfolded on all fours being sensually whipped by a dominatrix, or an orgy with three couples all crowded on a king size bed, or a voyeur couple watching another couple in the throes of passion. It was so enticing, and I felt ready for anything, often stepping into one of the bedrooms living out a sexual fantasy.

Drinking heavily again and indulging my hedonism caused me to forget to take my pills most of the time and my parents were getting sick of my late nights on the town. I would often come home drunk and didn't have the energy or focus to complete my studies. Even though I had only a year left, I dropped out of grad school. My parents put their foot down. I had to get a job and pay rent.

I found work at a personal injury law firm, which were a dime a dozen in Los Angeles. Car accidents happened so often that we had a steady stream of new clients as I did intakes, filed papers, made doctor appointments, and handled the reception desk. I felt like a machine. There was no philosophy to grapple with, no thoughtful essays to write, and nothing creative to explore. Hitting the liquor store before clocking in, I would buy those airplane bottles of vodka to swig in the bathroom while I worked just to cope with the misery.

And things got worse after the shocking victory Trump had over Hillary Clinton in the 2016 presidential election. That destroyed me. My guts overturned, and my glass heart shattered. This was a man who was so repulsive and vile that I lost all control of myself trying to numb the sorrow. I sank deeper into a depression and went with Darrell more often to after-parties, indulging in sexual escapades, so drunk and delusional that somehow it all made me feel better.

It was a warm summer Saturday when Darrell whisked me away to Santa Barbara for the weekend to attend his friend's wedding. The Tesla silently glided along the highway, and two hours later, we arrived at the Four Seasons by the beach. I loved the glitz and glamor of a fancy hotel, and I couldn't wait to indulge in the champagne, sex, and the spa. We checked into the luxurious San Miguel Suite and after the bellman unloaded our luggage, Darrell broke out a bag of cocaine and laid out a couple of lines on the glass coffee table with ornate iron legs. The balcony had a view of the pool, and we watched the women in their bikinis lounging in the sun as the rush from the cocaine took flight.

After soaking in the Jacuzzi, we dressed up in our sophisticated attire and hit the bar before the wedding began. Clinking glasses with other guests, martini after martini, we all felt at home sitting on barstools, bedazzled by the effect of the booze. The elegant glass shelves and mirror on the wall made the bottles sparkle behind the bartender who did his job with precision and grace. He wore a sly smile as he collected big tips, banking on the generosity of rich alcoholics to pay his mortgage and put his kids through college.

We basked in the Spanish Colonial charm as we strolled through the grounds on our way to the ceremony, surrounded by 75 different species of palms, and admired a splendid century-old fig tree spreading its roots above the topsoil. The beauty of this opulent hotel has entertained Hollywood's power players since the 1930s and hasn't stopped since, with some flying in via helicopter to their private bungalows. We located the area in the garden set up for the wedding with large pots of cream-colored flowers and chose seats in a row near the back.

As the wedding began, I watched the bride walk down the aisle. I admired the gorgeous couple sealing their vows with a kiss. They walked hand-in-hand out of the ceremony to take exquisite photos that would last a lifetime.

"Wana bump?" Darrell nudged his elbow into my side scooping out some cocaine from a vile with a tiny spoon.

"Sure," I said, ready to party, ignoring my desire for true love.

The reception was held at the La Pacifica Ballroom and Terrace along Butterfly Beach. The band was stellar, and champagne flowed freely from trays held by servers wearing black bow ties. I didn't count how many glasses I emptied. I never cared to know. Free alcohol tasted even sweeter than paying for it and drunkenness always motivated me to let loose on the dance floor. I had great rhythm and freely moved my body, attracting the attention I craved. I enjoyed dancing so much that I preferred it to making small talk or eating, even though the hors d'oeuvres were delicious. I kept on dancing, twirling my gold strapless dress that accentuated my tan. My hair was loose, shoulder length, and dyed blonde. I felt on top of the world as time passed and the band played everything from funk to disco to oldies. A whirling dervish, I was so lost in the music that I didn't notice when the bride stepped onto the dance floor. Darrell had been schmoozing with the Hollywood elite before noticing that people were trying to grab my attention, urging me to have a seat and calm down so the bride could have her dance. Oblivious to it all, I invited people at surrounding tables to join me. One by one, each person shook their head and looked embarrassed for me. It wasn't until the groom tapped me on the shoulder and asked me to leave the reception that I stopped dancing.

"Please, you are making me and my wife very uncomfortable," he said unapologetically. "Just leave, or I have to call security."

"I'm here with Darrell. Have you seen him?"

"No, I haven't. Please go back to your room and sleep it off," the groom said struggling to be polite.

"Fine, but can I have a bottle of champagne to take with me?"

Just then, two men approached and took me by the arms, escorting me away. I shook my arms out of their hands and walked off defiantly as they followed me out of the reception hall. Drunkenly grumbling under my breath, I cursed Hollywood and its uptight rich asses who didn't know how to have fun. I waited outside after bumming a cigarette, standing under a heat lamp, expecting Darrell to come out and join me. He didn't, so I went to the beach and skinny dipped in the ocean, howling at the night sky.

Darrell was quiet the next morning as he sped on the freeway all the way home. When we arrived at my mom's house, he said he didn't ever want to see me again.

"You embarrassed me in front of very important people," he said with a stern face.

"Sorry. I was drunk."

"You were acting like a fool."

"Whatever! You aren't that good of a fuck anyway," I snarled as I slammed the car door in his face.

When I approached the house and opened the front door, my girls came rushing out and hugged my hips. Suddenly, I felt like a terrible mother. I had become so selfish, flaming the wildfire of my unresolved youth, indulging in escapism, ignoring my responsibilities. With my priorities upside down, I was a sexual maniac and a full-blown alcoholic. I kissed and hugged my daughters, expressing my apologies silently. They were so pure and innocent; in contrast, I felt soiled. I resolved to take a cleansing shower and wash my tainted body.

It was Sunday and I didn't have to work, so I swam in the pool with my girls. We had fun splashing each other, playing tag, and singing Beach Boys songs. They took turns balancing on my shoulders and then dropping into the water. Being in the present moment, comforted by real love, satiated my usual longing for more. This was what I always wanted, my girls to hold and cherish.

After drying off and grabbing some snacks, we relaxed on the couch next to my mother, who was fiddling with the computer. Mom, who loved Facebook, had befriended Jessica, my friend from high school. She showed me a picture of Jessica holding her five-year chip from Alcoholics Anonymous with her arm around her girlfriend. She had come out and was getting ready to get married. She looked happy and beautiful. My mom told me I should contact her, but I was apprehensive. It had been so long.

I knew I needed a fundamental change, but didn't know where to start. My first thought was to try yoga, maybe that would stave off the booze and marijuana. The following weekend I bought a yoga mat, some new yoga pants, and found a local studio in the Valley. I was early, and there was a juice shop next door. Should I order celery, carrot, or a mixture of greens and fruit?

"Oh my God! Alika?" said a voice behind me, "Is that you?"

I turned around and there was Jessica. Same long dark curly hair. Still with her hourglass figure beaming through her yoga outfit. She looked healthy, clear as crystal.

"Jessica? After all these years!" Amazed, my mind's eye opened— the cosmos were obviously at work.

Surrender

Chapter 25

It is one thing to feel defeated, it is quite another to admit it out loud. After meeting at the yoga studio a couple of times, Jessica invited me to celebrate her 50th birthday at a Mexican restaurant. She didn't have to dig too deeply into my past before inviting me to my first AA meeting, because at her birthday party I ordered margaritas one after another. It was my norm, and I was having fun. I drove myself home, even after Jessica tried to call me an Uber. I shouldn't have been surprised when I got a call from her the next day asking me if I would join her at an AA meeting. Aghast, I didn't believe I had a problem. I functioned just fine. I did my job, took care of my kids, and paid my bills. I had never lived a more "normal" life.

"I've talked to your mom, Alika. She is very concerned about you," Jessica said over the phone. "I saw the way you ordered half a dozen drinks last night, and you didn't even care that you made my sober friends uncomfortable or that you drove home drunk."

"I'm sorry, I didn't realize..." I wasn't sure what to say.

"Listen, it's worth a shot. Come with me to a women's AA meeting tonight at seven o'clock. I'll text you the address. It's in North Hollywood, not too far from you. It's a great group of women. Have you ever been to one?"

"No. I haven't. Of course I've heard of AA, but I don't really know anything about it," I said, unsure if I wanted to know.

"If you want, I'll come pick you up."

"No, it's okay. Let me make sure my parents can watch the girls. I'll come if I can get them to babysit," I said, thinking about whether weed counted with AA people. I was dying to smoke my morning joint.

"Okay, see you later. I'll text you the address. Alika, my life has become so wonderful since I got sober. I just know in my gut that you can also live happy, joyous, and free."

I supposed this was AA lingo.

"Get there a little early, like 6:45, because it starts at 7 p.m. sharp. Just bring an open mind."

After clearing things with my parents, I summoned up the courage to go to this meeting, though I wondered if I was ready to change. There was a fear I didn't understand creeping up, but I pushed through and parked in the street in front of a church. I approached a group of women smoking cigarettes in the parking lot. Unable to find my Bic I asked for a light and made small talk before one of them asked my name. I introduced myself and told them that Jessica had invited me. They were welcoming and friendly which helped ease my anxiety as we walked toward the entrance.

I was offered some coffee and sat down next to Jessica in a squarish circle before the meeting began. People took turns reading paragraphs of words that felt foreign yet struck a chord. The leader introduced the speaker of the night, and she told her story. Aside from her multiple DUIs and her bouts with Child Protective Services, I could relate with her inability to stop after taking that first drink.

I couldn't remember ever having just one drink.

These women took turns expressing their gratitude at having taken the steps needed to change their lives. They spoke of events that led them to AA, demoralization, and a Higher Power. A pressure built up within me until I felt like I needed to share. But I still wasn't convinced that I was an alcoholic. I thought of Dario. He was way worse than I was, and the comparison kept me from owning my own experience. I wanted to talk about why I sat waiting in my car drinking a bottle of vodka a couple of weeks ago while my kids were in their pajamas enjoying a movie inside the elementary school auditorium, cuddled on their sleeping bags and eating popcorn. Why didn't I sit inside with the other parents and watch a Disney movie?

I stayed silent. I couldn't admit that I had a drinking problem, but I left the meeting with a big, blue hard-covered book in my hand anyway. Before I went home, I drove to the baseball fields and smoked a joint, staring at the Big Dipper, then Pleiades, and then the Moon. Fixated on the glowing orb half lit up, the other half shrouded in darkness, I teared up and cried for no apparent reason.

I did not go back to that AA meeting the next week. I just worked my dead-end job and brought the kids to and from elementary school. I helped them with their homework, poster board presentations, and their dioramas. I took them to ballet classes and cooked their meals. But I couldn't break free from the cycle of secretly getting high and drinking little airplane bottles of vodka each day. It was just enough to remain in denial, rationalizing that I needed it to get by. While putting up a front at work and at home, and after a couple years of the same old routine, along came 2020 and a city-wide shut down.

Covid-19 changed everything: no more work to go to, no more dropping the girls off at school. Staying home watching the news with my parents made me feel like I was stuck in a cage. My dealer stopped answering the phone, and it was hard to hide the effects of booze from my parents. I felt trapped.

Before Covid hit, I had been promising myself that each bag of weed was my last for a long time. Now sequestered, I was trying to keep those airplane bottles of vodka to just six a day: one in the morning, two at noon, and three at night. I wouldn't get drunk. I was compelled to feed the addiction. One day, I finally realized I was trying to manage something I had no control over. Just the fact that I had to monitor myself was proof enough. I was an alcoholic. And I had been for decades. One drink, even ten, was never enough. There was never enough alcohol to satisfy my craving, never enough of anything because down deep I felt like I wasn't enough.

Feeling a kind of panic set in, I needed some fresh air and went out to the back yard. Desperate, I looked up at the sky and called, "Help! I need help!" I prayed for a moment, but didn't feel worthy. I cried, feeling the sting of defeat. It had been so long since I called out to the power of the universe for help. I didn't want to fight anymore. I decided to ask God to take the addiction away from me. The word surrender popped into my mind. The time had finally come.

I cried and cried and thought of Grandma. She would have wanted me to live a better life. Immersed in self-pity, I thought about instances of self-sabotage and what a victim I had been. Something had to change. That's when I was nudged by a silent voice in my head, telling me to go to an online AA meeting.

It was almost 7 a.m. The website had a directory of Zoom meetings across Los Angeles, and I picked one called "Sunrise Steps" on a whim, because it started in a few minutes and gave me a sense of optimism inherent in the name. Dozens of little boxes appeared, and people chit-chatted before the meeting began. I sat in a swinging chair in the back yard with my laptop on my thighs. I looked at myself in my little Zoom box with overflowing tears falling down my face. I was sick and tired. Feeling vulnerable and ready to bare it all, it was time to be honest with myself, and I became willing to look at my moral compass and discover my truth. Was this the epiphany I'd been hoping for?

The format was the same as Jessica's women's meeting, reading after reading, but then they asked if anyone was in their first 24 hours of sobriety. I pushed the unmute button and spoke up this time. "I'm Alika, and I think I am an alcoholic."

"Welcome, Alika," said a woman leading the meeting. "You are in the right place."

Everyone silently clapped and smiled in their little boxes.

The people in the meeting were of various ages and sexes and came from a variety of backgrounds. The speaker was a woman who told her story for about 15 minutes with a message about the need to take it one day at a time, one step at a time, and to avoid future-tripping or dwelling on the past. The present moment was her focus, and the choices she made now were the most important. She spoke of "living the promises" and her gratitude for being sober, which filled her life with humility and joy. I still had the Big Book Jessica gave me a few years ago, the book I had never opened. After our early morning meeting, I was inspired to open this thick book and see what these promises were all about.

I continued going to that same online meeting day after day and soon I asked a woman to be my sponsor. She agreed and said she would meet me on Zoom to read the book together and start my steps. I was grateful, because I found many aspects of the writing to be pleasingly poetic, but also rather archaic. I needed some guidance to make sense of it all. She helped me to adapt some of the words so that the essence of the message became universal and avoided tripping up on the masculine angle of the text. I was taught to look at the similarities, not the differences, and was able to relate purely as a person who had been an alcoholic and addict for much of my life. I never thought that my propensity to drink and use was a roadblock to living a successful life, but everything was finally coming into focus. Plus, I was what they called "dual diagnosis" because of my bipolar disorder. I had been self-medicating all these years. Everything made so much sense, I dived right into the program.

In the meetings, some swore that they had recovered from alcoholism, some said they were in a constant state of recovery, but they all had found a solution to their problem. Each person had an individual concept of a Higher Power, which was the key to their success. I was free to choose my own Higher Power. Nobody told me to believe in a religion or follow some leader, it was my choice, and none of us had to agree. That rang true to me. We did not have to believe in the same God, we were free to create our own personal relationship with whatever worked for us. And mine was not a him or her, just God—an all-encompassing force.

The fact that I was powerless over alcohol, and in my case cannabis, tobacco, or anything else that was put in front of me, indicated that I needed a power greater than myself to overcome my lack of power. I just needed to be honest with myself and others to come clean in mind and body.

I started the steps and began working through the shame and regret, accepting my part in the circumstances of my life. The fourth step, doing a moral inventory and listing all my resentments, was a transformative experience and deeply therapeutic. Recognizing that

I had made bad choices, which sprang from the pain and confusion I experienced as a child, helped me come to terms with my responsibility for those choices.

Sahira was the freshest wound, and I felt guilty for putting my children in harm's way, but worked at forgiving her and myself. I prayed to forgive Danny, Ricardo, Tess, Dario, even the rapist in London, which was all easier than I thought, because time is a great healer. The bigger challenge was to forgive myself for the harm I had created and the years I had thrown away, the love lost with Diana, and especially my abortion. I learned that forgiveness is a virtue. I also discovered that being humble and honest with myself was an opportunity for growth.

My mind started processing differently. Negative thoughts and feelings were filtered through a spiritual siphon. With a humble heart, I read, wrote, and prayed every morning before the break of dawn. A new kind of routine, a daily practice that kept me both grounded and produced a new kind of freedom. My vulnerability allowed me to get in touch with my soul, and I started to notice that I was becoming the person I had always wanted to be. I strove to become a woman of integrity, finally realizing what that word meant after my teacher, Ms. Dearmore, had said it to me so many years ago, when I was 13, after the first time I got drunk.

I decided to give Jessica a call.

"Jessica? It's me Alika."

"Hey, Alika," said Jessica, chomping on an apple. "How's Covid treating you?"

"Actually, I've never been better. I finally joined AA for real. I am amazed by what is happening to me," I exclaimed.

"Oh, what good news! I'm so happy for you Alika! Sorry, I am just finishing up my lunch."

"Is this a bad time?"

"No, not at all." Jessica was all ears. "Tell me all about it."

"I have found a new freedom and a new happiness. The promises do come true!" I said using my AA lingo. "Thank you for planting this seed for me. Guess I'm a bit slow."

"Each in our own time," she said, and I could hear her smiling. "Alcohol is a killer, I'm just so glad you were finally ready to give it up."

"These steps have been so therapeutic, and getting through my moral inventory was so freeing. What a great way to become aware of all the complexities surrounding resentments. And then, to recognize my part in it was such a revelation!"

"I hear ya. AA is real, no doubt. It changed my life. How about recognizing character defects and being in acceptance?" Jessica sneezed. "Excuse me. What step are you on?"

"Bless you. The ninth. Making amends," I cleared my throat. "I need to tell you I am sorry for hurting you way back when we were teenagers. I know I could have been a better friend."

"Don't sweat it. We were fools back in the day, girl!" Jessica laughed. "Anyway, I'm the one who slept with your boyfriend!"

"Yeah, but I left you at that party in Malibu after slapping you across the face while drunk off my ass." I remembered.

"We were both a mess back then," Jessica paused. "But it's water under the bridge, Alika. The past is long gone."

"I will always love you, Jessica. Call me anytime," I paused. "And we've got to get together after Covid lets up!"

"Yes definitely! I love you too and stay sober!" Jessica exclaimed, before hanging up the phone.

By the time I received my six-month chip, I felt empowered to say no to anything that would threaten my sobriety. "No" was a word that had a whole new meaning to me. "No" helped me define my new identity. No more drunk Alika, no more self-sabotage, and no more running away to escape the truth. No more hurting the people I loved, and no more slacking on my medication. I like to use the word *miracle*, because I think they happen far more often than we give them credit for. Miracles, or unexpected events that fill me with wonder, have significantly changed the way I see the world, and more importantly, changed the way I think. Sobriety and working the Twelve Steps have been miracles in my life. They have allowed me to build confidence, take responsibility, be honest, and less self-centered. "Trust God, clean house, and be of service," is my sponsor's motto. I began to live by it.

Restrictions due to COVID-19 had lightened up when it was time for my first sober birthday. I was invited to the park where the Sunrise Steps meetings first started. My sponsor had arranged for me to lead the meeting and share my 15 minutes with the group, which was dozens of people on this sunny day. It was surreal and heartwarming to hug people I had only seen on a computer screen for the past year, those who had shared many personal stories. It was through this sharing with each other that we feel connected by relating to each other's behaviors and emotions. Unloading the past is therapeutic, whether sharing it with one person or a group. It shows us that we are inextricably linked. Our commonality, accompanied by our uniqueness, rings true as we bare our souls. We are not alone; we are singular, woven together like threads in one fine fabric, diverse and beautiful.

With half of the people still wearing masks that day at the park, it took a minute to recognize some of them. After the normal format of readings and handing out new chips, my sponsor presented me with a homemade cake. It had a stunning jellied mold made with an array of intricate flowers on top, which must have taken a lot of time.

"Wow! Thank you," I said with a tear in my eye, as the crowd sang "Happy Birthday."

"You're worth it," she said handing the gorgeous cake to me along with my one-year chip.

When it was my turn to speak, I felt myself tense up, but as I began to talk, the vulnerability started pouring out of me. "My childhood wasn't exactly ideal. I came from a broken home, there was verbal and physical abuse, and my propensity for drugs and alcohol started at a very young age, like 12 or 13. Actually, in elementary school, I used to hide in the back yard and swig a whole gallon of Hawaiian Punch as fast as I could because I liked the effect of being dizzy. Silly I know, but a sure sign that something was off. Before this program I never said "no" to any mind-altering substance. The crux of it all is that I lose control once I start, one drink or drug always turns into more than I can remember."

My nerves began to subside.

"I eloped with a raging alcoholic when I was 19 and traveled far and wide for many years. We always found people who liked to party the same way we did. Drugs and alcohol were practically worshiped. God forbid, we lose our stash! Disaster, right? The decades seemed to fly by and the whole time I was oblivious that I was an alcoholic. My life fell apart over and over again, sometimes directly related to alcohol and drugs, sometimes just because I was crazy, but always because I wasn't sober in mind and body. The miracle of sobriety is that it has changed the way I think. I choose to do things that benefit myself and others, rather than self-destruct or burn bridges. I choose to face obstacles head on instead of running away and ignoring the issue. I choose truth instead of utter denial. And for me, my truth is that I can rely on a higher power, who I choose to call God, for strength and for peace. Morning prayers straighten my head out each day and I meditate on honesty and love which guide me to live a better life today."

I wasn't sure what to talk about next. Usually, people tell a specific demoralizing story. Should I talk about the drunken night in the Army, or living on the streets of London with Dario, or Disneyland jail in high school? Then a more recent embarrassing story came to mind.

"I have a slew of demoralizing stories, but what immediately comes to mind happened in Key West, Florida. I was homeless and camping on the beach with my two toddlers. One night, I decided I had to have a drink. I had been living through a dry period while nursing my babies, but there was a fire under my ass that night which I couldn't control. I packed my sleeping babies in the car, left the campground, and drove to the district in town where bars lined the streets, but I couldn't find a place to park. There was a red zone at the end of a block where I decided it would be okay to park while I just had a couple of drinks since the girls were sleeping in the minivan behind darkened windows. Popping into a bar, I quickly felt that sweet relief that was so familiar whenever I sat on a barstool and ordered a double shot from the bartender. After shooting back another double vodka on ice with a lime, I had a hunch I needed to get back to the girls. As I walked briskly down the crowded sidewalk, I saw flashing lights in the distance where I had parked. It was a tow truck hooking onto my van! I ran to the driver and begged him to unhook his chain and hoped my girls would stay quiet. I had managed to squirm out of a hundred sticky situations in my life, and this was no exception. Like a typical alcoholic, I had an incredible ability to lie and wiggle my way out of trouble. The tow truck driver grew sick of my pleading and unhooked my car. I took the parking ticket off the windshield and drove away, still shaking. Pulling into an empty parking lot on the outskirts of town, I checked on the girls who were waking up, and I started to cry as their sweet baby faces looked back at me. I came so close to losing them. But even after this experience, it didn't occur to me that I was an alcoholic who made drinking a priority over my children's safety.

"As the years passed, my addiction would grow progressively worse before I admitted I was an alcoholic and addict. Forty years of what I considered partying had prevented my life from becoming what I wanted it to be. Well finally, I have arrived. Sobriety has changed everything for me. Today I am happy and at peace with myself. It brings me so much joy to witness the same miracle that I have experienced in another person. That is the magic of this program and how it continues to grow. AA is a force, a magnetic force drawing the sick and weary to find comfort and relief from torment. We are millions strong worldwide unified to combat addiction and alcoholism, and I am forever grateful. I have experienced a revolution of the mind; we rise anew, free from the constraint of living in denial. Honesty gives us a chance at a fulfilling life. If you are new, let go of your fear. Freedom is just around the corner. I have found that freedom gives me the power to live the life I have always wanted. It is never too late to change."

As I drove home after the meeting, I had the conviction that the girls and I had outgrown my parents' house. It was time for us to move on. Now that I was back at work and doing my job sober, I grew even more uncomfortable at the law firm and was determined to make some significant changes. The girls were so big now that we needed space, but rent across Los Angeles was skyrocketing. I could only afford a one-bedroom apartment in a junky neighborhood, and I didn't want that. I wanted a spacious house where I felt my girls were safe and the schools were great. I imagined a place where I could plant flowers and stay put, maybe even get a dog. It suddenly became clear that it was time to move out of L.A. and settle somewhere beautiful and more relaxed, where I could make a home. I was tired of living in a big city riddled with traffic, stress, and smoggy air. I set my sights on going north and thought of Oregon. It was a place where the seasons were distinct. I desired mountains and forests, a slower pace, and a more affordable lifestyle. I prayed for a miracle. There had to be a perfect place for us to live and thrive. A place where relaxation was a way of life and not partitioned strictly for vacations. A place where we could breathe fresh air and shop local; where small businesses thrive and participate in an intimate community.

Amid my drive, I pondered the essence of my existence and looked beyond this world to the origin and the destination. It was unknown by logic but known in my soul by faith. Conscious that we are all between the past and the future, only existing in this present moment, and that all troubles pass, I felt comfort. Realizing that the God of my understanding is the beginning and the ending, within every breath I take, and in every page I turn of my life's story, gave me the peace and security I had always wanted. Summer was approaching. The time was now.

900 Miles

Chapter 26

How marvelous it is when a heart's desire is set in motion and synchronicity shines!

I didn't want to live in Portland, too crowded. I considered Eugene and Salem, but decided I wanted something even smaller. I started researching and put the word out on Facebook to see if anyone knew about a moderately small town that would suit me and my girls. That weekend, a close friend reached out and told me that his cousin Harmony had a large house for rent in Golden City. Located in the northeastern part of Oregon, the town had a population of 10,000 people, and the house was only $1300 a month. I just had to see it!

I contacted Harmony and was impressed by the virtual tour on FaceTime. The house had fresh white paint on the inside walls with original dark wood molding and high ceilings, refurbished wood floors, and large new windows. The beveled glass with wrought iron designs remained intact on either side of the wide front door and the stained-glass light fixtures were in mint condition. There was a chandelier in the dining room, a large raised front porch with pillars, a brand-new AC/heating unit, and a 100-year-old pear tree on the side of the house. With 2,800 square feet, there was a bedroom for each of us, two bathrooms, a guest room, an office, a laundry room, storage, and an extra room for arts and crafts. After an hour-long call, Harmony said, "Because you know my cousin, I will hold it for you if you fly out here to see the house in person."

The following Friday after work I landed in Boise, Idaho, after an almost three-hour flight from LAX. Driving an economy rental car, late at night through a mountain pass, I arrived in Golden City two hours later, exhausted. I found the tall, white house with pine green trim on Main Street and met Harmony and her husband as they answered the door and invited me in. After a little small talk, they escorted me to a large blow-up mattress upstairs where I dozed off, excited to explore everything the next day.

In the morning, the owners and I enjoyed some delicious Hawaiian coffee and took a tour of the house. It seemed too big for the three of us, but I was smitten. The hunch I had felt all along was right—this house was a gift. I signed the lease and wrote a check for the deposit. Even though I did not have a job lined up yet, I wasn't worried because the rent was less than the price of a studio apartment in Los Angeles. I trusted that miracles were at play, and a job would fall into place.

The house was just two blocks away from the quaint city center. Main Street had an entrepreneurial spirit with small businesses lined up and down the street. There was a bakery, a specialty cheese shop, a botanical store, a homemade ice cream parlor, an independent bookstore, art galleries, vintage stores, a chocolatier, and a historic hotel built in the 1880s with a nice restaurant and a stained-glass ceiling. Old fashioned light posts and hanging pots of petunias lined Main Street with ornate century-old tuff stone and brick buildings standing strong on either side of the road. An American small town was a new experience for me, and I was excited for my girls to grow into their teenage years in a safe environment. They could ride their bikes, and I wouldn't have to worry about them as they bopped around town by themselves.

Returning home, I got to work planning the move. I had enough money saved to secure the house but because moving expenses were so high across state lines, I had to do *something* to get us there, so I started a GoFundMe campaign and put it on Facebook. Without shame, I put myself out there and sent the link to anyone I thought might help. I put my resume on Indeed and felt certain something would come up. Since I hardly had any furniture, my solution was to scour Los Angeles for free stuff advertised on Craigslist and pack it in the truck. Whether the truck was full or not, it would cost the same to move.

Every piece of free furniture was carefully chosen. I needed nearly everything, and I became very successful from the start. I was amazed at how many quality items were advertised. People going through divorce, moving to NYC and downsizing, or leaving the country altogether were abruptly letting go of their belongings. I ended up collecting an emerald-green chenille vintage couch, an elegant square glass and iron coffee table, beautiful antique ceramic lamps, dark wicker side tables, a seven-foot-long white modern desk, bedroom furniture for myself and my daughters, a proper dining table and chairs, a large distinctive mirror, and area rugs...the list went on. My mom and Ron were indispensable when it came time to help me gather the free houseful of stuff. They supported the move, knowing that I was committed to building a better life. I was so grateful when enough people contributed to the $5,000 bill from the mover. I had nearly reached my goal, and my parents pushed me over the finish line by making up the difference. Andrejs, an independent mover I found on Craigslist, packed the truck to the brim and would meet us at the new house after a two-day drive.

Before leaving on a Sunday in July, I met Kalani for coffee.

"I can't believe you are leaving!" said Kalani, sipping her cappuccino.

"I want you to know you are the best friend a girl could have," I told her, looking into her sincere brown eyes. "Thank you for all the years of love and support. No one has been more honest with me than you have."

"That's what friends are for, right?"

"It's no wonder you became a therapist," I said, choking up. "You've always given the best advice. Too bad it took me so long to listen. I'm going to miss you."

Setting down her coffee cup, Kalani acted serious, pushing back her tears, "You better come and visit once in a while, or I will track you down." Then she flashed a smile. "Who am I going to bum on the beach with?"

"Hey, I never gave my amends to you." I took Kalani's hand. "I am sorry for all the times I was drunk, outrageous, and embarrassed you."

"Thank you, because you *were* a pain in the ass sometimes." Kalani looked me directly in the eyes. "But to be honest, what hurt most was the secret you kept of just how bad the addictions were. I have always believed in you. I wanted you to believe in yourself as much as I did. I am so glad you are sober, and the medication is working better with your chemistry." She sat back in her chair, "I love you and will always be here when you need me. Don't hesitate to call."

With my girls settled in the car, I drove off in my white Kia which I named Ox, figuring we were in our modern day covered wagon headed to the Oregon Trail. Northbound, on smooth roads and without traffic, passing through deserts and mountain ranges, we admired the sights. Nine hundred miles, two days, and fourteen hours later, we rolled into the valley, admiring the Blue Mountains, as the twinkling lights lit up the town at twilight. Golden County sits on the 45th parallel, halfway between the equator and the north pole, signifying something—perhaps an energetic balance? Founded 150 years ago, Golden City was a gold rush town. I just knew I had struck proverbial gold myself.

Andrejs the mover was from Latvia, a strong and hardworking man. He texted that he had arrived and was staying overnight in a small motel by the highway. He would meet us at the house in the morning at seven sharp to start unloading. The girls and I stayed in an Airbnb downtown in the historic center. It was a rustic loft with brick walls that had all the modern fixings. After settling in, we went downstairs to a restaurant with fine woodworking indicative of the Old West. We filled our bellies with hearty burgers, and I drank a delicious ginger beer from the bottle, satisfied, knowing we had arrived.

At 7 a.m., Andrejs and I waited for the extra hands he hired to show up, but there was no sign of them, even after numerous phone calls. I decided to knock on the front doors of our new neighbors to ask if they knew anybody who'd like a job unloading the truck. There was no answer next door, but luckily a woman walking past with her dog volunteered her husband. Next, I walked up to another neighbor in her driveway who was opening her car door.

"Good morning, I'm Alika. I am moving in across the street and really need some help unloading the truck. Do you know anyone interested in a quick job for the day? We'll pay twenty-five dollars an hour."

"Good morning," she said. "I'm Sally. Welcome to the neighborhood. I was wondering who was going to move in across the street. Let me see. I could ask a handyman friend of mine from church. I'll put my groceries away and give him a call."

"Thank you so much. I've come 900 miles and can't stop now."

Much to my relief, two fellows, young and strong, showed up around 8 a.m. and we all unloaded the truck. My neighbor's husband, an older gentleman, assembled the bed frames and my gorgeous desk, while the rest of us placed furniture and boxes where I needed them. Directing them all up and down the stairs, we finished the job in just four hours. I wrote Andrejs a check with the final installment of $2,500, and he gave cash to the men who helped us. It was done. Andrejs drove away in the empty 26-foot-long moving truck as the girls and I waved goodbye from the raised porch next to the pear tree, which was exhibiting beautiful bulbs of fruit on its branches.

Finding a place for every piece of furniture, every framed photograph, every book, dish, and piece of art was thrilling to me. Making every angle pleasing to the eye and optimizing functionality, appreciating pockets of negative space, and filling in areas with pops of color was a joy. I hung embroidered green velvet drapes to match the sofa in the living room, and French flowery cotton curtains in the dining room. I bought large houseplants from the botanical store, bringing the corners to life, and a few smaller plants for the mantel with cascading green leaves exuding health and wellness. I discovered a great thrift store and some resale shops where I gathered the finishing touches to make the house a home. I was amazed at how many frames I found for fifty cents each. Frames that could hold new memories, adding to the baby pictures of my kids on the wall. I had everything I needed, and a home to call my own.

Interviews from Indeed started to line up—one with the grand historic hotel as an assistant manager, one at the Department of Human Services as an eligibility worker, and one at the local art center as a community art director. The pay was relatively the same for all these positions, so I'd just have to interview and see what happened. I prayed that I would become the art director, managing the gallery in the stately historic building built in 1906 next to City Hall. I registered my kids in school, which was only a few blocks away—they could walk to school if it was a nice day. Everything was falling into place. Gone were the days living in an overwhelmingly expensive and chaotic city. My sober life was suitable to my new environment, and I felt in harmony with the deep tone of bells ringing every hour from the tower of the tallest church in town.

I joined the gym at the YMCA and learned that there was a large, heated pool included with membership that opened early in the morning year-round where I could begin a swim routine each day. Eventually the snow would fall, and the brisk air would fill my lungs. Clean air, clean water, and a clean life became the essentials I enjoyed. I had always been able to adapt to new environments and this was no different. Here I could feel the serenity flow, swirling like magic dust, and peace swooping in, guiding my path.

Home

Chapter 27

The girls started at the middle school, Jane in 6th grade and Cora in 7th. They missed their friends, and I knew this was hard but surely, they would connect with teenage souls here in town and make memories to last a lifetime. I had interviewed for all three jobs and was offered positions at all of them! Turns out there were not enough people in town to fulfill the demand for employment, and many businesses were suffering because of it. A large part of the community was retired, and many of the kids who moved away for college didn't return.

The art director position was perfect. I started managing a beautiful art gallery with paintings on the walls and fine ceramics, wood, and metal sculptures on the shelves. Quilts and woven table runners, place mats, and felt work softened up the displays. The gallery represented the vibrant art scene in town and connected me to a community that I longed for.

The executive director and my coworkers were delightful. The art committee members I managed were experienced, some for 25 years at the art center, and welcomed me with the hope that I could bring a new life to their mission. As a nonprofit and respected entity in town, the Golden City Art Center provided classes and art events that gave me a sense of pride. Presenting a new exhibition for the ArtWalk every First Friday drove me to do my best, giving the gift of art to the community at large, free of charge. Another miracle had transformed my life. Trusting God had a boomerang effect. Meditation, positive thinking, conscientious action, gratitude, and patience fueled me to live my best life.

The girls and I loved the spacious house. The owners had said I would be the first in line to buy it if I chose, and that had planted the seed of home ownership in my brain. Could I one day purchase a home of my own? That idea swirled inside my mind, but I had time as I had been told that I could rent for a few years, until the girls finished school. We settled in and relaxed, waiting for the pears to ripen on the side of the house.

That summer, parades, fairs, and music in the park filled our weekends with opportunities to merge into the life of the small city. Summer quickly became autumn. The leaves turned gold and red, and booming splashes of color fell to the ground, resembling an elaborate carpet across town. Every business along Main Street opened its doors and handed out sweets on Halloween. Candy galore filled the bags of hundreds of costumed kids, big and small, walking along the main thoroughfare, which was closed off to cars, making a safe environment for them to collect their goodies.

Then the time came when tree branches and electrical wires were all topped with white lines under misty skies. Winter had me scraping the ice off my windshield every morning before I hit the pool. The weight of my boot prints on the blanket of snow made a crunching sound as snowflakes gently drifted down light as cotton. Each unique snowflake, shaped like the essence of stars, crushed under my feet. Fascinating frozen water, fused on the ground, was heavy when I shoveled the sidewalks. It is a customary gesture to make a path for mail carriers, people walking their dogs, and children walking to school. Being on a corner, I had to carve out time each morning to accomplish this feat before heading to work. But the cold didn't bother me. Today, coats, gloves, and boots solve that. It was something I didn't have when freezing in London winters.

Christmastime came and I bought a real tree, decorating it with ornaments and ribbon from the thrift shop. I made cookies for my neighbors, wrapped them in tissue paper and delivered them in tins. In return, I was handed fresh eggs and homemade jam, frozen elk steaks, honey, and some quilted pads for hot pans. This was a place in the world I didn't think existed. But here I was in a town where people kept bees and chickens, hunted for their meat, spent time on their sewing machines, and jammed up the plentiful fruit growing all around us.

The city was politically split blue and red, like much of the country. I kept close to my liberal artist friends and was pleased to live in a town where people respected one another. Whatever my neighbors believed in, religious or political, we were friendly above all else.

It was nearing a year in our new town when the owners informed me, in a text, that they were putting the house up for sale. Panic set in. I couldn't imagine having to move again. It turned out that rentals were almost impossible to find, so I started scrambling to see if I could be the buyer they were looking for. They were asking $425,000 and that number was difficult to grapple with. The house needed a new roof and siding, so the price was too high, but it got me thinking. What else was out there? I asked my new friends for referrals to a lender who could help me figure out a plan and investigated houses for sale in town. Houses out of town were significantly less expensive but Jane was terrified of living out in the country, surrounded by cattle, too far from the park and shops. Plus, the girls loved walking to and from school, petting neighborhood dogs along the way. The question was, how would I get the money?

The lender suggested that I pursue a VA loan. The debacle in the military could actually pay off. After applying, I was approved for $270,000! The hunt was on. My panic turned into excitement. After a transient life had me spinning for decades, here I had a chance at securing a home for my little family.

After looking through the listings on the internet, I found that most affordable houses were run down and needed work which I did not have the means for. I needed more money. I began searching for resources and found an organization that had grants for veteran first-time home buyers, and I applied. I was a perfect fit and my paperwork checked out. All I had to do was take some financial planning classes and sign a contract promising to pay the mortgage consistently for five years, and the loan would be forgiven. The organization had $30,000 left in their coffer and told me I was approved. With $300,000 I could find something that worked for us!

There was a white A-framed Craftsman house with a for sale sign on the way to school that had attracted me for months. It was on the corner with a big front porch. I had to see the inside. I called the realtor advertised on the sign planted in the front lawn and took a tour. The kitchen was gorgeous. Both bathrooms had been restored. There were big windows in the living room and pine ceilings throughout creating a homey and sophisticated feel. With three bedrooms, two bathrooms, a big kitchen, and an extra room for my big desk, I had to have it.

The lender was confident we could work something out, but the asking price was $320,000. I suggested we offer $300,000 and see what the sellers would say. They came back with $310,000 as their final price. Where was I going to get $10,000? My parents were supportive of my efforts and when I told them of my dilemma, they said they would give me the 10K and deduct it from my inheritance. Wow! Everything fell into place, and I started the process.

I kept thinking this house would be worth a couple million in Los Angeles, and here I was on the verge of buying an elegant home, just the right size, with fabulous new appliances in the large, gorgeous kitchen. The seller was desperate to move near her daughter in Boise, Idaho, after her husband had died. Nobody else was making an offer because it had no garage or back yard. But it was the house I wanted; we could live just fine exactly as it was.

My lender moved mountains and made it work. I signed the contract with the realtor, who worked as a dual agent, and I got a $1,000 check from the bank to give earnest money to the title company. Step by step, it fell into place, and with the funds from my parents, the loan from the VA, and the nonprofit money, I bought a house! I brought the girls with me to sign a stack of papers; the look on their faces was priceless. They were proud of me and so was I. Thrilled, after living a precarious life, I would have security at last. This manifestation of physical stability reflected the security I finally felt inside. Willingness to change, faith, and the aspiration for a better life unfolded when my thoughts elevated into a positive light. That wise guru from the yoga retreat many years ago was right. Our thoughts *are* very important.

I gave my notice to the owners of the rental. I would move at the end of my lease as summer flowers shone all over town. I couldn't wait to plant mine on the wide front porch. A porch that faced east and the rising sun. Neighbors and friends I had made in the art community generously offered to loan me their trucks and help me move. It was the first of July, and it was hot. Sweating, we packed up the furniture, boxes, plants, and odds and ends, moving into the house where I would plant my family.

I threw a big housewarming party on the weekend for all the people who helped me. The previous owner left behind a grill, so I decided to barbecue kabobs. I also made some salads and chocolate chip cookies for dessert. Stirring a summer punch with fresh lemon slices swirling on the surface, I thought about how jubilance and gratitude color the course of my life. I was so moved as guests arrived that a small well of tears accumulated on the bottom rims of my eyes without enough momentum to fall. I grabbed a tissue. Suddenly, the tautness of my heart strings tugged, stemming from the memories stored within, and reminded me of how far I had come.

Now we live in a beautiful house, fortifying my feelings of safety and accomplishment. Tenacious faith drove me to believe that we could live somewhere with a wholesome beauty, where joy resides, and comfort feeds our spirits. I had lacked purpose for decades, a boat without a rudder dragged wherever the stormy seas bade me. Finally, I am happy, regardless of the circumstances that life brings, because peace, like water, fills the crevices where self-doubt and regret used to live.

My bone-colored case has officially retired, now holding my sewing supplies, and my big, warm coat hangs on the coat rack ready to be useful during winter months. The town deer wander the neighborhood on the side of the house, creating a beautiful sight through the dining room window. Their big, dark eyes portray an innocence, and their tall, furry ears perk up at the soft music of wind chimes sounding from my front porch, as if angels were singing. With newfound freedom and immense gratitude, I thanked the force that spared me from death so long ago. I am, I thought to myself. I am.

Just as Grandma would polish clean a chicken bone,
So too would I feast on a gritty life down to the marrow.
A montage of scenes, alive like the lava
from Mauna Loa in Hawaii where I was born,
erupts from the mountaintop, while the rest of its body
lays hidden under the sea.
After living through extreme highs and lows,
I ultimately swim in the expanse of the ocean
Level and free, with my head above the moonlit water.

www.ingramcontent.com/pod-product-compliance
Lightning Source LLC
Chambersburg PA
CBHW021955130726
47903CB00014B/1456